POT POURRI:
Whistlings of an Idler

POT POURRI:
Whistlings of an Idler

A Novel by
EUGENIO CAMBACERES

Translated from the Spanish by
LISA DILLMAN

EDITED AND WITH AN INTRODUCTION BY
JOSEFINA LUDMER

OXFORD
UNIVERSITY PRESS

2003

OXFORD

UNIVERSITY PRESS

Oxford   New York

Auckland   Bangkok   Buenos Aires   Cape Town   Chennai
Dar es Salaam   Delhi   Hong Kong   Istanbul   Karachi   Kolkata
Kuala Lumpur   Madrid   Melbourne   Mexico City   Mumbai
Nairobi   São Paulo   Shanghai   Taipei   Tokyo   Toronto

Copyright © 2003 by Oxford University Press, Inc.

Published by Oxford University Press, Inc.
198 Madison Avenue, New York, New York 10016

www.oup.com

Oxford is a registered trademark of Oxford University Press

Library of Congress Cataloging-in-Publication Data
Cambaceres, Eugenio, 1843–1889.
[Pot pourri. English]
Pot pourri : whistlings of an idler : a novel / by Eugenio Cambaceres ;
translated from the Spanish by Lisa Dillman ;
edited and with an introduction by Josefina Ludmer.
p. cm.—(Library of Latin America)
ISBN 0-19-514464-3 (pbk.)—ISBN 0-19-514463-5 (cloth)
I. Ludmer, Josefina.
II. Title.
III. Series.
PQ 7796.C23P613 2003
863'.5—dc21
2002011006

1 3 5 7 9 8 6 4 2

Printed in the United States of America
on acid-free paper

Contents

Series Editors' General Introduction
vii

*Introduction: Modernization and the Boundaries of
the Periphery*
JOSEFINA LUDMER
xi

Acknowledgments
xxxix

Pot Pourri
EUGENIO CAMBACERES
I

Series Editors'
General Introduction

The Library of Latin America series makes available in translation major nineteenth-century authors whose work has been neglected in the English-speaking world. The titles for the translations from the Spanish and Portuguese were suggested by an editorial committee that included Jean Franco (general editor responsible for works in Spanish), Richard Graham (series editor responsible for works in Portuguese), Tulio Halperín Donghi (at the University of California, Berkeley), Iván Jaksić (at the University of Notre Dame), Naomi Lindstrom (at the University of Texas at Austin), Francine Masiello (at the University of California, Berkeley), and Eduardo Lozano of the Library at the University of Pittsburgh. The late Antonio Cornejo Polar of the University of California, Berkeley, was also one of the founding members of the committee. The translations have been funded thanks to the generosity of the Lampadia Foundation and the Andrew W. Mellon Foundation.

During the period of national formation between 1810 and into the early years of the twentieth century, the new nations of Latin America fashioned their identities, drew up constitutions, engaged in bitter struggles over territory, and debated questions of education, government, ethnicity, and culture. This was a unique period unlike the process of nation formation in Europe and one which should be more familiar than it is to students of comparative politics, history, and literature.

The image of the nation was envisioned by the lettered classes—a minority in countries in which indigenous, mestizo, black, or mulatto peasants and slaves predominated—although there were also alternative nationalisms at the grassroots level. The cultural elite were well educated in European thought and letters, but as statesmen, journalists, poets, and academics, they confronted the problem of the racial and linguistic heterogeneity of the continent and the difficulties of integrating the population into a modern nation-state. Some of the writers whose works will be translated in the Library of Latin America series played leading roles in politics. Fray Servando Teresa de Mier, a friar who translated Rousseau's *The Social Contract* and was one of the most colorful characters of the independence period, was faced with imprisonment and expulsion from Mexico for his heterodox beliefs; on his return, after independence, he was elected to the congress. Domingo Faustino Sarmiento, exiled from his native Argentina under the presidency of Rosas, wrote *Facundo: Civilización y barbarie*, a stinging denunciation of that government. He returned after Rosas' overthrow and was elected president in 1868. Andrés Bello was born in Venezuela, lived in London where he published poetry during the independence period, settled in Chile where he founded the University, wrote his grammar of the Spanish language, and drew up the country's legal code.

These post-independence intelligentsia were not simply dreaming castles in the air, but vitally contributed to the founding of nations and the shaping of culture. The advantage of hindsight may make us aware of problems they themselves did not foresee, but this should not affect our assessment of their truly astonishing energies and achievements. It is still surprising that the writing of Andrés Bello, who contributed fundamental works to so many different fields, has never been translated into English. Although there is a recent translation of Sarmiento's celebrated *Facundo*, there is no translation of his memoirs, *Recuerdos de provincia (Provincial Recollections)*. The predominance of memoirs in the Library of Latin America series is no accident—many of these offer entertaining insights into a vast and complex continent.

Nor have we neglected the novel. The series includes new translations of the outstanding Brazilian writer Joaquim Maria Machado de Assis's work, including *Dom Casmurro* and *The Posthumous Memoirs of Brás Cubas*. There is no reason why other novels and writers who are not so well known outside Latin America—the Peruvian novelist Clorinda Matto de Turner's *Aves sin nido*, Nataniel Aguirre's *Juan de la Rosa*, José de Alencar's *Iracema*, Juana Manuela Gorriti's short stories— should not be read with as much interest as the political novels of Anthony Trollope.

A series on nineteenth-century Latin America cannot, however, be limited to literary genres such as the novel, the poem, and the short story. The literature of independent Latin America was eclectic and strongly influenced by the periodical press newly liberated from scrutiny by colonial authorities and the Inquisition Newspapers were miscellanies of fiction, essays, poems, and translations from all manner of European writing. The novels written on the eve of Mexican Independence by José Joaquín Fernández de Lizardi included disquisitions on secular education and law, and denunciations of the evils of gaming and idleness. Other works, such as a well-known poem by Andrés Bello, "Ode to Tropical Agriculture," and novels such as *Amalia* by José Marmol and the Bolivian Nataniel Aguirre's *Juan de la Rosa*, were openly partisan. By the end of the century, sophisticated scholars were beginning to address the history of their countries, as did Joao Capistrano de Abreu in his *Capitulos de historia colonial*.

It is often in memoirs such as those by Fray Servando Teresa de Mier or Sarmiento that we find the descriptions of everyday life that in Europe were incorporated into the realist novel. Latin American literature at this time was seen largely as a pedagogical tool, a "light" alternative to speeches, sermons, and philosophical tracts—though, in fact, especially in the early part of the century, even the readership for novels was quite small because of the high rate of illiteracy. Nevertheless, the vigorous orally transmitted culture of the gaucho and the urban underclasses became the linguistic repertoire of some of the most interesting nineteenth-century writers—most notably José Hernández, author of the "gauchesque" poem "Martin Fierro," which enjoyed an unparalleled popularity. But for many writers the task was not to appropriate popular language but to civilize, and their literary works were strongly influenced by the high style of political oratory.

The editorial committee has not attempted to limit its selection to the better-known writers such as Machado de Assis; it has also selected many works that have never appeared in translation or writers whose work has not been translated recently. The series now makes these works available to the English-speaking public.

Because of the preferences of funding organizations, the series initially focuses on writing from Brazil, the Southern Cone, the Andean region, and Mexico. Each of our editions will have an introduction that places the work in its appropriate context and includes explanatory notes.

We owe special thanks to the late Robert Glynn of the Lampadia Foundation, whose initiative gave the project a jump start, and to Richard Ekman of the Andrew W. Mellon Foundation, which also generously supported the project. We also thank the Rockefeller Foundation for funding the 1996 symposium "Culture and Nation in Iberoamerica," organized by the editorial board of the Library of Latin America. The support of Edward Barry, formerly of Oxford University Press, was crucial, as has been the advice and help of Ellen Chodosh of Oxford University Press. The first volumes of the series were published after the untimely death, on July 3, 1997, of Maria C. Bulle, who, as an associate of the Lampadia Foundation, supported the idea from its beginning. We received substantial institutional support and personal encouragement from the Institute of Latin American Studies of the University of Texas at Austin.

—*Jean Franco*
—*Richard Graham*

Introduction

MODERNIZATION AND THE
BOUNDARIES OF THE PERIPHERY

A n examination of the period known as *El 80* in Argentina is essential to any study of Latin America's process of modernization. The 1880s represented a complete historical disjuncture: the annihilation of the Indians, the end of civil war, political and jurisdictional unification by the liberal state, and entry into the world market—the zenith of capitalism for a Latin American country. This constituted both enormous historical change and a modernizing leap taken by the state (in the peripheries, the state orders society from above, in the absence of a powerful, autonomous bourgeoisie).

But the 1880s also ushered in a new literature in Argentina, created by a group of young, university-educated writers (average age: 35; the country's president at the time was 38) whom critics called the Generation of 1880.[1] One thing that characterized the group was their appropriation of Western, particularly European, literature; this not only changed the relationship between Argentinian Spanish and foreign languages but also founded translation as a literary genre. These writers created fragmented, conversational, imaginative, Francophile, ironic, elegant, substantially cultured, and refined literature: "aristocratic," in short (yet in a Latin American country). The 1880 group founded national high culture. Their common ground included liberalism, positivism, the Club del Progreso, Colón Theater, *Sud-América* newspaper, and a few carnivals.

One of the key moments in the definitive formation of the Argentinian state occurred when lay education and civil registry legislation was proposed in 1883 and 1884 (and President Julio A. Roca defied the Church and expelled the papal nuncio). The Generation of 1880 was directly represented in the creation of this legislation via Eduardo Wilde, the most fractional and humorous member of the group, who was at the time Minister of Education. Later, when civil matrimony was legalized, he became Minister of the Interior under President Juárez Celman.

The members of *El 80* wrote sets of autobiographical "tales" based around these laws that were used by the liberal Latin American state to define itself, to take charge of the birth, education, marriage, and death of all of its subjects. These narratives included both reality and fiction—novels, stories, memoirs, autobiographies, biographies, notes, chronicles, and travelogues. The tales of education centered on specific school-age episodes that were written as autobiographies. (Classics like *Juvenilia* (1882) by Miguel Cané and *La gran aldea* (1884) by Lucio Vicente López, both from the group's patrician sector, are good examples.) And the tales of matrimony—told in a different space, time, person, or world—centered on the marital problems of a friend or relation close to the narrator.

New subjects—what we could term "the subjects of the liberal state"—appeared with this literature, alongside these tales of education and matrimony. The group's patrician writers, who held posts in the new state, adopted traditional postures and created first-person fiction about public identity, with subjects like the memoirist, the hero from Buenos Aires, the diplomat, and the columnist.

This was the height of capitalism in a Latin American country that was also in the midst of modernization: new subjects required new systems of taxonomy, and new fables of national identity had to be written. The present had to be narrated in a depoliticized, more specifically cultural, independent way. Literature that told other tales, "modern," "private" tales of education and matrimony, had to be written. With his avant-garde style, Eugenio Cambaceres (1843–89) wrote just that, inventing the modern Argentinian novel and the gazes of the dandy and of the man of science.[2]

Eugenio Cambaceres as the 1880 Vanguard, the Boundary of the Periphery

Cambaceres, a first-generation Argentine and member of the economic aristocracy (in his latter novels he portrayed land ownership and its attendant dramas), was unique among the writers of the 1880s because he constituted their literary and ideological vanguard. *Pot Pourri*, his first novel, presents the narrator as an anonymous actor playing a dandy who finally ends up "acting" as head of state. With this multiple subject, Cambaceres created a new literary language—an "aristocratic" Buenos Aires slang—and a new fable of identity for Argentina's high society.

Cambaceres was not a state civil servant, like many of the generation's writers (deputies, ministers, and diplomats), nor was he the son of exiles from the Rosas reign, like patricians Cané and López; rather he was the son and heir of a rancher—the point of entry into the world market—who became a millionaire during the Rosas era. His father was a young French chemist who met the Argentinian consul, Larrea, in Paris and came to Argentina in 1829 to invest his inheritance in land, slaughterhouses, and salteries.

Eugenio Cambaceres was a lawyer but never practiced law: he earned his degree in 1869, after writing a pragmatic, capitalist dissertation called *Utility, Value and Price*. By 1880 he was off the political scene, having proved himself too liberal—or too modern—to legislate in pre-1880 Latin America. As a young man he was a pure, Jacobin republican (who, according to Paul Groussac, was erroneously credited with a French grandfather: Jean Jacques Régis de Cambacérès, the famous legal adviser and delegate appointed foreign minister and duke of Parma by Napoleon I).[3] The "French" Cambaceres, like many others, was so radical that he had to abandon the political arena altogether. As a deputy in the Convention of Buenos Aires Province in 1871 he had presented, and lost, a proposal for the separation of church and state. The proposal was based on a strictly *economic* liberalism: why should the state maintain the Catholic church with taxes paid by citizens of all religions?[4] Then in 1874, as a national deputy and out of strictly *political* liberalism, he denounced the electoral fraud of his own party—yet was ignored. He had, at that point, hit the limits of the Argentinian or Latin American state; he renounced his seat and retired from politics in 1876. From then on he alternately lived at his Buenos Aires palace,[5] his ranch (El Quemado), and his Paris home. Cambaceres wrote four novels between 1881 and 1887 and died in Buenos Aires in 1889.

He didn't marry an Argentinian woman (as the "actor" from *Pot Pourri*'s stage asks: Why are women here not educated like they are in the United States? Why do we follow the ancient Spanish tradition?),[6] but rather, forever performing, he wed the Italian lyric singer Luisa Bacichi whom he met in Paris. She was 17 years his junior and died in 1924.

The vicissitudes of Cambaceres's life were indicative of one of the paradoxes of modern, liberal, post-Enlightenment thought in Latin America: just when these new ideas came to the fore in modern Latin American states, they were shown to be unworkable, and then shelved. And that was when Cambaceres closed the book on politics and opened a new one on literature.

At the ideological vanguard of the Generation of 1880, Cambaceres was the one who had lived out the differences between the Latin American, French, and North American liberal states. He himself had fought the boundaries and limitations of the periphery and, analogously, his fictional subject was one who failed at everything: "There is naught to be done about it, no matter how my pride screams: I am completely *raté*." So in the 1880s, when the liberal state was established, he made a clear-cut distinction between the political portion of his life—which he situated in the past and as failure—and the literary, "theatrical" part: *Pot Pourri* and the present, in which the "actor" is a depoliticized subject who ends up *enacting* political power as his final role.

Cambaceres Among El 80: Head of Colón Theater and Founder of the Modern Novel

The Generation of 1880's cultural coalition wove specific spaces and texts together into a common fabric.

Miguel Cané, referring to Cambaceres's role at the Colón Theater, said "Best seat in the house! Eugenio Cambaceres, with the allure of his talent, his artistic taste, his exquisite culture, his wealth, his looks, why he had it all; that man, who seemed to have been born under the protection of a fairy godmother, was *the undisputed boss*."[7]

A patrician—and a state civil servant—Cané proclaimed Cambaceres the "boss" of the Colón, to which *El 8o* men went with their wives or to look for wives. And he said Cambaceres had it all, because he was in charge of a purely cultural and artistic institution, of the representation that was the other face of the liberal state, its fiction, its other self. In the 1880s, when politics could no longer be equated with war, the Colón came along with its ludic, illusory space in which literature was acted out, and the coalition reproduced scenes from the liberal state.

Theater and performance—fictionalization, representation, simulation, and disguise—were not just used as a way of thinking about the liberal state and its politics of representation.[8] They were also a way of thinking about its new literature, and what Cambaceres founded was exactly that: the liberal state drama. *Pot Pourri: Whistlings of an Idler* first came out anonymously in 1882, with an Argentinian dandy (or gentleman, or *señorito*) as the subject of Cambaceres's autobiographical fiction. He called the dandy an "actor" and "small-time musician"; or inversely: he chose an "actor" and an "idler" who played a dandy as his subject. Using this multiple subject, he theatrically told a "tale of matrimony," and within it created the liberal Latin American fable of identity: private, "aristocratic," masculine.

Cané, in *Prosa ligera*, situates Cambaceres in "real life" at the Colón, using his name and presenting him as the man who "has it all." In the fictional *Pot Pourri*, Cambaceres's actor-narrator places Cané and the coalition at the Club del Progreso carnival ball, complete with real names, but chooses to remain anonymous himself; Cambaceres's characters receive generic names: Juan, María, Pepe. There at the Club, the women, the maskers, choose partners:

> In the immediate vicinity of the orchestra (and take note, as this is the most strategic point, the part of this human pond in which the most fishing is done), they spend the sleepless night like wallflowers on the prowl, without so much as a slap from the hand of God to say: "Take that, you miserable wretches!" and in exchange for dislocating their jaws, Miguel Cané, Lucio V. López, Manuel Láinez, Roque Sáenz Peña, and others of their lot—rascals and imbeciles one and all—mill about the salons, find themselves chased, assaulted, and fought over by the blessed maskers like flies on a pot of jam.
> Tell me with whom thou goest.... No comment. (pp. 85–86)

Compare Cané's tone in referring to Cambaceres at the Colón with Cambaceres's tone when referring to Cané and the Club's coalition. The patrician is eulogistic, solemn, and reverent; the dandy is—how to put it?—amused, and uses an exceedingly modern, oral language to laugh at the coalition. We might say that this difference is what separated the coalition's patricians from the vanguard dandies.

I would like to think that the Generation of 1880 did not forgive Cambaceres for poking fun at the boring, old wallflowers and for this reason did not welcome him into their ranks until 1885, after he published *Sin rumbo*—which lacks his prior satirical tone and "aristocratic" Buenos Aires slang—and after he was vehemently attacked by the Catholics. That was when Martín García Mérou, the coalition's official critic, called him "the founder of the national novel" in *Sud-América,* the state newspaper, writing: "The author of *Whistlings of an Idler* has founded, within our ranks, the contemporary national novel."9

The 1880 Literary Vanguard: A Theory

Cambaceres wrote the first theory of literary "modernity" when Argentina's liberal state was emerging in 1882. He was at the literary vanguard of the Generation of 1880 and founded the modern novel. In doing so he separated literature from party politics, radically autonomizing the former. He was the first Argentinian writer to use the liberal state as a metaphor for theater and performance. In *Pot Pourri*, while the anonymous dandy travels to his friend Juan's ranch on a British train, he "performs" politics as a four-act republican farce: act one, the election farce; act two, the low theater of the legislative assembly; act three, the military uprising simulacrum; and finally, act four, *the voice* of the people. (Recall Cambaceres's political cleanup campaign and proposal for the separation of church and state.)

Pot Pourri is a novel comprising every type of 1880s prose: memoirs, autobiographies, letters, travelogues, stories, and newspaper excerpts (all written in a theatrical, satirical, farcical style). Cambaceres was the cultural coalition's anti-fragmentary writer as well as the one who created a novel using fragments, pulverizing them into one piece. A tale of adultery, one of the central themes of contemporary French theater and fiction,10 strings together the series of fragments in a literarily modern fashion. (The history of the Latin American novel could be read as the history of sexuality in Latin America. As Foucault said, "The history of the novel cannot be understood as separate from the history of sexuality." But this is also true of the history of the state.) Adultery was seen as a breach of that all-important contract that upheld everything—all others being dependent upon it—and that maintained the entire system: I am here referring simultaneously to the text, the literary system, and the political-state system. Cambaceres's fictional adultery is located in the present, with the insolent language and gaze of the actor playing an Argentine dandy: a rich, cultured, idle, "aristocratic," jaded bachelor who had everything he could wish for (and who also appeared in Lucio Vicente López's 1884 *La gran aldea*).

Pot Pourri was the 1880s' first vanguard novel (and the first "theory") because, like Pirandello later, Cambaceres clearly separated author, actor, and character. But the book was also the first best-seller and the first literary scandal of Argentinian modernity. The author was at the forefront of the Generation of 1880 because he directly *Argentinized* contemporary European literature: French fin de siècle boulevard theater, realism, naturalism, and modernism-decadentism. He superimposed, exaggerated, and amassed styles. He did the same with foreign languages—Italian, French, Latin, and English—to invent a carefree, aristocratic, pompous orality: what Martín García Mérou called "*porteño* [Buenos Aires] slang" and Paul Groussac disdainfully referred to as a "creole-aristocrat dialect."

The coalition of *El 80* founded Argentine "high" culture and established translation as a literary genre; Cambaceres's stance was both different and the same because he plagiarized—imported ideas, sayings, attitudes, ways of narrating—European genres and postures, but he also put them all in an utterly Argentinian space, tone, and language, literarily "translating" them. He nationalized not only foreign languages, but everything he touched: the dandy (*Pot Pourri*, 1882), fin de siècle malaise and sexuality (*Música sentimental*, 1884, with the same dandy narrator), spleen, tedium, loss of faith, depression, and suicide (which he located on a ranch to which the hand set fire (*Sin rumbo*, 1885)). And he used naturalism and scientific laws of heredity to Argentinize second-generation immigrants and to tell the tale of their education and matrimony (*En la sangre*, 1887).

In *Pot Pourri*'s series of responses to high society's "private life," the dandy's stance oscillates between transgression/scandal after the first carnival ball (the "actor" places himself on the divide and exposes sexual inequality and injustice) and convention/conformity after the second (in "arranging" a solution to the adultery issue, he acts as "the law"). The subject's position—gentleman, dandy, caballero—and that of the Generation of 1880 vanguard are the poles between the two extremes of transgression and enactment of the law.

But Cambaceres not only wrote Argentina's first modern novel, he also leapt so far forward that his echoes can be read in Manuel Puig in the 1960s and 1970s. In Puig and his precursors, we see the specifically literary role of performance: for Cambaceres, the theater (Colón, Comédie Française, and boulevard theater); for Puig, Argentinian radio and North American cinema.

Both worked from a minimalist theory of representation, with fragments and a proliferation of discourses, dialogues, and quotations: "staged" dialogues, newspaper clippings, social gazettes, letters, advertisements, interior monologues and discourses, and footnotes. And they tied them all together with a "familiar" orality and a simple, melodramatic tale whose story line was taken from popular film or theater. Cambaceres invented both a theory of representation for contemporary high society and an "aristocratic" language and tone to express the anonymous subject's verbal detachment (Puig does the same for the middle classes), creating a language of clichés, sayings, proverbs, the most familiar aspects of the language of the people. So, really, to tell the tale of a breach of contract, Cambaceres wrote a discourse on the language and *on dit* of the 1880s.[11]

Pot Pourri: *Author, Actor, and Character*

First, the author of the farce. Cambaceres was 38 when his "slap in the face of good taste" came out. *Pot Pourri: Whistlings of an Idler* was first published anonymously in 1882 in Buenos Aires by Biedma. (*Música sentimental* was also published anonymously, but in Paris.) It was a spectacular success: the first "anonymous" book of the Generation of 1880 and the first best-seller, first scandal, first literary transgression. It was attacked, reprinted, and parodied.[12] The book sold out the first year and there followed a second edition; in 1883 the third edition was published (Paris, Denné), still anonymous but with "a few words from the author." The anonymous author was a wealthy man of leisure who referred to the *scandale* created by the first edition and to the fact that he had been called a criminal; he claimed not to be the *flâneur*, the whistling idler; he set out his avant-garde project to demolish institutions; and finally, he also presented himself as a failure (this time, as the "failed author" of a farce in which the "truth sings out clearly"). His rapid-fire, conversational language, simultaneously so creole, so native, and so French, was the picture of the "aristocratic" 1880s Argentine who has seen it all, the new subject of the liberal state:

> One morning I awoke feeling adventurous and, fed up to the gills with the tedious routine of my life (rise at noon, luncheon at one, wander aimlessly along Calle Florida, eat wherever I chanced to be at the appointed time, play a hand of bezique at the Club, set off for the theater, etc.), I thought I might well fancy a change in direction, inventing something new—the first thing that popped into my head—so long as it took my mind off this beastly ennui, whereupon I was struck by an idea as absurd as any: that I should contribute to the enrichment of the nation's literature.
>
> To contribute to the enrichment of the nation's literature, I told myself, one need only be in possession of pen, ink, and paper, and not know how to write Spanish; I discretely meet all of these prerequisites, and thus there is no reason why I should not contribute to the enrichment of the nation's literature.
>
> And in my spare moments—in between yawning wide as an ocean and smoking a packet of Caporal—I managed to fabricate the concatenation of nonsense with which you are already familiar and which has raised such a storm, such an outcry, such furore against a certain third-rate specimen of humanity: the author.
>
> Frankly, it wasn't worth it: *le jeu n'en valait pas la chandelle*. (pp. 1–2)

> But you see, one does not dig trenches or take up a pickax to mine the foundations of an edifice with impunity, even if it threatens to collapse and one works with the Christian intention of preventing—should it suddenly come crashing down—broken arms and legs, of avoiding the owner's becoming churlish, complaining that his chattels are being assaulted and his home violated. (p. 6)

> But, really, I never imagined that they would take it so seriously and would shout themselves hoarse, crying: *à la garde, au voleur, à l'assassin!* before a defenseless fellow, an unhappy player who steps out into the open with

his hat in his hand, who does not flee from justice as he is neither thief nor assassin and whose only crime is to have written a farce, to have composed a *pot pourri* in which the truth sings out clearly.

I conclude.

I tried to induce laughter and instead induced rage.

Total fiasco; that was not the aim.

Like all mocked maestros, I want to smash my instrument against the floor . . . and yet . . . the love of the art . . .

Will I offend again?

Who can say? (p. 6)

Of course he offended again. This was the failed author who, with his truthful farce, reached the limits, hit the literary boundaries of the periphery, somewhere between transgression and "verbal crime." The public could not comprehend the avant-garde contract: to "mine the foundations of an edifice . . . even if it threatens to collapse." They did not grasp the fact that the contract's truth was what held the whole thing up.

Next, the farce's "actor." *Pot Pourri* was the first autobiography-manifesto by a multiple, anonymous subject (or a subject who was anonymous because he was multiple) who seemed always to be the same (Cambaceres himself): an "aristocrat" who inherited a great fortune, a *rentier* like Flaubert (Cambaceres also liked to *épater le bourgeois* and later, in exasperation, liked using free, indirect discourse to put himself in other selves without giving them a true voice), and an idler who "germinated" because he had a drama: personal realization. He was heir and *rentier* of the family who thwarted his plans to traipse the boards.

"Yes, sir; I was born to act," he says, and tells not only of his calling but of his perfect actor's talent: plagiaristic intelligence, a bohemian inclination to seek out life's pleasures, good looks, and an ability to interpret "any manner of outpourings of the soul." But, "Unfortunately, the high social standing of my family coupled with the scorn the world heaps onto a thespian—an absurd remnant of the times in which the mask of the buffoon degraded the practice of this noble art—assaulted my natural impulses, whereupon I was forced to renounce my most cherished predilection." (p. 8)

This anonymous subject, who tells of his education, does not have a political identity—as do characters in the tales of education by the impoverished patricians Cané and López—but rather an economic and social one. The two fictionalities—one of the failed author and the other of the frustrated actor—come together in the fable of identity of the new subject of the liberal state: torn between the economic and the social in peripheral, marginal regions, he finally becomes a writer. (Interestingly, this was also the position Victoria Ocampo set out in her autobiography, in a different set of relationships between cultural coalitions and liberal Latin American states. For her, too, adultery and anonymous, passionate love formed the center around which the system's fragments were articulated.)

The Dandy's Gaze

Like Prince Machiavelli, the actor—who plays the dandy who is perpetually performing and sees the world as a stage—uses different masks. This act transgresses the family prohibition of his entry into the theater. But his stance is simple; he places himself above and beyond conflict (refusing to marry),[13] and oscillates between two opposing poles (or between the boundaries or limits of the periphery).

At the magnificent dance held by society's élite in chapter III, the be-gloved dandy—having seen it all before—disdainfully watches the drama of Argentine high society unfold before him, feeling "gossip's evil spirit" overcome him. Part of the "theory of the dandy," this is a traditional characteristic of the historical dandy: Baudelaire's "aristocratic pleasure of displeasure." "I was then experiencing just such an ill-fated moment, and gossip's evil spirit was goading me on.

I felt an evil disposition, caustic and biting, awaken within me; I would have sunk my teeth into the virgin's white tunic to tear it asunder, and through the frenzied desire to wreak harm that assailed me, I saw everything round me painted in the most odious of manners." (p. 18)

The dandy-actor's gaze and stance constitute the Argentinization-translation (parody?) of the historical dandy, who is ascetic, malicious, misogynist and androgynous, distant, frivolous, impertinent, intelligent, provocative: somewhere between cynical and sadistic.[14] Lashing out against members of Argentinian high society, this dandy exhibits a fundamental trait of Argentinian high culture: the critique of his own culture, cultural self-criticism. That criticism from within, that stance (the position and voice), lies between two extremes, two boundaries or languages: on the divide between masculine and feminine. The feminine belongs to a "woman-friend" who is "commonly known as a viper-tongue" and "has made up vile deeds, told disgraceful tales, concocted atrocities." He listens to her tales and, a rhetorical-verbal accomplice to the crime, he watches various characters parade by. The viper-tongue's cultural criticism uses metaphors involving the theater, actors, and the stage—showing liberalism as theater's double—to touch on hypocrisy, farce, and crime in the private lives of the "aristocratic" guests there present. She shows what is behind the beautiful exterior of the middle classes: a vile, utilitarian spirit, vulgarity, and conformity.

Later we see the other extreme. When the narrator becomes disgusted by his friend's stories, he leaves her behind and then happens to see a young journalist. "Overflowing with talent from head to toe, he is as brilliant, dangerous, and sharp as a straight-edge razor," his "eyes sparkled with a pernicious mischief," and his "expression, quite peculiar to himself, was one of permanent sarcasm." At the end of the chapter, the dandy takes him by the hand and the pair go for a "breath of the fresh night air." Lying somewhere between the vindictiveness of the two genders, the dandy's proof of cultural modernity is his critique *of* the culture of modernity. Or, to put it another way, what defines his cultural modernity is the rejection of *bourgeois* modernity. Of course, this ideology has both leftist and rightist connotations; it can also fluctuate between two languages, two extremes.

The "character" who plays the dandy (or the dandy who plays the actor) is an exasperatingly eccentric "spiritual aristocrat" who places himself above the marriage conflict so that he can tell the truth about (depoliticized) modern private life. In doing so, he invents a masculine, "aristocratic" fable of identity and a gender code for the liberal state's marriage contract. This then allows him to fulfill another of the coalition's aims: to formulate a "private," "aristocratic" (sexual) identity to oppose the public, national, patrician fictions of identity.

The Tale of Matrimony

The dandy tells Juan and María's tale of matrimony in this order. First, his "research trip" to the ranch at which they spent their honeymoon (and where María was already getting bored). Second, the first carnival ball, at which María suspiciously exchanges cloaks with a friend and then disappears. Third, the second carnival ball where the oafish Taniete (the dandy's servant-cum-spy) follows María and discovers that Pepe, Juan's confidant and secretary, is the "intruder." And fourth, his own intervention on two occasions: first by writing a letter to María, and second by naming Pepe consul in Monaco.

The strategy he adopts to resolve the María-Pepe problem for Juan involves multiple steps and several oscillations, depending on to whom he's talking. He swings between the boundaries of "feminine" and "masculine," "left" and "right," moving between transgression and representation of the law, like the Argentinian vanguard of 1880.

First, the transgression. Amongst equals (i.e., male friends), he tells the truth about sex: he shows the natural equality and social inequality between the sexes (he transgresses, puts himself in the "feminine" position). He speaks with Juan after the first carnival ball, once he is already suspicious of María:

> "It's fine that man marries and together with his wife traverses the path of life, but really! Up to a certain point!
>
> "Man is like a horse: from time to time he needs to take to the fields, twitch his tail, frolic and roll around in the mud, if there's no sand around."
>
> "If man is like a horse, then of course woman must be like a mare, who switches her tail, frolics, and rolls around as well.
>
> "What would you say if your wife used your logic?"
>
> "Stop right there! Man is man and woman is woman; she dons skirts and he wears the trousers."
>
> "Oh, how we men, made in the image and likeness of our Lord, mete out justice in this vale of tears!" (p. 102)

Second, the law. After the second carnival ball he writes to María, calls her a trollop, and tells her that if she doesn't forget about Pepe he'll tell all to Juan. He delivers the letter to her and then in a monologue which he mentally directs to María, he tells her "the truth," reformulated in a "male" version and from a purely economic, liberalist perspective. Thus he explains the new civil marriage contract:

> Do you know what you have done by getting married?
>
> You have transferred the use of your person, you have signed a rental agreement; that is exactly what you have done, as if you were a dwelling;

it is a contract in which you cannot be occupied by any objects aside from those your tenant chooses.

Juan has taken you in order to inhabit you, and as Juan possesses his fortune one can only suppose that he does not want to share you with anyone else, especially when the intruder is not even paying rent and is, moreover, actually cheating him out of it like a swine.

In a word, you are not your own but another's chattel, and having usufructed yourself clandestinely by a third party you fall—under the precepts of the aforementioned Astete Code—into mortal sin, committing the offence of robbery; and therefore you are naught but a thieving sinner who deserves no pardon from our Lord. (p. 135)

So *El 80*'s first "anonymous" book, first best-seller, is the first literary scandal, the first offense. One of the main reasons for the scandal was Cambaceres's purely economic liberalism in his discourse on the separation of church and state, in view of the "legal" marriage contract. Feminine sexuality became the biological equivalent of capitalism: woman's body was property—furniture or chattel—and robbery, the maximum breach of contract.[15] Only Juan, he imagines telling María, is *naturally* free, and equates time and money:

But let us admit for a moment that as a son of Adam, it runs in the family, and he will often be of a mind to close the book of matrimonial duties and decree his time off and his holiday periods.

Where is the harm in that? How can it wound you?

Do you fear, perhaps, that your husband might forget you or love you less?

Nonsense, señora! Men's hearts are very large: there is comfortably room for many of you within them, simultaneously.

Our Lord Father and Mother Nature, in their infinite knowledge, have made it so. Why, look no further than cocks and other quadrupeds for proof of what I say.

I once met a man, *verbi gratia*, who used to spend his nights at his mistress's house and yet, one fine day, to save his father-in-law from a fraudulent bankruptcy, he gave his entire fortune to his wife.

To his lover his time, to his wife his money; and since time is money, it made no difference which; and since love is measured according to the benefits it brings, then by giving to both of them he loved both of them in equal measure. (pp. 135–36)

He thus resolves the money-sex-marriage equation with liberal capitalism, thanks to his position as "legal representative."

Head of State and the Solution

Pot Pourri, with its actor and his performance, acts complicitly as the state's double. Theater becomes the state's other, its fiction, its transgression, and also itself: the actor *represents* it, he *performs* its functions. Speaking in both the masculine and the feminine, in the end he comes to embody the head of state who wards off the threat to Juan's marriage by elegantly expelling the "intruder" Pepe from "the nation." Juan will never be the wiser.

But first Pepe is given the option of taking the honorable route and fighting a duel with Juan. If he owns up to the affair ("if it is serious and the flames of passion burn intensely within your soul"), the dandy will call Juan, tell him everything, and give each of them a revolver so that Pepe cannot claim he was "shot like a defenseless dog." Or, if he "couldn't give a bean about the woman," if he has no honor and is a coward—which is the case—then *l'état, c'est moi*, and he will be expelled from the country, from "home":

> "I have foreseen the event and fitted myself out with this case, containing one thousand francs in cash in twenty-franc denominations, this passport in your name—ordering the national authorities and begging the foreign ones to place no obstacle in the way of your transit—and finally, this appointment for your distinguished self to occupy the demanding post of Argentine consul in . . . Monaco.
>
> "Go, my young friend, go and join the ranks of those who, with a few honorable exceptions, nobly and worthily represent the republic abroad.
>
> "I recommend roulette in Monte Carlo." (pp. 142–43)

Thus, with the actor-dandy *enacting* his role as head of the liberal state, the literary vanguard novel of the 1880s is founded and draws to a close. This new subject is perhaps the most powerful—the one who has it all, the head of the Colón—the only one who dared to "represent" the head of state. He can name consuls and ambassadors because his position—both the physical distance and the gaze that separates him from the rest of the world—assures his control.

The liberal state is the limit of this subjectivity and this fable of identity. And the 1880s Argentinian dandy acts as a constant transgressor of limits, thereby making him part of the liberal state's cultural coalition: their legal subjectivities have a boundary that is occupied by the state itself (its representative, its "actor"). By hitting that boundary, reaching the limits, the dandy reformulates the masculine code of honor: an "aristocratic" code that places the caballero, the gentleman (the "high" masculinity of Juan and the dandy's own ascetic masculinity[16]) on one side, and Pepe's "low" masculinity (or that of any old Pepe[17]), that of the coward and traitor (after all, Juan paid for his education!) on the other. What we have here is a (Latin American) masculine pyramid of patronage, a means of defining the "true gentleman."

So the dandy's fiction is, in short, both the representation of gender codes in the legal, economic marriage contract of the liberal state, and a fable of private, "aristocratic," masculine (sexual) identity, as opposed to the national, public identity of the patricians.

Dandies and the Exclusions of the 1880s

Marriage-adultery—the contract and breach of contract that threatens social order, trespasses borders, and implies contamination and pollution[18]—became the central narrative institution of the Argentine novel in the 1880s. Analogous to civil law, this binary marked the abandoning of politics and stressed the precedence of private life, constructing a purely cultural and social universe. It also furnished themes, events, and ways of opening and closing stories. *Pot Pourri*'s tale of matrimony provided a whole series of narrative links that were later seen in other Generation of 1880 texts (*La gran aldea* from 1884, for example): announcing a marriage at the beginning of the story (for Cambaceres, the autobiographical subject is the groom's friend; for López, the nephew); committing adultery by switching costumes or dominoes during carnival celebrations (doubles representing both feminine transgression and liberal theater); and resolving the dilemma by evicting the "intruders." The new dandy subjects in *Pot Pourri* and *La gran aldea*—embodying honor and the aristocratic masculine code—banish different characters not only from the realms of honor and truth, but also from the nation. Acting as the president who names foreign civil servants, Cambaceres's actor-dandy banishes the secretary who broke into Juan's house—and robbed him of his honor, after everything Juan had done for him!—from the country. The womanizing "gentleman" in *La gran aldea* similarly evicts the Jew—in whose cave his friend-protégé may lose his honor—from truth, honor, masculine distinction, and Latin American "aristocratic" culture. He, too, is expelled from the country. With the Jew representing money, a clear distinction is also drawn between material wealth and honor.

These new subjects, founded in tales of matrimony, depict a private, marital space alongside a purely social, cultural, public space that serves as a map, fiction, or specter of the liberal state. They portray contemporary writers at social events: at the Club del Progreso, the Colón, carnival balls, and wedding parties. They criticize modern culture from within for the inauthenticity of its values, its utilitarianism and hypocrisy. And they provide alternatives ("solutions") to the scandals of adultery, sexuality, and money, creating a new fable of (private, gendered) identity for the coalition and the state. An "aristocratic," masculine fable for the liberal Latin American state that evicts those who are licentious or threaten honor—Pepes and Jews—from the nation, from their homes. The Generation of 1880 dandies show a depoliticized, masculine subject who displays exemplary ethics with regards to money, honor, and truth; thus they culturally represent the state and, by extension, its exclusions. The theater of private life, therefore, becomes the only adequate arena in which to act out "domestic" issues that the nation-states sideline.

—*Josefina Ludmer*

NOTES

1. Argentina's so-called "Generation of 1880" was made up of minor writers who were classics within national borders but almost entirely unknown outside them, since peripheral cultures only tend to transcend borders with a quota of two or three "masterpieces" per country, or per century per country. The inverse, of course, is not true: secondary classic writers from dominant cultures are, in general, read and admired in peripheral countries, and being familiar with them is seen as a sign of "high" culture. Borges was one Argentine writer who advocated reading secondary classic writers from dominant cultures.

These 1880 writers, founders of Argentina's "high" culture, were diplomats, deputies, ministers and senators, and they wrote political tracts, memoirs, stories, fragments, travelogues and cultural chronicles. In my book *El cuerpo del delito. Un Manual* (Buenos Aires, Perfil, 1999) I call them "the liberal state's cultural coalition" and analyze their writings as state fictions created by "subjects of the liberal state." This coalition was comprised of a patrician sector, including Miguel Cané and Lucio Vicente López; dandies like Eugenio Cambaceres and Lucio V. Mansilla; and a scientific sector, including Manuel Podestá and other medical writers like José María Ramos Mejía.

2. Cambaceres wrote four novels: *Pot pourri* (1882), *Música sentimental* (1884), *Sin rumbo* (1885) and *En la sangre* (1887). He used two narrative stances as vehicles for the protagonists in these books, both linked to theater performance: the dandy in the first two and the scientific naturalist in the last two. The dandy's theater or balcony, where the "self" is enormous and absolute, and the scientist's laboratory, which has no "self." In both cases, the subjects' gazes are distanced, one "aesthetic" the other "scientific"; the difference lies in what he sees: the dandy looks only at what is around him, at members of the high life, and the scientist looks down on those below.

3. Paul Groussac referred to that "lie that was concocted in far-off lands" and then immediately attacked the writer: "having pretended to be a novelist with the publication of scandalous anecdotes, told, as if sitting around the club, in an *aristocratic-creole dialect*, he was naive enough to want to carry on—with the success he imagined—in this literary vein, as artificial as his old-world nobility." ("Trois pionniers du progrès," *Le Courrier de la Plata*, December 16, 1917, quoted in Claude Cymerman, 53).

I have taken Cambaceres' biographical information from works by Claude Cymerman ("Para un mejor conocimiento de Eugenio Cambacérès," *Cuadernos del idioma*. Buenos Aires, year 3, no. 11, 1969: 62) and Rodolfo A. Borello ("Para la biografía de Eugenio Cambacérès," in *Revista de Educación*, La Plata, Semester A, 1960).

4. Taken from "Separación de la Iglesia y del Estado. Discurso del Sr. Dr. D. Eugenio Cambacérès. En la sesión de la Convención de la Provincia para la reforma de su Constitución del 18 de julio de 1871" (in *Revista del Río de la Plata*, no. 2, 1871: 275–289).

In a plea for total religious freedom, free from favoritism, Cambaceres said:

That political miscarriage known as state religion must not be legitimized in the eyes of the Republic!

What is the state? indeed, Mr. President:—in its political sense, the state is the assembly of public powers; and since those powers are constituted by delegates, by the leaders of the people, the state is no more than the expression, the manifestation, as it were, of the people themselves.— Starting from this point and given that people profess, as they do, different religious beliefs, what right does the Legislator have to declare an official religion? How can the state be legally justified in saying, I am Catholic,

Protestant, Jewish or Mohammedan? How can it then, in turn, represent the Catholics, Protestants, Jews and Mohammedans?—Clearly, sir, such a declaration presents the most tangible of contradictions, and with flawed foundations, the consequences will also be flawed.

If this is not so, then justify supporting the Catholic faith, paying their ministers, building and repairing their temples, etc., with the people's money.—Prove that it is fair and just to tell a Protestant, for example, who is as much a citizen as a Catholic: you have the power to be Protestant, if you wish, but at the same time *you must pay taxes and all sorts of contributions that will subsidize a religion that is not yours*; so, purchase your right to be Protestant by paying the Catholic tab.—No, Mr. President, the very articulation of such a doctrine, consecrated in the same law that grants each citizen the right to freedom of worship, is itself the most eloquent refutation of it that one could provide.

And he concluded:

Based on these considerations and adhering to a deep conviction, I propose to the Honorable Convention an amendment to the article under discussion, adding the following words, or words to this effect: "the state neither has nor subsidizes any religion."

According to Cymerman this proposal "made him an enemy of the entire Catholic party, led by Estrada and Goyena," to such a degree that *La Unión* newspaper, their press organ, requested on November 1, 1885, that *Sin rumbo* be banned and its author be fined. And Cymerman quotes from the Catholic *La Unión* (p. 1, col. 6): "The Mayor . . . has taken no measures designed to block the sale of don Eugenio Cambaceres's new book, *Sin rumbo*, regardless of the fact that it is a highly immoral publication. . . ." The paper went on to demand that the author be fined and that "the copies currently on sale in all the Capital's bookstores" (p. 48) be removed from the shelves.

When the "Catholic party" demanded the prohibition and confiscation of *Sin rumbo* (and when Cambaceres relinquished his satirical tone and fragmented novels), in 1885, the patrician cultural coalition welcomed him into their literary ranks with open arms.

5. Cymerman (p. 57) notes that a description of Cambaceres's palatial home appeared in *Sud-America* (p. 1, col. 5) on July 15, 1886: the house, which stood just where Calle de Buen Orden, now called Bernardo de Irigoyen, turned into Avenida Montes de Oca, looked

just like a miniature castle sitting atop a hill. . . . Its marble staircase leads into a salon covered in beautiful Gobelin tapestries; a painting here; an invaluable piece of furniture there; a splendid Venetian mirror further on;

armchairs and furnishings that induce the sweet voluptuousness of true languor; yonder a window covered by heavy, luxurious curtains . . . Cambaceres leads a life that is simultaneously active and subdued—he has the sybaritic tastes and nervous habits of an industrial entrepreneur; he is a mixture of wealthy gentleman and poor chap fighting his luck to eke out a fortune. The fortune he is now in search of, clearly, is fame, which he very nearly conquered with his previous books, and which will crescendo marvelously with successive ones.

6. While watching a young Argentinian woman at an élite ball, *Pot Pourri's* dandy says:

His dance partner was a lovely creature some fifteen years of age who possessed all the charming graces and southern spirits of a native-born girl but who was hollow, superficial and ignorant in the manner typical of Argentinian women, whose intelligence is a veritable swamp thanks to the tender and exemplary concerns of the paterfamilias. (p. 21)
Yet draw closer with the aim of passing but one half hour in her amiable company; either you shan't make it ten minutes, pummeled by boredom as if by a club, or you will be obliged to partake in utter triviality: providing merriments or receiving them of her; prattling on about boyfriends, about who says that So-and-so is courting such-and-such a girl and shall ask her hand; discussing who left some other boy high and dry; or, as a last recourse, drawing out the knife and stabbing it repeatedly into the back of whomever's path it should cross.
And as if woman were a weed in the park, something well-nigh indifferent that should hold no sway over the family and, therefore, over society and its improvement, this is how we try to raise her moral standard.
What do we care if in other places—in the United States, for example, which we are proud to ape—often with neither rhyme nor reason, monkey-like, they award her the dignity of worrying about her political rights and allowing her to be a lofty public servant, doctor, lawyer, etc?
It suits us to have her know her place and station, hang it! And that is the way we want to keep it, by god.
Why?
Because. Because routine is a vice that flows through our bloodstreams and because that was the tried and true custom of our Spanish forefathers. You made your bed, now lie in it; let the dance continue, and long live the revolution! (pp. 21–22)

7. Miguel Cané, "La primera de Don Juan en Buenos Aires," in *Prosa ligera*, Buenos Aires, "La cultura argentina," Vaccaro, 1919: 89 (though the text is

from 1897, these are Cané's recollections; Cambaceres was already dead when the piece was written).

In Lucio Vicente López's novel, *La gran aldea* (1884), we read: "A night of classic opera at the Colón draws the cream of Buenos Aires's men and women. Just cast a glance round the salon's semicircle: president, ministers, capitalists, lawyers and celebrities, they're all there." (Buenos Aires, Eudeba, 1960: 142)

8. Eduardo Rinesi (*Ciudades, teatros y balcones. Un ensayo sobre la representación política.* Buenos Aires, Paradiso Ediciones, 1994) analyzes the concept of liberalism as representation (both political and theatrical). His basic thesis is that "the theater metaphor is a purely functional way to think of politics within a certain hugely important Modern philosophical-political tradition: liberalism" (p. 63). Rinesi analyzes the logic of privatization inherent in the metaphor and critiques the representationalist, theatrical paradigm, because there is no truth or reality behind the vision; what one sees is not hiding anything, it is reality (p. 106). So, "to think against the theater-politics analogy is to think in favor of democracy." (p. 65)

9. Martín García Mérou's study, "La novela en el Plata -*Pot pourri-Silbidos de un vago -Música sentimental -Sin rumbo* (study) by Eugenio Cambacérès" appeared in *Sud-América* on December 7, 1885 (p. 1, cols. 2–5). The following year it also appeared in *Libros y autores* by the same author (Buenos Aires, Félix Lajouane Editor, 1886: 71–90) with the title "Las novelas de Cambacérès."

Martín García Mérou says that *Pot Pourri*:

. . . has roused our emotions and literarily charmed us. . . . What originality this profoundly human book displays: so vivid, like an endless string of humorous paradoxes and bizarre reflections! Society, politics and the press file by, life is shown buzzing around us, and it is all reproduced like an unrelenting daguerreotype! . . . The most outstanding quality of Cambacérès's writing is the strength, the vigor of both thought and word! . . . His incisive, cutting, harsh, sharp-tongued paragraphs possess an icy spirit, terrible satire, and an almost dithyrambic hatred.

To conclude, let us mention two overriding characteristics seen in the works that concern us. First, the style. The author of *Whistlings of an Idler* has founded, within our ranks, the contemporary national novel . . . Second, the language. It is true *porteño* [Buenos Aires] *slang*, as a clever, young critic has noted. The most familiar locutions, terms we currently use in conversation, local jargon, like semi-French, semi-indigenous *upper-class argot*, are the bits and pieces that comprise the intrigue of the picturesque, *genuinely national*, expertly handled language of these books. . . . Cambacérès, in short, is an original literary personality, endowed with true talent. He is destined to play an important role in our limited intellectual life and to blaze the future trail of the Argentinian novel. (p. 89, my emphasis)

García Mérou's article was written in 1885, after the publication of Cambaceres's third novel. It is an absolutely fundamental critique in that it openly indicates that the writer has been adopted by the coalition, by the Generation of 1880. *Sud-América* was the coalition's official organ. Founded by Lucio V. López and others (Pellegrini, Gallo, etc.) in 1884 to back J. Celman's candidacy, the paper serialized En la sangre, Cambaceres's final novel, in 1887 after a publicity campaign. According to Claude Cymerman: "Between March and September 1887, *Sud-América* announced the impending publication, repeatedly postponed, of *En la sangre*, thus piquing readers' curiosity." Cambaceres received 5,000 pesos for the rights, which was a considerable sum at the time.

10. Contemporary French drama gave Cambaceres the themes of adultery and money. Lucio V. López, in *Recuerdos de viaje* (1881), the Generation of 1880's first travelogue (Buenos Aires, La Cultura Argentina, 1917), wrote in "La Comedia Francesa" (dated August 19, 1880 in Vichy): The Molière school inspired modern drama. . . . *Adultery* was Alejandro Dumas' muse, and Augier's heroines were *cocottes*." But he criticized the "dramatic literature of our day" because, he said, the theater of Sandeau, Feuillet, Augier and Sardou was a "school of moral decadence. These men who are supposedly going to rebuild society start by demolishing what we already have without rebuilding anything in its place." According to López, Sandeau's *Le gendre de Monsieur Poirier*, very similar to Cambaceres's *En la sangre*, was about a "repugnant scoundrel who marries a delicate woman he does not love just to get at Monsieur Poirier's millions." And he asks: why attack the *bourgeoisie* and not the Jesuits or the tabloids—who fan the flames of 1871—if they want social and political battles? (pp. 184–86).

11. The only complete study of the language of *Pot Pourri* is Marta Cisneros's *Según decimos en criollo . . . (Un "pot pourri" de Eugenio Cambaceres)*. Río Cuarto (Argentina) Fundación Universidad Nacional de Río Cuarto, 2000. She surveys all of *Pot Pourri*'s speech-related phrases: as it were, as they say, as they now insist on calling it, as the saying goes, as the Italians say, as the rude women say, as tenors say, as old women say, etc. Cisneros highlights the text's self-referentiality (and linguistic self-awareness), the number of discourses present—journalistic, political, epistolary, poetic, euphemistic, rural—and the way they coexist. She makes a study of *Pot Pourri*'s informal and "vulgar" language (sayings, proverbs, idioms, clauses, terms, vocabulary, barbarisms, foreign words, syntactic features) and a survey of textual expressions (pp. 107–152). Her hypothesis is that the book's tone is delineated by speech and not by the literary tradition of the written word (pp. 34–37), and that this constitutes another "literary language." Cisneros also establishes Cambaceres's literary modernity, his

avant-garde character in Argentinian literature (maintaining that he was a pre-cursor to Julio Cortázar, Leopoldo Marechal, Arturo Cancela, and Juan Filloy). Finally, she comments on the relationship between *Pot Pourri*—a re-working— and *The Cuckold* by Charles Paul de Kock, a "second-rate" French *feuilleton* writer.

I would add that *Pot Pourri* critics do not mention Voltaire's *Pot Pourri* (1765), one of his *Contes* written in the form of a pamphlet, which compares Christianity to a puppet-making factory. The central character, Polichinelle, goes on tour with a troup of puppeteers, putting on farces in country towns. See Voltaire, *Romans et contes*. Paris, Garnier, 1960: 408–423.

12. Attacked: Cymerman repeats what the limited number of earlier critics and biographers had said (Carlos A. Leumann, E.M.S. Danero, Alberto Oscar Blasi): that Cambaceres was called a "Mason, a heathen and an atheist." And he adds that he was surrounded by "scandalous unconformity" and a bad rep-utation in the "bourgeois, prudish mood of the times."

Parodied: critics mention the author Suárez Orozco, who using the pseu-donym "Rascame-Bec" published *Música celestial* (193 pages, París, José Jola, 1885). See Cymerman, *op. cit.*, 51.

13. I shan't marry, says the dandy:

"That is a cross I could not bear!

"To bring a strange being into my home, some Joan of Arc to share my things, my table, my bath and, far more serious, my bed, where . . . armed with her legitimate title . . . she would attempt to sleep every night and every day without my having recourse to kick her out when it struck my fancy were I not in the mood for her company." (p. 71)

14. The "actor" presents himself as a classic or historical dandy. So, is his translation, his Argentinization, a parody? Does importing that European cul-tural myth to Latin America change its function? Does it attack the model, or mix in local traits that corrode it from within? Perhaps the difference lies in the lack of a true aristocracy in Latin America, the presence of which is what allows the European version to make sense.

Gloria Ortiz (*The Dandy and the Señorito. Eros and Social Class in the Nineteenth-Century Novel*. New York & London, Garland Publishing, Inc., 1991) separates the historical dandy ("the quintessential dandy") who she says was not a seductor, from the Spanish and Latin American señorito who, with rare exception, is. In the señorito's case, Ortiz says, the dandy's legacy was confined to clothing, appearance and a leisurely lifestyle. Pampered and narcis-sistic, he is an active seductor who conquers women to feed his self-esteem. She adds that the señorito tends to be young; he has an aversion to work; he sometimes has a job requiring minimal effort, such as some political appointment or other acquired through connections; he places huge importance on clothes and relies on them to give an appearance of economic well-being and social distinction that are sometimes fading or nonexistent. Being a señorito seems to be more of a mental state that implies falsifying one's worth, Ortiz concludes.

Nineteenth-century dandyism is above all *an intellectual stance* which is presented as the "destiny of the modern artist" says Hans Hinterhäuser (*Fin de siècle. Gestalten und Mythe.* Fink: München, 1977. *Fin de siglo. Figuras y mitos.* Trans. by María Teresa Martínez. Barcelona, Taurus, 1980).

In essays by Balzac ("Traité de la vie élégante," 1830), Barbey d'Aurevilly (*Du dandysme et de George Brummell*, 1844), and Baudelaire (*Un peintre de la vie moderne*, 1859) the dandy is seen as a person who embodies social protest and rebels against hypocrisy and conformity, against the masses hostile to art and the spirit. Though these three versions of the French dandy differ we can synthesize their traits into a "philosophy of dandyism" as determined by them and as set out in the classic anthology by Emilien Carassus, *Le mythe du dandy* (Paris, Armand Colin, 1971), which contains an introduction and the most important works by and about dandies—Balzac, Barbey d'Aurevilly, Théophile Gautier, Byron, Baudelaire, Huysmans, Albert Camus, Jean-Paul Sartre and Roland Barthes, amongst others.

Jessica R. Feldman (*Gender on the Divide. The Dandy in Modernist Literature.* Ithaca and London, Cornell University Press, 1993) says: "Dandyism exists in the field of force between two opposing, irreconcilable notions about gender. First, the (male) dandy defines himself by attacking women. Second, so crucial are female characteristics to the dandy's self-creation that he defines himself by embracing women, appropriating their characteristics" (p. 6). Feldman's central point is that in a culture that places genders in binary opposition, dandies "poise precisely upon, or rather within, this divide: the violence of such self-placement generates the energy of dandyism as a cultural form" (p. 7).

Feldman examines European dandies in the works of Gautier, Barbey d'Aurevilly, Baudelaire, and North American dandies in the works of Willa Cather, Wallace Stevens and Nabokov, and shows that these writers simultaneously reject and pursue women because they take on a self-dividing project: "living within dominant cultural forms while imagining new forms taking shape in some unspecifiable beyond" (p. 7). The cultural shift might begin, Feldman says, with these individuals who see things in a "new (and often illogical or crazy-seeming) way" (p. 7).

"In fact, the literature of dandyism challenges the very concept of two separate genders. Its male heroes . . . relocate dandyism within the feminine realm in order to move beyond the male and the female, beyond gender dichotomy itself." This requires us to understand "the dandy as neither wholly male nor wholly female, but as the figure who blurs these distinctions, irrevocably" (p. 11).

15. Walter Benn Michaels (*The Gold Standard and the Logic of Naturalism. American Literature at the Turn of the Century.* Berkeley, University of California Press, 1987) establishes a series of relationships between the self as property and the feminine body "as the utopian body of the market economy, imagined as a scene of circulation" (p. 13). In late nineteenth-century, North American naturalism (for example, in Frank Norris's "corporate fiction" *The Octopus*—and the octopus that closes Julián Martel's Argentinian novel *La Bolsa* (1890)—and Theodore Dreiser's *The Financier*) Michaels establishes a series of relationships between capitalism, a specific system of representation—the photo or daguerreotype—and woman (or slave) treated like property. Female sexuality becomes the biological equivalent of capitalism and the marriage contract, what Michaels calls "the phenomenology of the contract," becomes a strategy to contain (and repress) her disorder, because desire can subvert social order and is a threat to realist fiction (p. 125 and following).

16. James Eli Adams (*Dandies and Desert Saints. Styles of Victorian Masculinity.* Ithaca and London, Cornell University Press, 1995) refers to Carlyle's hero in *Sartor Resartus* and says that ". . . the persistence of the *dandy as a shadow of both prophet and capitalist* reflects a paradox within the regime of what Weber called inner-worldly asceticism." The dandy, "like the desert eremite, . . . is constantly on display even in the midst of solitude. . . . Ascetic discipline dictates the presence of an audience. . . . [so] from this point of view dandyism is an exemplary asceticism. In Baudelaire's canny description it is 'a kind of religion' governed by discipline 'strict as any monastic rule,' but one that openly acknowledges a public gaze. . . . And it is for this reason that the dandy is such a tenacious and central presence in Carlyle's writings—as in so many Victorian discourses of *middle-class* masculine self-fashioning" (p. 35, my emphasis).

These struggles for masculine authority have a still more mundane and pervasive analogue in the incessant Victorian preoccupation with *defining a true gentleman* . . . [and] *distinguishing between sincerity and performance*. If the status of gentleman is not secured by inherited distinctions of family and rank, but is realized instead through behavior, how does one distinguish the "true" gentleman from the aspirant who is merely "acting" the part? This was less of a challenge for the Augustan age, not only because of more circumscribed social mobility, but also because the gentleman's role accommodated *a degree of theatricality*," says James Eli Adams (p. 53, my emphasis).

17. The narrator's adolescent visit to the Pepes' household clearly shows the difference in status implied by names. This is the only time that "Pepe" is pluralized, with Doña Pepa, Don Pepe and their daughters. Pepe, of course, is also the man held in confidence by Juan, the dandy's friend and protégé, who

broke into Juan's house to get to his wife. When the dandy, as a teen, goes to "the Pepes'," in a Chaplinesque foray, the situation degenerates into bodies, smells and ridicule. At the Pepes' he sees: "Kidskin boots with Louis XV heels, low-cut necklines, teeny little gloves for great big hands and every other imaginable high-life flourish of the times: it was a *tour de force* of finery unlike anything seen nowadays." Especially noteworthy is the Pepes' family library, where the young dandy tries to pull down a copy of *Don Quijote* in order to quote from it and ends up demolishing the entire "library": it was nothing but a "cheap decoy."

18. Tony Tanner (*Adultery in the Novel. Contract and Transgression.* Baltimore and London, The Johns Hopkins University Press, 1979) says that although eighteenth- and nineteenth-century novels tended toward marriage and genealogical continuity, their narrative force was derived from an energy that threatened to break the family stability seen as forming the basis of society. It is therefore paradoxical that a text could subvert what it seems to celebrate, because adultery, the act of transgression that threatens the family, is "an attempt to establish *an extracontractual contract, or indeed an anticontract, that threatens precisely those continuations, distinctions and securities*" (p. 6, my emphasis). What is worth exploring, Tanner says, are the relationships between a specific type of sexual act, type of society, and type of narration (pp. 3–6). Adultery as a phenomenon has appeared in literature since the start, as in Homer, and Tanner maintains that "the unstable triangularity of adultery, rather than the static symmetry of marriage, is the generative form of Western literature" (p. 11). It is the dominant trait in the *chivalrous* novel and in the works of Shakespeare, but it *"takes on a very special importance in the late-eighteenth- and nineteenth-century novel"* (p. 12, my emphasis). Many of the nineteenth-century novels that have been canonized (Rousseau's *La nouvelle Héloïse*, Flaubert's *Madame Bovary*, Tolstoy's *The Kreutzer Sonata*, and *Anna Karenina*) have adultery as their central theme. In these novels, marriage is the "all-subsuming, all-organizing contract, . . . the structure that maintains the Structure." By confronting adultery and marital problems, Tanner says, the novel must confront not only the provisional character of law and social structures, but also that of its own procedures and affirmations. Because when marriage is seen as man's invention, and the central contract upon which others depend in some way, adultery becomes not an incidental deviation from the social system, but a frontal assault on it. Divorce is the way society confronts adultery, but it is worth noting that in none of these novels is there ever a divorce, "nor is it felt to offer any *radical* solutions to the problems that have arisen," Tanner writes (pp. 14–18).

BIBLIOGRAPHY

Blasi, Alberto Oscar. *Los Fundadores: Cambacérès, Martel, Sicardi.* Buenos Aires, Ediciones Culturales Argentinas, 1962.

Borello, Rodolfo A. *Habla y literatura en la Argentina (Sarmiento, Hernández, Mansilla, Cambaceres, Fray Mocho, Borges, Marechal, Cortázar).* Tucumán (Argentina), Facultad de Filosofía y Letras de la Universidad de Tucumán, 1975.

———— "Para la biografía de Eugenio Cambacérès," in *Revista de Educación,* La Plata, Semester A, 1960.

Cané, Miguel. "La primera de Don Juan en Buenos Aires," in *Prosa ligera,* Buenos Aires, "La cultura argentina," Vaccaro, 1919: 89.

Cisneros, Marta. *"Según decimos en criollo . . ." (Un "pot pourri" de Eugenio Cambaceres).* Río Cuarto (Argentina), Editorial de la Fundación Universidad Nacional de Río Cuarto, 2000.

———— "Cuestiones de re-lectura: *Pot pourri* de Eugenio Cambaceres." *Borradores,* year 1, no. 1, Departamento de Lengua y Literatura, Universidad Nacional de Río Cuarto, 1991.

———— "Del texto a la problemática literaria," Actas IV Congreso Nacional de Literatura Argentina, Universidad Nacional de Mendoza, 1986.

Cymerman, Claude. "Para un mejor conocimiento de Eugenio Cambacérès." *Cuadernos del idioma.* Buenos Aires, year 3, no. 11, 1969: 62).

García Mérou, Martín. "La novela en el Plata—*Pot pourri-Silbidos de un vago -Música sentimental -Sin rumbo* (estudio) por Eugenio Cambacérès" appeared in *Sud-América* December 7, 1885 (p. 1, cols. 2–5). It also appeared the following year in *Libros y autores* by the same author (Buenos Aires, Félix Lajouane Editor, 1886: 71–90) with the title "Las novelas de Cambacérès."

Jitrik, Noé. *El 80 y su mundo. Presentación de una época.* Buenos Aires, Jorge Alvarez, 1968.

———— *Ensayos y estudios de literatura argentina.* Buenos Aires, Galerna, 1970.

Laera, Alejandra. "Sin olor a pueblo: la polémica sobre el naturalismo en la literatura argentina," *Revista Iberoamericana,* University of Pittsburgh, vol. LXVI, no. 190, Jan–Mar 2000: 139–46.

———— "Familias en la pampa (la novela de Cambaceres sale de la ciudad)," in *Las maravillas de lo real,* Instituto de Literatura Hispanoamericana— Facultad de Filosofía y Letras, UBA, 2000: 39–47.

Ludmer, Josefina. *El cuerpo del delito. Un Manual.* Buenos Aires, Perfil, 1999: 46–74.

Panesi, Jorge. "Cambaceres, un narrador chismoso," in *Críticas*. Buenos Aires, Norma, 2000: 275–85.

Viñas, David. "El escritor *gentleman*"; "Infancia, rincones y mirada"; "De la sacralidad a la defensa: Cané," in *Literatura argentina y realidad política. De Sarmiento a Cortázar.* Buenos Aires, Siglo Veinte, 1971.

——— *Literatura argentina y política. De los jacobinos porteños a la bohemia anarquista.* Buenos Aires, Sudamericana, 1995.

Acknowledgments

To Alejandra Laera, who did the research for and writing of the historical notes for this edition of *Pot Pourri*.

To Susana Anaine (assistant director), Armando V. Minguzzi (researcher) and Santiago Kalinowski, Federico Plager, Mercedes Paz and Pedro Rodríguez Rodríguez, assistants in the Department of Philological Investigations at the Argentinian Academy of Letters. They kindly helped solve some of the text's many tricky linguistic issues.

POT POURRI:

Whistlings of an Idler

A Few Words from the Author

When some poor devil strolling peacefully down the path of life with a song on his lips finds that his chosen tune rankles certain diseased ears; when he senses himself suddenly set upon by an angry mob who advance on him, catch up to him, hound him, struggle to snatch his billfold and rob him of name, fame, and reputation—as those banknotes he has earned with his sweat are otherwise known—what is he to do?

In the attempt to avoid a savage beating, he hides quickly—albeit against a corner of the wall used by the indecent public as a urinal—he wields a cane righteously, or if they catch him unawares, lacking an alternative form of refuge, he takes up his umbrella in the manner of a sword and crouches behind it to fend off the fists of the big boys and the fingernails of the little ones who—like puppies at a dogfight—try to get a leg up and join in the action as well.

Such is the case at hand.

One morning I awoke feeling adventurous and, fed up to the gills with the tedious routine of my life (rise at noon, luncheon at one, wander aimlessly along Calle Florida, eat wherever I chanced to be at the appointed time, play a hand of bezique at the Club,* set off for the

*Founded in May 1852, the Club del Progreso, which Cambaceres presided over as vice-president in the 1870s, was the cardinal social center of its time. The focal point

theater, etc.), I thought I might well fancy a change in direction, inventing something new—the first thing that popped into my head—so long as it took my mind off this beastly ennui, whereupon I was struck by an idea as absurd as any: that I should contribute to the enrichment of the nation's literature.

To contribute to the enrichment of the nation's literature, I told myself, one need only be in possession of pen, ink, and paper, and not know how to write Spanish; I discretely meet all of these prerequisites, and so there is no reason why I should not contribute to the enrichment of the nation's literature.

And in my spare moments—in between yawning wide as an ocean and smoking a packet of Caporal—I managed to fabricate the concatenation of nonsense with which you are already familiar and which has raised such a storm, such an outcry, such a furore against a certain third-rate specimen of humanity: the author.

Frankly, it wasn't worth it: *le jeu n'en valait pas la chandelle.*

But since they fell upon me with no warning, and since, when they fall upon you, you are free to raise a stink, as we natives say, then I ask you to grant me a few words, not of correction but of explanation.

I have no desire to justify myself as I feel I have committed no crime.

I simply wish to set the record straight.

The characters in chapter II are fictitious.

Nothing could have been further from my aim than trying to portray the diction of Mr. and Mrs. So-and-so, real flesh and blood human beings.

Mine are characters who exist, or could exist, as easily in Buenos Aires as in France, in Cochinchina, or in hell, and whom I have allowed myself to present to you as part of the show, to bring out on stage stark naked because—like the followers of the realist school—I think the mere display of those blemishes now corrupting the social organism is the most potent antidote that can be employed against them.

Do I say the same about my models at the Club del Progreso?

No; here I have followed the example set by industrialists in daguerreotype and photography; I have copied from the original, as is my right.

---

for the cadre of élite Buenos Aires men, it reached its greatest period of splendor in the 1880s. In addition to all-male social gatherings and political meetings, the Club also held elegant parties and carnival balls. There are other references to the Club in chapters VII, XIII, and XVIII, and the action in chapter XIV takes place there.

Ever since Aristophanes found no one who wanted to play the role of Socrates he'd brought to the boards, without so much as changing his name, and so played the role himself; ever since Shakespeare uncloaked his sybaritic Falstaff in broad daylight and served him up to the audience just as he was; ever since Racine hung Louis XIV in Haman's mind, and Molière helped Monsieur de Montespan patiently endure his sad fate as a cuckold, affirming in *Amphitryon* that a *partage* with Jupiter had no shame; since Balzac said that traipsing on rooftops was for madmen, and Gautier turned George Sand into a Camille Maupin; and more recently, since Zola used Excellency Rougon to tell a few home truths about his Excellency Rouher, what have the masters of the trade done but flay their fellow men, since time immemorial? Since when has anyone who knows which way the north winds blow ever thought to paint Thalia and her sisters, cheeky creatures if ever there were, as prim and proper, prudish ladies?

Let us be frank, then, and do away with the exaggerated, hypocritical, ridiculous fuss, since what makes them cry *scandale*, shouting out to the heavens, are naught but the building blocks, the ABCs of art the world over, and especially here where—over and over again—any old fool can take on another man just because it strikes his fancy, fight him tooth and nail and thrash him in the public eye.

I proceed.

As I was saying, I had the material before me, but it being carnival time, when everything is transfigured and becomes distorted, my lenses were probably also distorted, leading to slightly altered negatives with a dash too much shade.

Like those crystal balls one puts in the garden: a figure of beauty gazes in, a wretch is cast back.

A qui la faute?

No one is to blame: not the creator, nor the beauty, nor the crystal ball.

*Vis interna verum.**

Besides, what more could be expected at a time when everything is topsy-turvy, when women turn into men, old men into boys, madmen into sane ones, and night into day?

It's obvious; the whole business was bound to come out twisted.

Result: some of my subjects, they say, rail against me.

Believing I might perchance be wrong after all and that maybe my

*The truth lies within.

3

hand had indeed slipped (that's how accidents happen!) I returned to examine and then reexamine the pages, not as the one who had written them or who sees himself reflected within them, but as one who reads them from outside, dispassionately and without preconceived notions.

So then, may the seven plagues cripple me if I found therein the remotest hint, even, of an attack on private dignity.

Either I am an absolute imbecile, or the others are absolutely fatuous.

Their vanity and pride may have taken a blow; their reputations, never.

But, decidedly, I must be in the doghouse, because if the right hand doesn't get you, the left hand will: when it's not one, it's many, and *seul contre* many, *que voulez-vous* me to do?

As I have also learned, one part—in particular the female part—of the respectable public has discovered in the pages of my book the most flagrant of offenses, the most obscene of insults, flung brutally in the face of society.

After each sentence, each word, each comma, and even in the blank margins, instead of the carefree whistlings of a *flâneur*, they have heard, *horresco referens!*, the whizzing of poisoned darts that I, perverse bastard son, have plunged with parricidal hands into the bowels of our common mother.

Scrumptious, my word of honor, scrumptious!

He who wrote this, said one who was indubitably wheezing over his wound, can be none other than a degenerate who believes in neither divinity nor humanity, a skeptic, an unbeliever without God or law or conscience, a pervert whose audacity leads him to the cynical act of depicting himself.

He who wrote this, brayed the flock of chime-along sheep, can be none other than a degenerate who believes in neither divinity nor humanity, a skeptic, an unbeliever without God or law or conscience, a pervert whose audacity leads him to the cynical act of depicting himself.

Excusez moi.

That is very kind of you, and I am beholden, but it is also a falsehood and I need not light a candle to find the proof.

First point: no one was within his rights to make assumptions that the author of an anonymous book, and a *vraiment* modest individual *par le fait*, would be petulant enough to pretend to be the life of the party, shouting out at the top of his voice: Yoo-hoo, over here, here I am! It's me, Rousseau—just like that—and these are my confessions!

No one had such a right, I repeat, if only because I granted it to no one; but as these gentlemen pretend otherwise, let us give them the pleasure and begin to assume.

We shall suppose, then, that the idler in question *c'est moi* and not one of many others who wear the same shoes and inhabit the same world; and let's suppose that he who writes eavesdrops on their affairs, makes them his by right of conquest, renders them in print, and enters them into circulation because that is his assignment or his profit, or for no better reason than that it simply takes his fancy.

Now let the facts speak for themselves.

He who seethes—to the extent of feeling his blood boil as it courses through his veins—because he sees wickedness, and vents, not against his mother, his wife, his sister, his friend, nor any relation, but against one linked to him only through the vile and wretched bond of humanity;

He who kneels down at the altar of friendship with the saintly devotion inspired only by faith;

He who beneath an iron glove conceals an open hand and behind an armor chest plate reveals a heart that beats to the unrelenting call of duty;

He who lives out the waning days of his life without the poisoned breath of the world having rotted him from within, no matter how scarred his skin be;

He who feels, thinks, and acts thus, he, this very man, is the one they call abject and depraved?

Please! Stop trying my patience and don't talk rubbish, to put it politely.

Here he stands before you.

If you do not believe it, you are cretins; if you pretend you do not believe it, you are wretched.

And in either case, I do not propose to have those men accept my ardent salutations.

But enough of these gratuitous suppositions; I do not care to continue calling myself every name in the book.

I am not the idler, nor did I work alone to sketch the profile of my characters, fill in their contours, and detail their finishing touches.

Hate it as you might, you have all lent a hand, placing the paint within reach of my brush.

Be it the noble and delicate colors, the pure and simple hues seen in Juan and in the nature of the idler himself—prey upon him though you might—or be it the shades of black that served to allow me to paint the bas-relief of social vices and miseries.

The whole score, I repeat, was carried out without identifying individuals. No one has *posé* in my studio, except for certain serious or humoristic tones that I have brought to the picture without distorting the model. The only exception is one blood-red stroke, just one, that ripped the canvas because I tore it as with a pickax, I confess, purposely, willfully, heaping on patriotism and bile.

Of course I knew that it was a hairy affair, that more than one would find himself reflected on stage, that the book would bring me a fair number of enemies, and as for friends, none at all.

But you see, one does not dig trenches or take up a pickax to mine the foundations of an edifice with impunity, even if it threatens to collapse and one works with the Christian intention of preventing— should it suddenly come crashing down—broken arms and legs, of avoiding the owner's becoming churlish, complaining that his chattels are being assaulted and his home violated.

Such are logic and human gratitude.

But, really, I never imagined that they would take it so seriously and would shout themselves hoarse, crying: *à la garde, au voleur, à l'assassin!* before a defenseless fellow, an unhappy player who steps out into the open with his hat in his hand, who does not flee from justice as he is neither thief nor assassin and whose only crime is to have written a farce, to have composed a *pot pourri* in which the truth sings out clearly.

I conclude.

I tried to induce laughter and instead induced rage.

Total fiasco; that was not the aim.

Like all mocked maestros, I want to smash my instrument against the floor . . . and yet . . . the love of the art . . . *

Will I offend again?

Who can say?

I live off my riches and have no obligations.

I cast my eyes about to kill time and I write.

---

*This is a reference to José Hernández's hugely popular epic poem *Martín Fierro*, in which the gaucho poet finally smashes his guitar against the ground so as not to be "tempted" to continue his song.

Therefore:

He who hopes to find serious studies, the fruits of assiduous labor, within the pages of this book must, to be sure, slam it shut immediately.

I cannot nor do I wish to undertake anything serious.

The most trifling of intellectual endeavors exhausts me.

I live for the sake of living, or better yet: I germinate.

Buried amongst my many defects, nonetheless, I do hold some assets.

I possess, for example, undeniable stores of honesty: that is why I promise nothing, for I have nothing to give.

You know, then, what to expect of me.

Many are the times I have asked myself: What in heaven's name might I be good for? What is my calling? In which of the many branches of human activity am I destined to make my name?

In the theater are the words that have fatefully pressed themselves to my lips: I have turned myself over time and again, examined myself with care, studied my size, my guise, my contours, the manifold nuances of my color and my intrinsic value; in short, I have looked as one does at a piece of wood, covered with painted paper and strewn *pêle-mêle* across the table, which one finally places in the only position possible in order to complete the landscapes and paintings in so-called games of patience.

Yes, sir; I was born to act.

Ever since childhood, I have felt strongly drawn toward the stage. Never once did it occur to me to follow the poor example set by the ragamuffins of my time playing truant from school, whether alone or en masse.

My truancies were of another class entirely.

For my part, I would purchase the favors of the illustrious descendent of Pelayo, our concierge, by way of sacrificing the sum of one peso in full, current coinage, given to me by my mother on Sundays and holidays as a treat; and when the dear woman thought me to be slumbering peacefully like a babe in my bed, I'd already scampered from betwixt the sheets, made myself scarce, and scurried down the street. In two shakes of a lamb's tail, I'd covered the distance separating me from the Teatro de la Victoria, into which I would slip, concealed between the legs of a party of theatergoers to escape the vigilance of the ushers.

Through the light of the greasy kerosene lamps that supposedly illuminated the stage, the whole scene struck me as sublime.

I found that I possessed, in my unconscious childish yearning, an admiration that bordered on worship for the dramatic talents of the mulatto Quijano and the musical gifts of Señora Merea.

Mind you, this was not hard to do!

My penchant for the theater became more and more pronounced.

As an adolescent, I was on various occasions at the point of casting off the yokes of paternal authority, damning both family and social proprieties and striking out on my own, beginning to make headway in *my career* across God's green earth.

Imagine, if you will, a clear, subtle, crafty intelligence, skillful in the art of assimilating others' talents, yet barren in its own production, simply reflecting external light: a plagiaristic intelligence, in short.

An *avenant* physique, elevated stature, social graces both correct and of distinction, vivacious expression, loose and limber physiognomy, capable of uncanny performances and interpretations of any manner of outpourings of the soul.

Add to these manifold elements of my composition, homogeneous and fashioned expressly for each other, a genuine calling—nourished by the most pronounced inclination for the bohemian lifestyle and the pleasures on which it is based—and you have before you the makings of an actor through and through.

Yours truly.

Unfortunately, the high social standing of my family coupled with the scorn the world heaps on a thespian—an absurd remnant of the times in which the mask of the buffoon degraded the practice of this noble art—assaulted my natural impulses, whereupon I was forced to renounce my most cherished predilection.

My most excellent mother was at pains to make a lawyer of me.

Loving her to the point of delirium, I couldn't find within myself the courage to oppose her will, which I held sacred, so I studied law.

But do let's be perfectly clear.

More than a life of study, mine was one dedicated to the pursuit of pleasure and enjoyment.

Pampered by my parents, supplied with endless funds and the most absolute of free wills, I regularly frequented salons, theaters, and promenades, while the Pandects of Rome, the Codes of Alphonse the Wise, and Canon Law all lay in pitiful, dust-covered oblivion.

And so it was for ten months.

Pride, which would have been a quality of mine had it not degenerated into such vanity as to become an unattractive defect, then began to put a stop to this heretofore uninterrupted series of earthly pleasures. The shame of possible reprobation forced me to react in such a way that I spent, in the course of the following two months, eight or even ten hours each day studying, which allowed me not only to sit my final examinations, but to acquit myself of them triumphantly.

But, alas! Easy come, easy go. Two months prior to the bar, I had known nothing, and two months later . . . ditto.

The science I had acquired in a trice to thrust me along life's path, evaporated in my head as quickly as spirals of steam vaporize once they've acted upon the red-hot valves of an engine.

Armed with this liability of knowledge, then, I was admitted to the bar, opened a *bureau*, and offered my professional services to the respectable public; not, I hasten to repeat, out of any sort of pecuniary necessity, as I have felt none at any point in my lifetime, but rather as the inescapable and logical by-product of my newly gained professional qualification.

I felt like the *aficionado* of Offenbach and Lecocq operettas who, though prone to falling asleep upright while listening to Beethoven's Ninth or a Haydn quartet, feels himself nonetheless obliged to attend a classical concert because he's bought an orchestra box for the season.

Meanwhile, arriving on a scene that was decidedly not mine, utterly *dépaysé*, the very force at play cast me out once again.

My spirit, like a bird in need of freedom and space in order to live, was asphyxiating while imprisoned in the stifling, depraved atmosphere inhabited by judges, lawyers, court clerks, solicitors, and other sundry courtiers.

The mere appearance of a case file compelled me to avert my gaze with indescribable distaste; handling one became a task quite beyond my capabilities, and an insurmountable feeling of disgust took hold of me at the slightest hint of a visit from a client or, worse still, a *cliente*— the female litigant, an irksome creature if ever there was—whose frightfully tedious banter I was ill-equipped to endure without yawning continually and drooping my eyelids over bloodshot, sorrowful eyes in an expression of cretinism befitting the poor wretch who has truly plumbed the depths of ennui.

On the verge of going down, a supreme act of self-preservation might just save me.

One winter morn, cold and gray as the funk prevailing over me, I arose resolved to take extreme measures in order to have done with my afflictions. I locked the doors to my office and posted upon them the following sign: Closed due to encroaching idiocy. Then I proceeded, without further ado, to distribute my clientele amongst fellow practitioners of law more destitute and famished than myself, as one would the meat of a tame ox amongst the cages of wild animals and birds of prey in a zoo.

All in the name of quashing grievances and setting wrongs to right for the greater glory of God and the greater good of humanity.

Myself once more, with no duties to enslave me, no obligations to fulfill, master of my own time, I dedicated myself fully to the easy life, of whose frivolous pleasures I partook many a time and oft.

An easily explained change in attitude, however, must have overcome me.

Feeling emptiness all around me, ashamed at the barrenness of my existence, I searched out more fertile ground where I might put my means to use in order to bring my share of sweat and labor to bear.

Once there was a time when the title of doctor acted as a safe-conduct, a sort of *passe-partout* that turned its bearer, whether he were called Dr. Innocent or Dr. Gullible, into the perfect man, indispensable to fill the panoply of life's noble callings.

Perhaps you were looking for a man in the field of politics, science, the arts?

You most certainly and irrevocably found him preceded by the fourth and eighteenth letters of the alphabet.

The members of parliament were doctors, the government was made up of doctors, as were literary and scientific academies, political and social clubs; and if, perchance, a commission were to be appointed without their inclusion, were its sole aim merely to double the land's yield, or to improve the bovine, equine, or ovine breeds, the indignant public would protest, exclaiming:

"Who on earth dares appoint a commission comprised of a bunch of animals: Imagine! Not one doctor in the lot!"

As if to interpret a text, to indict one on charges of contempt of court, to amputate a leg or administer an emetic were to seal one's fate as omniscient, were the panacea without which society would be irrevocably condemned to downfall and ruination.

Meanwhile, the real, solidly cultivated talents, the practical and sensible spirits who could have been of tremendous help in the administration of public affairs, stagnated in a cloud of oblivion.

In order to become something in this blessed land, one positively had to possess the license of a mischief maker or a quack.

It was thence that we saw the halls of our faculties of law and medicine brim with young people who might otherwise have applied their aptitudes to a more serviceable branch of human knowledge, to the benefit of themselves and others.

The university in particular, a new gate of hell, vomited forth this veritable social plague of begowned devils by the hundreds, continuing to pummel us with their production at a rate inversely proportionate to market needs; it would have been entirely plausible to discover that even the most humble post of deputy mayor in the most humble of border towns was filled by a doctor.

Common sense, providentially, has undergone a sea change and we are today able to exclaim along with Cervantes, freshly applying his witty observation to the case:

"Titles are like rags: good for naught."

And so it was that, as a doctor, I found all doors open, and a long, smooth road stretched out before me.

The vast field of public life struck my fancy, whereupon I flung myself headlong into its thoroughfares with fervent spirit, inspired by the most sincere and worthy aims.

I held a variety of public posts without begging any of them off cronies, without political affiliation, that is, without ever tacitly or expressly entering into any agreement that would curtail my personal freedom, sacrifice my convictions, or, as a matter of political consequence, make me a blind instrument of more or less monstrous iniquities.

My very independence led me to believe for a time that it was my calling to pitch in—in the limited sphere of my importance—by working for the well-being and happiness of my fellow man.

But, alas! When in a moment of weakness, on touching upon one of those burning issues, in the midst of one of the most arduous struggles ever recorded in the annals of our political woe—alarmed at the abject depravity of the parties—I ventured to erect defenses against the torrent that threatened to overflow and sweep away the painstaking work brought to bear by patriotism and by the times; when—having a premonition of the tremendous disturbance about to rock the very foundations of the social edifice—I tried to close off access to the Temple of Law, to save it from the corruption beating at its doors, I was rewarded by utter condemnation from all sides.

Guelphs and Ghibellines alike rained their formidable wrath upon me! The sovereign people who had listened to me embarked on the most frightful booing and hissing ever to ring out in any theater of the world!

And yet, God knows that the blessedness of my country was my only aim, my conscience the only means of attaining it!

One side, in its sublime love for the fatherland, did not hesitate to resort to the most vile and despicable of stratagems, engaging in fraud, violence, and bribery and thereby contending with the adversaries for the very proclamation made against them: "bankrupt fraudsters, enslaved to foreigners, ever wheedling the exchequer, leeches on the people's bloodstream."

The other, in its fervent patriotism, dared to brandish the selfsame weapons in the cold light of day, for the mere chance to denigrate the enemy with these words: "villainous swine, recruited from the dregs of society!"

Both boasted of their blessed unselfishness in the name of greater public good until the shame of their own degradation was complete, until they had wholly sacrificed their honor, which in the foolish naïveté of my youth I believed man should strive to salvage intact, first and foremost, in order to pass it on to his progeny as the most precious of legacies!

What generosity, what grandeur, what noble examples of civic value for the generations to come!

Woe is me! It required tremendous strength of character to admit: I was not, by any means, of the same moral standing as the political leaders of my time!

I am cowardly enough to confess: I couldn't find the courage within me to march in the ranks of such valiant champions.

I felt a pygmy in battle against giants.

One dream less, one disappointment more.

Access to the courthouse and the capitol, like the stage door, remained forever blocked against my entry.

Decidedly, I was not carving out a career.

Prostrate to the point of humiliation, utterly mindful of my own ineptitude—where to look? What new endeavor might still be mine to make?

Could I perhaps turn back and, a bad lawyer and a worse politician, make of myself an engineer, a man of letters, a military man, or a doctor or a priest, or at least a rancher, so that I too could write, like Señor Lima, some treatise on practical stockbreeding?

All in vain; there is a time for everything in this life, and I was too old a dog for new tricks.

You see, I might have ended up like the painter who, wishing to sketch a horse, made something which more resembled a mule and, unhappy with his work, drew a line of charcoal through it to begin again and ended up making an ass.

There is naught to be done about it, no matter how my pride screams: I am completely *raté*.

Chassez le naturel, il revient au galop. They say you can drive out nature with a pitchfork, but she keeps on coming back.

Ah! The theater, the theater!

Universal pulpit to whose doors the masses flock and in whose precincts they learn, grow, elevate and transform themselves, become the heat that transmits the inextinguishable fire of art, opening the mysteries of the soul to the eternal notions of the good and noble!

Veritable ministry for regenerating the populace, what greater glory for the ambitious man who aspires to great heights than to dominate you as lord and absolute master!

Ah! The theater, the theater!

How many times, lost in deep self-contemplation, have I lovingly reached out to caress my life's golden dream!

I was transported by my imagination, by that crazy, restless passion, to the magnificent pavilion bathed in light and flooded with people.

I would embody one of Shakespeare's sublime creations.

A spark of the eternal flame shone upon my forehead.

Under the spell cast by my lips, the bad man came good, the good man better, and this one and that and many and all; the whole of the crowd brought to heel, hanging on my every word, fought with my courage, triumphed with my glories, cried with my tears, suffered with my pain and—swept away by the force of my genius—leapt over the fence that separated us and came to me to live the ideal that I had created as real life!

That is the vision of beauty that the artist discloses before the eyes of the crowd—vivid, pure, dazzling—the vision that enraptures and captivates, that imposes itself with the strength of deeds and penetrates so deeply as to wound the fibers of one's very heart!

If it were not so, a thousand voices would not together cry out to hail it!

The irresistible influence of truth!

The magical trance of art!

The incomparable triumph of the man of the cloth!

For, what is all the world if not one great stage, with its lead roles, a few outstanding performers, and a collection of greater or lesser opera singers, dancers, speakers, chorus girls, extras, and other assorted rabble?

What is society but a vast theater in which millions of farces are ceaselessly performed, at times bloody and grotesque, and nearly always ridiculous!

The difference between the two resides in the fact that fictitious theater—for which one purchases a ticket with a banknote, thereby acquiring the right to applaud or to boo at the puppeteer or the player bedecked in tinsel but able, perhaps, to run rings around him who judges him in matters of honesty—is what it ought to be, while real theater, in which the common man acts in confusion, is what it is.

If a more or less strict moral trajectory does not obey the prescribed rules of conduct, the work in the former is booed.

But the absence of all morality might be deemed a requisite in the latter, in order to curry favor with the public.

In the former, success is measured by merit.

In the latter, merit depends upon success.

Ill-fated actors floundering on the boards are ferociously heckled by the public.

But the rogue who prospers receives frenetic applause.

Il s'agit de réussir: tout est là. And, for my part, asked to choose between the theater of Corneille and that of Napoleon, I declare that I most indubitably select that of Corneille.

Turn the page and lend your ears to a collection of melodies, proof and testament to my thesis, that have been arranged as a concerto for whistles, a *pot pourri* of whistlings and catcalls composed by ear and on impulse—*sans* embellishment or variation—from the monumental music of the world.

I

"What do you think of my fiancée?" Juan asked, striking a match to light his cigarette as we departed, at midnight on the eve of his wedding, from his future wife's home. He had just officially introduced me as one of his best friends.

"Very pretty," I replied.

"And dutiful," he added, taking my arm as we carried on our way. "How she adores me, poor thing!

"If, as they say, marriage is a gamble, then I can assure you that I've hit the jackpot.

"Marrying a girl like María, the odds are ninety-nine to one that I will be the happiest of men."

"Right-oh. That's grand," I replied calmly.

"What do you mean it's grand? Oh, the sangfroid and tranquillity with which your excellency rejoins! Perhaps you are of a differing opinion?"

"Yes, my dear friend, like you I believe that your fiancée is a darling creature, good, adoring, and loves you the way a seventeen-year-old girl is likely to love a young, handsome chap: with the intensity of all her passions; she thinks of nothing but you; her sole dream is to make you happy; she is overcome by the purest of sentiments; and your name and fortune made not a blind bit of difference when she swore to be yours; she would deem herself the world's luckiest being if she were to spend the rest of her life on a ranch eating sheep stew with mush and stale bread so long as you were to share it with her.

"You see to what degree I concede that your wife-to-be embodies a veritable assemblage of perfections for you, but . . ."

"Ah! There's a but?"

"One moment. You know that getting married has never crossed my mind. What is more, that I have always fled from the temptation like a Greek from an Englishman, like a cat from cold water: it's a question of temperament; but you also know that I accept and justify marriage as a social necessity and I am the first to applaud when others are wed.

"Allow me, nevertheless, given that it is you we speak of and given my fondness for you, to maintain that I am not in love, do not share in the enthusiasm, nor do I wish to make a snap judgment, nor try to force the issue.

"He who marries sets sail aboard a ship, and he who sets sail courts danger," I added sententiously.

"Yes, but he who does not set sail does not cross the sea."

"Better to leave it uncrossed than to drown in its depths."

"That is nothing but an odious platitude. You are a coward, a castle builder, and an unbeliever."

"No, I am a prudent man; nothing more."

"I presume that your prudence will not compel you to abandon me cowardly at the supreme hour of danger and that you will gladly accept your involvement in the crime, honoring my wedding with your presence."

"Indeed I shall help kill you, fervently wishing all of heaven's blessings are lavished upon you."

We had reached the corner of my house.

"See you tomorrow, then," Juan said, shaking my hand firmly.

"See you tomorrow, my dear Juan."

Poor boy, I thought: the past belongs to him, the present to his fiancée. To whom shall his future belong: God or the devil?

With body in tailcoat and neck in white tie—or rather, imprisoned in the straitjacket with which society still subdues lunatics like me who flee from the company of other lunatics, and sane but bashful men who love spending long winters in an armchair in front of the hearth—I took out my watch: it was seven seconds past eleven o'clock in the evening.

A first-rate *mise en scène.*

In the presence of a legion public comprising relations, friends, and—in the main—curious onlookers, and subsequent to the formalities called for by the occasion: vows, banns, and so forth, once concluded the *toilette* of the condemned man, if you will, the executor of the noble deed gave commence to his ministry.

Four minutes and twenty-eight seconds later, my friend Juan had passed on to a better life.

He had died, or rather, he had married, which amounts to much the same thing.

Heaven above, I cried *ab imo pectore* in my benevolent fervor, let not the soul of this poor devil wander errantly and come to dwell in the body of some cuckold!

I then chanced to see an edifying behind-the-scenes family episode, to which I was admitted in the capacity of close friend of the beneficiary.

A sobbing mess, the mother-in-law had taken to smothering her daughter in kisses, then collapsing into the arms of her spouse, her brother, her cousin, Juan's father, and, finally, even into my own waistcoat, where alas she decided to deplete her last reserves of tears, exclaiming as they all do:

"My poor, darling daughter, my precious angel!"

I understand it is required behavior, but I cannot abide.

And in truth: albeit colossal and deserved the discredit that, in the face of world opinion, the respectable phalanx of mothers-in-law has fallen into, it must be hard even for a mother-in-law to bear, raise, and educate a daughter, running the risk of finding that when she least expects it, and for a sacrifice no greater than the modest sum of two hundred pesos cash—which, at the end of the day, if one is quite thrifty, is no more than the cost of the ceremony itself—any old pompous dolt can come along and marry her.

A moment later, the bride and groom had gone up in a puff of smoke, a result of the high temperatures produced by the burning passions of their love.

A train as swift as their desire to arrive was taking them to spend their exquisite honeymoon on his grandparents' idyllic ranch.

I I I

Having patiently spent half an hour in front of the mirror and then adorned myself with the added touch of a pair of gloves, I wanted to get my *argent's* worth and slipped once again into the ballrooms overrun by society's élite.

A most magnificent dance was taking place within their walls.

The idea of removing my person from center stage, occupying the place of honor in the ranks of the passive, struck me as prudent.

Which is to say, I sat down in the far corner.

Carried along by my habitually jovial character, I was preparing to spend the next little while encountering the gay, ridiculous side of humanity, when suddenly I was overcome by one of those brusque changes that tend to befall men who, having reached a certain age, have derived both pleasuring and suffering in vast quantities.

The memory of tantalizing delights and distressing pains brings on a profound disenchantment and, as a consequence, perverse sentiments are roused, sentiments that shock and horrify, after the daze wears off.

I was then experiencing just such an ill-fated moment, and gossip's evil spirit was goading me on.

I felt an evil disposition, caustic and biting, awaken within me; I would have sunk my teeth into the virgin's white tunic to tear it asunder, and through the frenzied desire to wreak harm that assailed me, I saw everything round me painted in the most odious of manners.

Just then one of those fellows that one finds ten to the dozen, neither good nor bad, chanced to walk by.

They can be deemed neither roguish nor honorable, in the absolute sense of the word, because their honor is elastic: it stretches and recoils, adapting to the measure of profit perceived and according to the intelligence that, to form judgment, offers a false sense of morality inherited by default from their breeding.

The subject to whom I refer is a merchant, which means that if trusted with a sum of money as a deposit, he refrains unconditionally from touching it and religiously returns the entire sum intact, notwithstanding the many years that may have transpired; he is categorically incapable of putting his hand in the pocket of a fellow man to purloin one peso or ten million, but craftily stings him like a bee, making him believe that he sells for a hundred pesos what cost him a thousand, when it cost not ten and is worth not one.

It matters little that the poor devil he swindles loses the shirt off his back and brings his entire family to ruination, reducing them to dire poverty and its accompanying horrors.

Do not believe that our man, for his deed, will lose even a minute of sleep.

His conscience is clear; he has lied, he has cheated, he has falsified and has done as much harm as the thief who breaks open the safe and absconds with the treasure therein; but what does it matter to him, if it was neither illicit nor illegal?

He has committed, it is true, an injustice, but that goes by the name—in his milieu—of meeting a commercial contract, making a good deal. He was in his rights.

If the operation has ruined the other party, if misfortune has thence befallen him, is the merchant, perchance, to blame?

Of course not. That's sound business.

Well, at that precise moment, possessed as I was by the aberrant influence that governed me, I would have cheerfully condemned that merchant, that man and others of his ilk whom the world—in which they enjoy untainted reputations—receives, reveres, and respects; I would have sentenced them all to three thousand lashes or to be shot in the head, without even the most minute pang of regret.

"What a charming couple!" exclaimed my neighbor, a passive soldier like myself. "Do you not agree, sir?" he added, bored, no doubt, of the silent abyss that yawned before us and wishing to shoot the breeze with me.

"Delightful, indeed," I replied, half turning my back on him, little disposed to engage in any intellectual trade with the *primer venu*.

He was referring to two young things who, entwined in the steps of a dainty waltz, had just spun by, brushing our legs.

The young man is what one would refer to as a molly coddled rich boy.

His father, believing whole heartedly that there could be no educational establishment in the land worthy of his illustrious offspring and dreaming of a brilliant future in the sciences for his son, sent him as an adolescent to finish his studies in Europe.

Once in Paris, and under the pretext of setting himself up decently, as befits a young boy from a good family in the Americas, with the aim of establishing his name and with the excuse of the increasing sums he was forced to invest in the fees charged by his professors—princes of science one and all—in his quotidian needs that were so consummately costly, in unexpected, extraordinary expenses, etc., he sent home letters, one after the other, requesting yet more capital.

The good father, proud of his son's progress, would answer these missives with letters of exchange, to the great satisfaction of the young man and the female friends of the *demi-mondaine* society in whose midst he lived and who incessantly exclaimed, with joyful rapture:

"Oh! le charmant p'tit père que t'as là!

With no one to clip his wings and the world as his oyster, he would have been cretinous to choose the austere campus of Charlemagne or Louis-le-Grand college over the *tours de Lac* in a *coupé* and suppers at the Maison-Dorée or the Café Anglais, the nasal, hollow words of a professor during a more or less soporific lecture over the sweet voices of *ces mignonnes*, murmuring *mon ange chéri* and *mon petit bibi adoré* into his ear!

Our hero, therefore, quite rightly threw himself wholeheartedly into that freewheeling lifestyle that drains away the contents of one's *poches*, degrades the body, and corrupts the soul, until one fine day, having entirely depleted the reserves of paternal largesse and spent the last franc, destitution itself drove the impudent boy to race hell for leather back to his homeland, where people remarked on the astonishing chic thought to emanate from his person, though he was somewhat shabby and just as simple as he had been when he left.

Desperate at seeing all of his golden hopes dashed, one by one, and finding himself obliged to finally face the facts, his father opted for the last resort all fathers in this country opt for in such circumstances: stockbreeding, the final retreat for barbarians and half-wits.

You can't make a silk purse out of a sow's ear, so to speak.

Daddy dreamt of a wise man and awoke with an ass.

And they send their children off to Europe for an education!

His dance partner was a lovely creature some 15 years of age who possessed all the charming graces and southern spirits of a native-born girl but who was hollow, superficial, and ignorant in the manner typical of Argentinian women, whose intelligence is a veritable swamp thanks to the tender and exemplary concerns of the paterfamilias.

At the age of eight, she was sent to the school of one such Doña Telésfora, not because the establishment of this nonentity—held in exceedingly high repute—could provide a decent moral and physical education worthy of any woman who later had to make her way in life—these matters were taken into low esteem—but by virtue of other facts, such as: Doña Telésfora's mother, it was said, had been a close friend of grandmamma.

Doña Telésfora was a poor soul; it was right to protect the unfortunate creature.

She had opened her school just round the corner, on the same block.

It was right that the girl study nearby, in case she should fall ill; besides, as she was thus not required to cross any streets, her mother could rest easy in the assurance that she would not be run over by a carriage, etc.

It mattered little that, in order to found her school, the aforementioned Doña Telésfora should have begun at the beginning, that is to say, by learning whatever it was she intended on teaching. Let time sail on, let the girl pitifully waste her best years and, at twelve, pretending to be a lady, let her leave on Doña Telésfora's word of faith with her education concluded, banging out a pathetic "Look, oh! Norma" on the piano to the lament of others' sensitive ears, and writing *dear* with two e's and *ciao* with a w in the amorous epistles she exchanged with one of the neighborhood scamps in some doorway, a rascal who played truant and hung about smoking cigarettes round the lamppost across from Don Juan the Genoan's shop.

And so it was that, at the age of fourteen, she had ascended to the ranks of womanhood, and here she was, living out the solemn consecration of the passionately longed for and endlessly rehearsed wearing of her first ball gown; and at fifteen, she was cast into the whirlwind of this earth, lioness of haute couture, queen of high society.

Yet draw closer with the aim of passing but one half hour in her amiable company; either you shan't survive ten minutes, pummeled by boredom as if by a club, or you will be obliged to partake in utter triviality: providing merriments or receiving them of her; prattling on about boyfriends, about who says that So-and-so is courting such-and-such a girl and shall ask her hand; discussing who left some other boy high and dry; or, as a last recourse, drawing out the knife and stabbing it repeatedly into the back of whomever's path it should cross.

And as if woman were a weed in the park, something well-nigh indifferent that should hold no sway over the family and, therefore, over society and its improvement, this is how we try to raise her moral standard.

What do we care if in other lands—in the United States, for example, which we are proud to ape—often with neither rhyme nor reason, monkey-like, they award her the dignity of worrying about her political rights and allowing her to be a lofty public servant, doctor, lawyer, etc.?

It suits us to have her know her place and station, hang it! And that is the way we want to keep it, by god.

Why?

Because. Because routine is a vice that flows through our bloodstreams and because that was the tried and true custom of our Spanish forefathers. You made your bed, now lie in it; let the dance continue, and long live the revolution!

Just at that moment, a woman friend of mine chanced to enter, and nevermind upon whose arm; you needn't know.

She was, this dear and beloved friend of mine, what is commonly known as a viper-tongue.

If she sank in her fangs, she mortally poisoned her victim.

She has spent her life like the poet's specters, setting traps and digging holes beneath the feet of humanity. Never for her has a virtuous woman or an honorable man walked upon the earth.

She has exploited misfortune, turning faults into offenses, offenses into crimes.

A veritable sentinel of scandal, when truth has not encouraged her to ravage her victim, already wounded by others, she has sated her lowly passions on the most monstrous of lies.

She has made up vile deeds, told disgraceful tales, concocted atrocities.

Matrons, virgins, and old men have all yielded to her venomous tongue.

Not even the exalted peace of the sepulchre has reined in her frenzied

22

profanity and, driven on by her jackal-like instincts, she has, like a beast, fed upon the cadavers she dug up to desecrate the dead.

Is that not enough?

Add to it, then, an aptitude for understanding as quick as her will to harm, as open to understanding as her disposition is to evil; an imagination as fertile as freshly manured fields; the subtle, biting spirit found in women, capable of bringing a stone to life, combined with the crude and dogged audacity characteristic of men: there you have a rough sketch of her profile, a pallid reflection of her reality.

The coincidence between the accidental state of my mood and her natural character, doubtlessly, attracted me to her with irresistible force.

I sat, therefore, beside her, seeking out in that burning light of perversity—as a cat seeks out the stove or a bee the flower—a fresh inducement to slander.

"But my dear, is that you? It's been so long since I've had the pleasure of seeing you! Maybe the wolf has turned into a sheep and to atone for past sins you have been overwhelmed by fanciful notions of asceticism; or maybe you have resolved to take a sacred vow in a religious order somewhere and the devil now goes about masquerading as a monk."

"Neither the former nor the latter, madam," I replied. "I think true talent lies in knowing when to quit the stage.

"The honorable public already had me pegged.

"Having squandered my resources over the years, I would have been forced to resort to the hateful *trucs* of frail mortals in their autumn days, in the final hour of *dégringolade* that, unhappily, had befallen me; and wishing to avoid compassion at any cost and the ridicule with which the world rightly upbraids old fops, I resolved to settle my accounts and spend the rest of my days peacefully confined within the four walls of my house.

"Was I right? Or was I wrong?

"I am certain that no one better than yourself, my friend and contemporary, might appreciate the prudence of my conduct."

"You did perfectly well," she said; and then, piqued no doubt by my last words and in pursuit of revenge, "How time flies!" she exclaimed, staring fixedly and with marked intentions. "You are emaciated and have aged so, my dear friend."

"If emaciation and aging were objects of desire," I replied, "I should think you spoke out of sheer envy.

"But, woe betide me! I must concede it. Only the noblest sentiments of your kind soul can have inspired your interest in me and the compassion I see on your face.

"Believe me, I am profoundly grateful.

"Funny, I, on the other hand, find you as fair and youthful as ever.

"One could say that time has not passed for you, and yet," I insisted, "I had the pleasure of making your acquaintance and counting myself as one of your many close friends so long ago.

"Do you remember? It was in the fifties, fifty-something, wasn't it?

"We were so wild back then . . ."

"I have always had such an appalling memory for dates," she interrupted, visibly vexed.

"And yet you cannot have lost it entirely, you being you, regardless of the fact that I am, I confess, speaking of events which have begun to fade into oblivion.

"I was saying," I added with the intentional aim of pricking her and making her crack, "that a trifling twenty-some years ago (and of course you must have already been at least twenty back then) . . ."

"Tch! Let up, by god!" she exclaimed with a nod of impatience and anger flashing in her eyes, "turn the page; enough is enough.

"Allow me to say that in your pathetic attempts to avenge yourself of what, by perverting the sense of my words, you take to be wickedness but was in fact nothing more—God as my witness—than a perhaps brutal but frank and spontaneous manifestation, if you will, of the friendly interest you awaken in me, you clearly lack gallantry and run the risk, if you carry on in this vein, of becoming obnoxious and even impertinent."

And then with marked irony:

"If I have offended you I beg a thousand pardons," she added, "but do not be cruel; do not prey on a poor defenseless woman and, from the heights of your grandeur, grant me a tiny morsel of peace or, at least, respite from ill-intentioned japes."

"Madam, you confound me. It is I who ought humbly beg your forgiveness if I have chanced to cause you any displeasure.

"Peace, my gracious friend, peace; I am the first to implore on bended knee and to bow down to pay you the most exquisite homage . . ."

"Peace, then," she said, stretching out her hand to me.

Vanitas, vanitatis . . .

This doggedly organized mind and hard, superior, implacable, great nature, that one would have thought inaccessible to human weaknesses in its infernal grandeur, in the act of destruction brought on by misfortune in fact presented a soft and vulnerable underbelly; so much so that a simple cliché, an ill-intentioned jape, as she herself called it, made her quiver with rage and pain like a serpent whose tail is trod upon.

Et omnia vanitas.*

After a moment of silence she seemed to recover her habitual aplomb.

"Do you not think," she said smiling, "that rather than scratching each other like petulant children, it would be more fitting and diverting to play with these windup dolls dancing here before us, in the same way that they themselves play with their own toys?"

That was where it hurt; in no time flat, the cat's claws were out.

"*Après vous*, my dear friend; open fire and cut them to shreds at will. Nothing could bring me greater pleasure."

She needed no further encouragement:

"Do you see," she asked, "that placid-faced fellow whose long sideburns are combed *à l'anglaise* and whose big, blue eyes, sweet and tranquil, would make one think of a pure soul, while his dignified airs and the distinction of his manners seem to be those of a perfect caballero?"

"Yes; so?"

"So, though many take him for a man and, what is more, for a decent one at that, he is far from deserving such status.

"If you scratch the surface a bit, you shall find a fungus that spreads and contaminates though one cannot see how; a poisonous weed imported from God knows where, that attaches itself to the indigenous plant, works its way in until you cannot distinguish the two, and ends up putting down roots and even flourishing thanks to the natural and bountiful fertility of this blessed land; a Greek gift; an adventurer, or a gentleman of industry, which amount to one and the same.

"Common as John Bull himself, possessing the gold lavishly afforded him by his audacity and by the senseless candor of the family into whose bosom he has insinuated himself like a bloodsucking vampire, he dreams of vanity and of ambition.

"Like a rash, he disappears for a spell and then crops up again unexpectedly, flaunting any old title such as count or marquis, which he

---

*This biblical expression (*Eccles. 1:2*) used to express total despair also closes Thackeray's *Vanity Fair*, an earlier novel that, like *Pot Pourri*, took a harsh view of the prevailing, wealthy society of the day.

has paid for with the money brought in by his meek and none-too-sharp father-in-law's ranches, in some secondhand clothes shop in Italy or Portugal, where this type of sham is easily undertaken at bargain prices.

"And how fortunate that the hungry crowd tires of its prey and is not compelled by its ferocious appetite to leave the sumptuous feast tabula rasa!

"How long, by god," she added, "will nobility continue to mask the idiocy of men; how long will you sit back and watch this rabble wickedly exploit the generously open door, the patriarchal hospitality offered to them!"

"You are quite right," I hastened to say, egged on, against my will, by the force of her words.

"It is time now for gentiles to be expelled from the temple and the doors of our homes to be closed to intruders profaning its sanctity!"

"Home, home . . ." she murmured, as if regretting an outburst of nobility alien to her character.

"But do not take it so seriously. Remember there is only one step from the sublime to the ridiculous and, in particular, that all that glitters is not gold . . ."

"Home . . . castle! . . . I advise you to avail yourself of a lantern and take inspiration from the example set by Job in order to find it in the society we inhabit.

"I shall prove it. Approach the woman that our man has on his arm, and if you can resist the rankness emanating from her person for just two minutes, I want you to come and tell me."

"But that woman," I observed, "is, they say, a saint, a rare specimen of conjugal self-abnegation, likened to the angel of charity who alleviates the sufferings of the miserable, of the deformed and repulsive, the wretched of the earth."

"And yet that angel is but a fallen angel, a woman of rare beauty but shrewd, heartless, free from any of the sensitivity characteristic of her sex; exquisite, delicate beyond measure, made of marble, in short, steeped in the spirit of her century, endowed with a preciosity so breathtaking that, as a girl, she did not hesitate to sacrifice her virgin charms to the golden calf—bedded by a disfigured man, a millionaire ten times over.

"The repulsive spectacle of that wretch whose body, from which all life flees in horror, bends double ever more drastically, until one day it blends in with the earth from which it should never have risen and, beside it, the venal creature, the speculator, the figures-woman who counts the beats of his heart and calculates the hours he has left, awaiting the moment his body is laid out on the floor to line her pockets with his riches, to snatch away the golden blanket that covers him, as a *chimango* vulture awaits the death of the lamb to devour its eyes.

"There you have it, the sweet and peaceful portrait of home life, and there are many others like it: there, look no further," she said all of a sudden, pointing toward one corner of the ballroom.

"Do you know that couple?" she asked.

She was referring to a man and wife who, speaking softly, had just passed before us.

"One would have to have come down with the last rainfall or live in Thebes not to know them," I replied.

"Don't brag, my friend, don't brag; watch your step.

"One learns something new every day and, God forgive me, I believe that in this instance something remains for you to learn.

"Would you like me to tell you an extraordinary story? Listen and be enlightened.

"Years ago a man gave his hand to a common woman and, spurred on by his noble and generous character, he made her his before the altar, when nothing would have prevented him from doing so behind it.

"Now you know that though one may well find protection against steel bullets, they have yet to invent any able to resist the old gold bullet, particularly any able to shelter us poor, fragile women.

"From the hovel in which she lived with her family in the slums, our heroine, reeking of disinfectant, moved to the splendid mansion that her husband had destined for her on one of the aristocratic streets in the center of town.

"Do you think she was in love when she married or, at least, that the benefits she and hers derived from the generous goodness of her husband—his affections for her, the considerations that she be surrounded by comforts and riches, the lucrative post given to her father, the schooling of her siblings paid for—awoke in her sentiments of gratitude, leading her to the path of righteousness?

"Nonsense, my friend!

"She married for money and without education, or conscience, or morals, or religion, naturally inclined toward evil and happy to devote herself even to crime, once rich, to pleasures, luxuries, completely absorbed by idleness and splendor.

"As a matter of course there was, as there always is, one of those perverted creatures who, in the capacity of relative, or associate, or doctor, slips into the house, takes possession of it, takes over all of its avenues bit by bit and, hiding behind the mask of friendship, even manages to make his way into the wife's bed, to caress her with one sly hand while the other effusively shakes that of the good and trusting husband unsuspecting of the deceit (because he is unable to commit it himself) as his honor is robbed in the most vile of manners.

"The same old story, my friend: the family doctor became the wife's lover and of that unlawful union were born several children of honorable name and bastard blood.

"One fine day, society was sorrowfully moved by the death of the husband who had finally succumbed to a long and painful illness, and one year later the news went round that the widow had entered into a new union with the doctor in question.

"Now on the surface there is nothing to remark upon in all this.

"The demands of the world had been met.

"She had spent a year in mourning. And she was still young and beautiful, so nothing was more natural than, though having loved her husband dearly—as Christian resignation had carried his soul to rest in peace—for time to heal the wounds of her heart and for her not to live voluntarily condemned to a life of perpetual widowhood.

"The union was enacted, thus, and today the pair are an exemplary wedded couple.

"He, a distinguished doctor, has numerous patients and enjoys an enviable reputation as a gentleman and sage.

"The voice of misfortune has never rung at his door in vain, for he attends graciously to the beds of the rich and the cots of the poor alike.

"She, a woman of utmost virtue, member of every philanthropic institution there be amidst us, whose abundant material riches cannot compare to the immense treasures of charity of her soul, such and so great are the acts of beneficence she bestows.

"Both live gay and content, in the blessed happiness of the righteous that rests on the full weight of virtue.

"That is what is taken by the public to be gospel, is it not?

"But would you care to know where the truth lies and to what degree the voice of the people is a fabrication; do you wish to probe their consciences, search their home, draw back the curtain that covers the sanctuary and find out what type of saints occupy those niches?

"Go and ask the practitioner who was called in, no doubt for form's sake, to the deathbed of the first husband.

"He shall whisper into your ear—taking care to look round first and asking that mum be the word—that all that cures, kills, depending on the measure in which it is delivered and that fate, having taken part in the game, had it that the doctor and the wife's hand slipped with the arsenic."

A sudden, surprised gesture was my first reaction upon hearing the tale of such a grim deed.

A moment later my conscience cried out, refusing to give credit to these last words; my shock turned to outrage against she who had perpetuated the slander, inventing it herself or echoing the tale of other prevaricators.

"That is a vicious lie!" I said brusquely, feeling the blood rush to my face.

"Lie!" she exclaimed with a dry cackle that, more than a laugh, was a nervous twitch.

"How behind on the news of the day is my friend!

"One would think you were an angel in heaven.

"Decidedly, the hand of God is no longer with you."

And then, staring at me fixedly:

"Why," she added, "you've gone all red; shame and anger have colored your cheeks so!

"Illustrious champion, worthy of the most heroic times!

"Why do you not close shop, put down your sword, and flounce off to right the wrongs of this world, once and for all?" she added with the most scornful acumen she could muster.

"You would no longer find, it is true, any windmills against which to charge, lance extended, but you could, if you like, crack your head against the enchanted castle of ridicule and get smacked in the mouth by a bunch of schoolboys."

"As you like," I replied gruffly, resolved to put an end to the scene that was becoming unbearably hateful, as the funk that had clouded my reason began to clear and I regained possession, bit by bit, of my *me*.

"Between my role as ridiculous old fool, however, and yours that I could but choose not to name, I need not add that I much prefer to stick with my own," I said.

"You wretch!" she cried, giving particularly irate emphasis to this last word. "What can you be made of, if you are scandalized by such a trifle?

"In this day and age things a thousand times worse are common currency that all society takes for legal tender without so much as suspecting it as counterfeit.

"What world must you inhabit, my poor friend!

"And look," she continued, "this incident serves perfectly to prove to you that I am indeed right and that you are nothing but a poor, gapemouthed innocent.

"Look at that creature over yonder, dancing amongst that band of Don Juans.

"I have no need to tell you she is fair, with locks as golden as summer dew and as heavenly as the angels.

"One would say that an exquisite *parfum* of innocence emanates from her supple curves and impregnates the air she breathes.

"You can see it yourself.

"But what you do not know, and what I want you to know so that you dare not go about feeling pity and acting a perfect . . . innocent, is what caused her family to disappear of a sudden last year."

"The lady's poor health; she was ordered by the doctor to spend an interlude in the country.

"At least that is what I heard."

"Yes, that is what was said. But it is true or was it just a pretext?

"Was the mother in fact unwell, as was claimed, suffering the effects of such a curious illness that the doctor sent her to the frontier in the month of June; or was it really to do with the daughter, with a secret so scandalous that it had to be silenced by a terrible event which must have occurred a few month's later, and which would have brought shame upon the entire family?

"The coarse mulatto, the scrounger of the house, the life of the party, is the one best prepared to shed light on that mystery."

Oh! To make a perverse, degraded creature of a matron and a tart of a virgin was the height of iniquity!

Every wholesome, honorable fiber in my body stood out in the face of such monstrous evil.

I would have wished that woman a man so as first to slap his face and then to kill him . . .

I became like a drunkard who, seizing the bottle and roused by its golden liquid, takes one drink, then another and another, until his stomach revolts in a terrible fit of anxieties.

Thirsty for scandal, I too had become intoxicated by that woman's— or rather that demon's—nasty respiration until the excessive venom digested reached my soul, which rebelled indignantly, causing me to retain a most unpleasant, sickening memory of that scene.

From amongst a group of people stationed on the other side of the salon rose the tall silhouette of a young journalist whose eyes sparkled with pernicious mischief and whose expression, quite peculiar to himself, was one of permanent sarcasm.

One could not look at him without being overcome by a vague sense of mistrust and fear at the same time as, inexplicably, feeling attracted to him in heartfelt sympathy, by the *je ne sais quoi* at once seductive and captivating, emanating from every pore of his being.

Overflowing with talent from head to toe, he is as brilliant, dangerous, and sharp as a straight-edge razor.

If handled with care, it leaves your skin smooth, terse, and soft as a kidskin glove; but if your hand slips even slightly, it will sting, smart, cut, draw blood, and even gash the flesh deeply, profoundly.

Implacable with his enemies, neither misfortune, nor punishment, nor time suffice to diminish his ill will; his pen could be engraved thus: *Qu'y s'y frotte, s'y pique.*

His was, at that instant, the only face I recognized.

I headed off suddenly in his direction and, taking him by the arm, said, "Come and have a smoke with me. I just had a nasty turn; I feel light-headed and need a breath of the fresh night air."

I V

Allow me the pleasure of introducing you to Don Juan José Taniete—whom we will encounter on more than one occasion in successive pages—illustrious descendent of the doughty Pelayo, conceived round about 1821, more or less, by poor but *hon-ra-bul* parents in the town of Lestemoño (patron saint: San Vicente de Lagraña), located seven leagues from La Coruña.

Don Juan José Taniete fulfills the delicate functions of concierge and confidant to my royal self, as well as being my bootblack.

And I say *Don* Juan because he himself uses the title.

The day he entered into my services, upon receiving him:

"What is your name?" I asked.

"Name's Don Juan José Taniete," he answered, displaying one of the squarest heads I had ever had occasion to lay eyes upon, and thereupon beginning to list the aforementioned et ceteras.

"Enough, commoner, enough!" I exclaimed.

I need no further details, the mystery cleared up: problem solved: answers received—a priori—to the three time-honored questions:

Who are you?

A beast.

Where do you come from?

From Galicia, the blessed land where such fruits are reaped in abundance.

Where are you off to?

To give you a hard time, turn your hair gray, poison your life, and perhaps annoy you to death.

In our first exchanges, a grave and serious conflict arose, a deep rift over the *Don* threatened to spoil the calm of our mutual relations.

"Let us average it out," I said:

> You try to cling to the Don
> I insist upon Pepe or Juan
> So I'll call you Taniete; it's wise
> To look on it as compromise.

And thus the thorny question of etiquette was resolved for both.

Taniete, then.

Would you care for a sample, just one, but a truly characteristic, typical example of the utter pricelessness of my treasure of a man?

Pray note that this is not an ordinary Galician-immigrant story, or rather, one of those stories people invent to make fun of Galicians; this is perfectly historical and its merit lies, precisely, in its veracity.

Here goes.

It was 7:30 of an evening.

I had just supped, when Taniete walked in with a copy of *El Nacional** under his arm.

"Light the fire," I said, indicating the chandelier hanging above the dining-room table.

---

* One of Argentina's most important dailies in the second half of the nineteenth century (1853–93). Though it was initially seen as a political organ of Domingo F. Sarmiento, who was also one of the main writers, the paper later began covering broader stories that were free of the partisan struggles of the early days.

"Whadju say?"

Taniete is deaf; he is not in the habit of acknowledging receipt of orders until they are repeated.

"I said, light the fire!" I bellowed, causing the windows to rattle.

"I'll a-git raht on it."

He matter-of-factly drew out a match, struck it, and, with all the aplomb of a man who knows what he is doing, held it to one of the spouts, without hitherto having troubled himself to open the valve, and stood steadfastly thus for nothing short of a minute.

He would have been quite capable of remaining in said position, undaunted, for all eternity.

Seeing no flame forthcoming, he put his noggin to work and seemed to believe he had hit the nail on the head.

He slapped his hand to his forehead, quitted the room, climbed down the stairs at a leisurely pace, climbed back up a moment later, entered the room once again, and—quite self-satisfied—fell to repeating the match ceremony once more.

In vain, said task; still the same negative result; still the same darkness surrounding us!

Decidedly, the fire was not lighting.

And note that, this time, he clean forgot the precautionary measure of turning the lever.

How was it going to light if, believing the gas meter closed when in fact it had been open, his effort to turn it on had in fact turned it off, the stupid oaf.

"Sir, this is broke," he said, finally, disconcerted. "The clock don' work" (said mechanism being known in common parlance as a meter).

"So while I goes for the ingineer, you'd best laht a candle."

"What I ought to do is light a rocket up your backside, stupid beast, for doing everything back to front!"

That is quite enough, is it not? You have made the acquaintance of Taniete.

And so it was that I was *en train de* undertaking one of the most deliciously sensual pleasures I know, the only form of exercise I tolerate or allow, which accommodates itself to my tastes.

Lying as I was, face up on my bed, arms forming an O, framing my head with my wrists meeting just above it, eyes voluptuously half-closed and the most ineffable current of delectation running through my body, I was tensing my muscular apparatus vigorously; that is to say that, between yawns, I was stretching with all the wiles of a cat when suddenly there appeared at the threshold of the door first a hand (which, for its size, seemed to be more of a glover's sample than a real one); through the jamb, then, came a foot wide as three bricks and, little by little, Taniete's stout corpulence entered, bearing a letter for me.

I ripped open the envelope at once, upon recognizing Juan's writing, and discovered the soft, sweet idyll, the veritable country pot of honey that I now allow myself to offer you.

Los Tres Médanos, December

Indra's idea of blessed paradise, promised to believers of Oriental fanaticism is, I swear to you, my dear friend, but a *maigre appât* compared to the immense rapture now flooding every waking hour of my life.

I live in seventh heaven or, in what is much the same thing, in Los Tres Médanos with its nine leagues of magnificent countryside, acquired by my grandfather in exchange for a few cents, back when this area was a consolidated center of savages* and which today can be considered worth a fortune.

My wife is a saint.

Pure as the air I breathe (it is at present six o'clock in the morning and I write you from the porch), her divine touch purifies and cleanses the blemishes that any contact with men leaves on one's conscience.

At her side it is impossible to be bad. One's spirit is lifted by the strength of her virtue and the beatitude expressed in just one of her looks, wrested from God himself so that this treasure could lie in the eyes of my María; she is a blessed fountain of inspiration in which even the poisoned soul of a parricide could drink of her renewing balsam, one sip of which would bestow a new way of life upon him.

I love her more than humanly possible.

Someone might have loved to this degree in the past, but no one has ever loved more, not even those who, like the heroes of Shakespeare and Walter Scott, commit suicide, unable to bear the burden of living after the death of their beloveds.

If I were to lose mine, I should need no weapon; the pain alone would kill me.

What I feel for her is passion, idolatry, frenzy; and the excess of my affection, the violence of my love, my rash imagination delight in creating

*South of Buenos Aires Province, the land on which the farm is located was taken from the indigenous population established there before or during Juan Manuel de Rosas's 1833 "desert" military campaign. The offensive came to a close in 1879, when the expedition led by Julio Argentino Roca ended in the extermination of virtually all native inhabitants.

apparitions, giving them life, shape, and color, only to destroy them again afterward.

Why just yesterday, seduced by the melancholy that the pampas solitude brings on in the late afternoon, we sat down together upon the old *ombú* trunk that you well know.

Her golden head lay resting against my shoulders; my lips touched her lips; my eyes drank in her eyes; and our sealed hearts spoke to one another, through the flesh that divides them, in the mysterious language of their beating; and their voices blended together and became confused as to whose was whose, when suddenly the sweet rapture that overpowered me was shattered by a harsh and bitter shriek that broke the magic spell.

What have I ever done, I asked myself, to merit such blessings from heaven?

Why has He not chosen one of His, but lavished this supreme, fulfilling felicity upon me?

But I am unworthy of her and God is just, so what befalls me must be untrue; it is but a dream that overpowers all my senses, and the more beautiful the present visions which beguile me, the more cruel shall be my eventual awakening!

Yes, yes, this must end: this spell that transports me and enchants me will vanish in the face of reality just as the life-giving dew on the morning grass evaporates when the south winds blow through the pampas.

Woe is me! Woe betide my life, my future!

The anguish, my dear friend! Ay, the terrible heartache of that moment!

By great fortune, the sweet voice of María, twixt kisses, whispered through her warm, perfumed breath, "How I love you! How I do! Yes, I am yours, yours for all eternity!" And as these words reached my ears, like a caress and a consolation, the fanciful peril that had terrified my spirit was calmed.

Impossible! I thought then; she is mine, I am her husband; her fortune is tied up with mine. If misfortune were to befall me, if He were to punish me, she too would be condemned, she too would be bound into the punishment. Nay, that could not be; it would be blasphemy: my María is an angel and God in His infinite mercy does not desire, must not desire, cannot desire to punish angels!

Well, dear friend, by telling you that I am head over heels in love, I tell all; do not wonder, then, that love causes me to think and write like a madman.

Shall I tell you the story of our pastoral life, whose hours fly by with vertiginous speed?

At five o'clock in the morn the first rays of sun, which come through the window and fall on our pillows, awaken us.

What's this about "our pillows?" I hear you ask: so, Don Juan has followed my advice, the advice of a wise old man, *un vieux de la vielle*, as you would say, or he who best knows where the shoe pinches.

It is true, I confess my sin humbly; it is an act of contrition and I kneel down before you and beg you to absolve me.

I was spurred on, as you know, by the best of intentions; so much so that I refused, on purpose, to include a double bed in the belongings sent down, as I resolved to abide by the ancient bedsteads of our forefathers, which would hardly accommodate a beanpole comfortably.

But what can I say?

Of course, the first night we must not speak of, for several reasons; let us strike it through.

The following night, María was afraid of robbers, poor thing, and I was afraid, too . . . of not being able to sleep without her.

This, then, was the second edition of the previous night, which threatened to be repeated on the third.

It was essential, however, to put an end to this quite alarming state of affairs so as not to allow use to degenerate into abuse and the general relaxing of morals.

I adopted, therefore, as a fair and conciliatory compromise, the following measure: I pushed our two beds together.

That way, I told myself, by undergoing a sweet indignity, the intention remains intact by any reckoning, I do not break my promise and I resolve the delicate issue of fear, all in one.

But oh, brother of mine! Man proposes and the devil disposes!

In spite of everything, one of the blasted beds seemed always to awake alone and vulnerable: mine, on the whole.

To insist was a waste of time; like preaching in the desert or putting a poultice on a wooden leg.

All roads lead to Rome, you know!

So I plucked up my courage and got down to work. Thus I negotiated the mattresses, rejecting the solution of incongruent continuity in the longitudinal sense; I cut one of my neckties into two equal lengths; with each I tied two of the beds' legs together so they should not move apart, creating a valley between us, and thus managed to crown my efforts to transform them into one, compact, more or less comfortable bed.

There is no turning back now.

Asking me to sleep without my wife is like asking the glove not to fit the hand or a shadow not to follow a man.

And finally, so that you shall leave me in peace, I exclaim like Hélêne: *ce n'est pas ma faute, mon cher Calchas, que veux-tu; c'est la fatalité!*

In my weakness lies my excuse; in my impotence, my justification.

As I was saying, we wake at five.

After an hour or so, which I assure you is not spent idly lying about, we each drink between four and eight glasses of milk, standing beside the cow, and then go out on horseback or in the carriage, depending upon our state of exhaustion or the extent of prostration resulting from the previous eve's exercise.

We go out for a turn, ride past the small farms, entertaining our ears as a dilettante would entertain his with Aramburo's "Spirto gentil" or Gayarre's "L'Africana" (such is the manner in which luck is predisposed to benevolence), with the lowing of the cows, the whinnying of the colts, the bleating of the sheep, the cry of the birds, and even the barking of the dogs and sobbing of the ranch hand's children who, together with the pack of dogs, half-naked as they are and sworn enemies of soap and water—though healthy and robust and rounder than balls of dough—come out to greet us at the tethering post and surround the carriage or the horses' hooves, with eyes wide as saucers and expressions of suspicious curiosity shared by man and beast alike.

The clock strikes ten and we head back, rushed on by our voracious hunger.

With the malicious aim of whetting your carnivorous appetite, making your mouth water, since I know you like the back of my hand, I shall include our lunch menu for your delectation:

Potage: Beef broth.
Entrée: Beef stew.
Légumes: Struck off (why bother?).
Viande: Barbecued beef.
Entremets sucrés: Corn pudding. Rice pudding.
Desserts: Toffee. Fresh cheese. Mountain peaches.
Hors d'oeuvres: Café con leche. Chocolate. Butter, etc.

The whole of it is deliciously prepared in the local style by the mulatta Jacinta, daughter of black Marta, my mother's slave and cordon bleu by profession.

After luncheon, our uncontrollable passion and the heat of the day strip us of our clothes, the bed cries out to us and siesta overcomes us until four o'clock in the afternoon.

At five, table is laid again with a second edition of luncheon, which also includes a traditional homemade pie, steamed or roasted corn cakes, Jacinta having been notified that she would be severely punished if she were to dip into the pantry: foie gras, mortadella, asparagus, and the like, which are only here for *pompam et ostentationem*; Bazille wines, advantageously replaced by *frappée* well water, and excellent Geronimo hams that grow old and rot out of boredom and abandon upon finding themselves relegated to the hindmost shelves of oblivion.

37

It is the hour of poetry, the time-honored moment of celestial music that Love—the most wily-tongued of gods—dedicated to the female inhabitants of Parnassus, according to Racine, who wanted to gain access to the aforementioned mountain.

At six o'clock we appear, still stuck together like Siamese twins, perhaps on the paths of the garden, perhaps on a hilltop, at the edge of the lagoon, or along the creek, telling one another, for a change, what we always say, in every tone and half-tone imaginable, accompanied by much kissing and hugging: I adore you; and I, you.

From eight until nine in the evening, a game of hearts and a round of Black Lady and at nine to bed, but not before finishing off every last drop of milk left for *notre intention* in the dining room cupboard by the kind-hearted, devoted Jacinta.

Et voilà.

Does our daily routine not entice you?

Do you not feel tempted, as well, to join in the show?

Would you be capable of brushing the dust off your bachelor's ways and opening an eight-day parenthesis in the tedium of your existence?

Oh Croquefer! if that were the case, I would beg of you to entrust the illustrious Taniete, solicitous treasure of yours, with the keys to the dilapidated tower in which you nest away like a bird of ill omen, struggling to keep your stale and tarnished *célibataire* banner raised.

Come to us, poor famished one!

You shall find two charitable souls, two Christian hearts ready to fling you the crumbs of the splendid banquet of their fortune.

Get up at five, take the train at six, and arrive the very same day to be greeted by the open arms of your friend, awaiting you like an obtuse angle.

V

Three Caporal cigs, smoked one after the other in no time flat, had just wreaked havoc on my empty stomach, thereby contributing, additionally, to my attendant vile temper, brought on by having had to get up at five o'clock in the morn when I am bred to do so between eleven and midday.

Choking back the saliva that filled my mouth, eyes as puffy as a hen before she lays, stomach jumping round uncontrollably, and wearing an expression of utter disgust brought on by frowning one's brow, wrinkling one's nose, and stretching one's lips toward one's ears like the strings of a double bass, I cursed Juan and his tastes, his wife, myself, the bloody English who make one get up at dawn as if one were a hen or a frontline soldier,* cursed an Italian bun vendor who came and tried to peddle me his dreadful goods, and even cursed Taniete, whom I deplored for not having broken a bone when, in carrying out his orders, he deigned to enter my room at such an unseasonable hour to rouse me from the deep slumber in which I had hitherto reposed.

Mise-en-scène: a Sur Railways train carriage, moments before pulling out to take me to spend eight days with my friend and his wife.

Why on earth, on whose account, since when was I—comfort-loving by instinct and by conviction, moored to my ways as a post to the ground—throwing my principles to the wind and casting myself into a life of adventures?

Not even I could explain it with certainty.

Was it my affections for Juan and my desire to please him?

Not likely! I have never been one to fashion myself to the will of others.

Was it selfish curiosity?

Rather more plausible: I wanted to feel the effects of the oft-lauded paradise ranch at *Los Tres Médanos* for myself.

If only, I said to myself, trying to paint a less somber picture of my situation, they would leave me in peace, leave me alone, not oblige me to endure a bunch of hillbillies (ever in attendance round these parts) making a hash of things at all times: opening the windows when I want them closed; closing them when I prefer a bit of air; causing the floor to be awash with pools of saliva, spit out quick as the lash of a whip from between their incisors; forcing my boots up into my nose as they stretch out to their hearts' content and spread out as they please; or what is ten times worse, on the pretext of their painful corns, taking off a boot or two as if it were the most natural thing on the planet; or doing any other crude and coarse thing to enrage me and vex me and try my patience.

I looked at the station clock: 6:13 *ante meridiem*.

A second later we would be on our way.

---

*Sur Railways, a new venture in the 1880s, was English-owned.

The station guard's whistle gave a sharp *mi*, the locomotive responded with a deep *doh*, the engine driver took hold of the starting crank, the steam acted upon the valves, the train was on the move at last . . .

"Praise God," I cried, "I am saved!"

Who would have thought?

Just then one bundle of leather and another of flesh came flying like a bat out of hell through the door, opened with a clatter, and a man and a case—such as the two were, blurred together as one indistinct shape—suddenly slammed into the wall opposite me.

"That was a close call; I almost missed it," he exclaimed with a triumphant smile, straightening up to brush off the dust from his collision.

"Heaven knows I wish that you had, you bl . . . undering idiot," I thought to myself furiously.

Would you care to hear the stupefying, miraculous life story of this gentleman without being obliged to ask a single question in order to earn the pleasure?

He's the son of an old foreman or overseer—or some post holder or other—in any old cow town in Anchorena or Dorrego or some such place.

He spent his early years moving between the hearth in the kitchen and the back of some weary, old animal probably left crippled by the encounter; that is, with his feet planted firmly on the floor or his toes gripping a sheep's shanks and a raw leather strip for a stirrup.

He could lasso a colt, herd cows to the milking yard, find a teruteru's nest, kill a partridge with the crack of a whip, capture a wild animal with his bare hands, and polish off two dozen fry cakes on Daddy's saint's day; but at twelve years of age, that was all he could do.

His father, swayed by the advice of his boss, resolved at the time to send him to the neighboring village's school twice a week (in Chascomús or some such place—what's in a name?) where he learned to read poorly and write worse, while being slapped and strapped with a belt: in those days, one learned letters by blood; the schoolteachers were Spaniards.

A dozen years later, the old countryman's little farm with its hundred cows and its team of horses had become a prosperous and valuable ranch—by the grace of God as well as sheer animal reproduction—so that when the father died this lackey found himself coming into a considerable fortune and being elevated to the ranks of influential member of the community, whose lofty appointments he carried out successfully and to the general applause of his subjects.

As justice of the peace, amongst the stackload of barbarous acts he sententiously begat, the crowning glory, his shining moment in the noble apostate of magistracy, was to demand proof of some poor devil who had taken the liberty of calling the pharmacist's wife a whore, and, upon hearing it, although she was the wife of a big shot, to absolve the accused of guilt and charges due to—in his opinion—the satisfactory evidence provided, whereupon the integrity of his character and rectitude of his deportment as a judge became manifest before the general public.

As president of the municipality, he lent all of his aesthetic weight to the embellishment of the town square and public buildings.

Columns, door frames, and cornices were six parts gravel and one part lime; capitals, moldings, rosettes, and other useless adornments of plaster; friezes, quoins and sashes of shiny white and sky blue tiles, symbolizing the "pure white and celestial status of our Pavilion"; and atop the pillars that surrounded the square (traversed by heavenly streets in a crisscross pattern), fat, crude little pineapples painted green and red, whose detail allowed one to divine the work of the town architect (commonly acknowledged as mediocre), a son of *bella Italia* and also a fanatic of the "*bianco, rosso e verde della nostra bandiera.*"

As president of the social club, he organized a smashing party in honor of both the patron saint and the inauguration of the chapel's new building, and it is still the talk of the town.

All of the salons' decorations (wallpaper, curtains, paper, etc.) were chosen, purchased, and sent by him personally from Buenos Aires, where he troubled himself to go with the singular and exclusive aim of acquiring the items personally and at his fancy, and spent a total of $12,350 Argentine pesos, the sum of the raffle tickets sold to the community on May 25 and July 9.*

The list includes:

An English shag carpet, double breadth, bought at Pereda's bazaar and adorned with regal Havana balusters on a white background, combined with luxuriant leaf and flower motifs of every mortally clashing

*Independence Day and Revolution Day.

color in creation, the mere sight of which—even from a quick sidelong glance caught whilst walking past a half-open door—was a slap in the face of good taste and enough to leave one cross-eyed;

Gilt wallpaper with horns of plenty on a red background with green trim and four pompous, allegorical (also paper) figures stuck in the corners: the Republic, Freedom, Industry, and Commerce, a purchase transacted in Sur Painting and Decorating on Calle Buen Orden;

Some sort of pastel concoction on the ceiling, transformed by the sheer genius of the artist—a young Piedmontese compatriot under the tutelage of the architect in question—into (theoretically) a brilliant sky smattered in the direction of the zenith with groups of monsters, chains of little angels that one could make out in a clearing adroitly arranged around a bower covered in flowers and foliage;

Damask, bright purple wool furniture, straight from Shaw's showroom, white curtains at 200 pesos a pair with their corresponding yellow tin rods and, lastly, two triumphant patriotic flags to complete the ornate decor of the salon.

As for the soldiers' salon, transformed into a great dining hall in honor of the party, if the furnishings were not brilliant—everyone runs out of steam at some point—the meal itself had potential.

Suckling pig and roast turkey, sliced rolled beef, cold meats, a pyramid of macaroons in the middle of the table and two pyramids of caramelized oranges on either end, endless supplies of egg-yolk sweets, selections of pastries, and shiny candies. Château-Biré, Carlón on tap, etc., etc., all of which was prepared and served by the hotel's proprietor and his silent partner, the confectioner, with *maté* and rose liqueur flowing freely.

Now, on to the event itself.

The orchestra was comprised of one marimba-clavichord—a truly formidable instrument when it comes to breaking eardrums. At the merest hint of the *mazurka* danced by the mulatto hired ad hoc in Buenos Aires, it unleashed torrents of "harmony" that could easily induce one to steer clear of the whole affair to avoid having to partake, even if one were wearing one's patriotic hat.

Just imagine the eyesore presented by this spectacular function— overrun by the town's long-haired dandies, from amongst whom our man shone out like a general before battle—filled to capacity with the cream of local lassies reeking of cheap cologne (the dark-skinned ones dressed in green and blue; the fair ones in red and yellow, a mass of fake flowers like deadweights atop their heads, and wearing red bone earrings, *doublé* brooches, kidskin gloves, and little elastic prunella socks).

That night, my companion truly surpassed himself.

Elected master of ceremonies by acclamation, he was determined to please everyone, enjoining the mulatto to dance first a habanera then a *chotis*, or whatever was requested by any friend attempting to curry favor with whichever lassie he was courting.

It was as if he were many people, attending to everything and everyone with the air of regal protection and hospitality peculiar to a small-town magnate, a fact that did not prevent him from being a show-off, blowing smoke from time to time, or from lingering with the daughter of the commander, a real desert flower to whom he became engaged a few months later.

Napoleon knew what he was talking about when he said that ambition is one of the human heart's fiercest passions.

Elevated from a nobody to the pinnacle of grandeur, one would have thought our hero had nothing left to do or want for but to rest on his laurels or, what is one and the same, on the veranda of his house, sipping a *maté* in his shirtsleeves; and yet, one fine day, he was struck by the thought that his town—his country, as a provincial deputy would call it—was but one tiny corner of the world, and what is more, the most remote tiny corner on earth.

The sight of the main street, the church vestibule, the plaza; the society inhabited by his father-in-law the commander, his friends, the doctor, and the priest; the power he wielded over his neighbors, their high opinion of him—in short, everything that made up his lovely life as an ace in that deck called county-town community—proved insufficient to satisfy the import of his aspirations and, a small-town player, he aspired to act on the stage of the capital.

His wife, for her part, dreamed of a house in Concepción, a carriage to take her to Palermo, and a box seat at the Alegría Theater, not because she was put off by the idea of displaying her weight and girth in a balcony at the Colón* but simply because: what was the point of going to a Huguenot play if she didn't speak Italian?

---

*The Concepción area, close to the center of the city if one heads south, was a favorite with wealthy families; Palermo, in the very north, became a popular place for Buenos Aires high society after it was turned into a park. As for the two theaters, there is a distinct opposition between them: the Colón was, between 1855 and 1908, a place for European opera performances; the Alegría, which put on comedies and variety shows, was frequented by those with few musical pretensions and by the general public.

Los Madgiares and *The Seven Degrees of Crime*: now that was *vraiment fantastique*!

With a full purse, the pair therefore decided to move to another neighborhood and to take their possessions on up to Calle Independencia or Calle Estados Unidos, between Calle Chacabuco and Calle Lima.

There they established themselves, there they started their family, and there they live still.

She, taking great, swift strides toward obesity, from sheer contentment and complacency at having seen her dream realized: she has her house, her carriage, her box seat, and relations with all of the decent families in the neighborhood, whom every year—give or take a few months—she informs of her acquisition of some new servant to order around.

He, a man of influence both in city and country—where he has at his disposal friends quick to serve him—a member of the Rural Society,* the parish Health Commission, and some political club or other, in whose ranks he militates in the capacity and rank of heartfelt republican.

V I

D id I say republican?
Yes, but let us set the record straight—a homegrown republican, for whom republicanism boils down to the following: calling this poor country "República Argentina," calling the executive power "Government," calling the head of government "President," and periodically performing the following political farce, played out in four acts, that consolidates the ideal of our republican existence.

---

*An Argentinian stockbreeding cooperative, the Rural Society was inaugurated in 1866 to help combat the recession affecting the livestock industry.

Act I

Colossal scandal disguised as popular election in which absolutely everyone casts a vote; that is, every native son there ever was and ever will be, including the dead who, from the graves where they rot in Recoleta or Chacarita,* frequently lend their names and votes to bribery.

To carry it off, all that is needed is for the group leader or parish caudillo to have a registry office enrollment receipt filled out in the candidate's name in his pocket, and for the candidate in turn to have a ballot paper from the national guard, notwithstanding his utter penury and his time spent in the penitentiary (where he paid for his profusion of crimes by lolling about on the national bankroll in a well-ventilated, comfortable room, with recreational time spent in the gardens, and his hearty portions of food, roast meat, and bread baked especially for him), on the battalion line (where he did whatever struck his fancy, and simply upped and left if the role of defender of the nation's honor and dignity did not suit him), and in the brothels and taverns in which he finally perfected his republican education.

For the month prior to the ruckus he lives with others of his kind *en famille*, on a ranch behind closed doors (just in case), with those in charge of the salaries and profits of the candidates. Who lies with dogs, wakes with fleas.

When the time comes, the somber moment arrives and the master of ceremonies, with some of the puppeteers, props him up to carry out his sovereign duties, such as voting for five pesos without knowing for what or whom, once, twice, or thrice if he can get away with it; first under the name of Juan, then as Pedro, then Diego; first bearded, then clean-shaven, with a beret on his head or a straw hat pulled down to his eyes; perhaps he will even raise Cain, fire a few shots, and stab a few people, stealing the ballots from the box if the caudillo sees it not going in his favor and gives the signal.

---

*Cemeteries in Buenos Aires. The first, wealthier and more traditional, is in the north; the second, not opened until 1871, lies in the northeast.

Act II

The republican tableau, or rather, the bloody, shameful farce, then stops centering on the extras and is performed in the lofty theater of the Chamber of Deputies.

Here, before opening the doors to the public, with the theater in darkness, the buffoons, that is, the play-actors—or, if you prefer, the fathers of the fatherland, with all due respect—furtively hold their highfalutin sessions, their corresponding rehearsals at which, with much sleight of hand and wheeling and dealing, they shred the script. They encourage the collaboration of fools who—playing the part of political integrity and purity of suffrage—have given a seal of legality and justice (adding a bit here, taking some away there, cutting and slashing yonder) until they have transformed something bad into something worse, into an indigestion-provoking hash concocted by patriotism, a sickening mess that appeals only to hawks and vultures, depending on whether the enemies are hawks or vultures and whether they themselves are vultures or hawks.

When the long-awaited day of the première arrives, after taking all necessary precautions in case of mayhem, with the police and a few company lines forewarned in case all hell breaks loose, the venerable house of worship is overrun by a huge, select crowd . . . the last dregs of society: murderers, thieves, bums, drunks, and bullies; out-and-out rogues, pistols tucked into their trousers and knives in their suspenders, recruited and rounded up ad hoc to solemnify the occasion with their presence, which represents the majesty of the sovereign people.

The scene opens with the appearance of a star player, the leading man let us say, dressed up as a young democrat, a champion of civil liberties, a deputy by profession, dark, frowning, stern-faced on penalty of death by starvation, hair tucked behind his ear, and wearing the uniform of his vocation, that is, meticulously attired in black cashmere.

He assumes a decorous, dignified air, looks round menacingly, gets up, puts on airs and then intones the following monologue, which lasts three quarters of an hour:

"Suffrage, freedom, justice, truth, right, constitution, sovereignty, beacon, law, independence, epic, country, people!" (Riotous applause from the audience, mixed in with loud whistles.)

"Democracy, honesty, fire, patriotism, light, sword, abnegation, republic, apostle, glory, peace, honor, propriety, life: us!"

"Excellent, superb, bravo, *bravissimo!*" (from the right).

"Git offa stage an' be gone wit' ya!" (from the left).

"Silence, you brutes!" (from the old man dressed as Papa Jupin, both the oldest and coincidentally the most useless of the lot, from the back of the stage that represents Olympus).

"Be quiet, you booby!" (a falsetto voice).

"Violence," the voice persists, "robbery, ill will, fraud, conscious grafting, bribery, interference, falsification, obscurantism, disorder, ruin, darkness, abyss, death: them!" (Prolonged, thunderous applause from the right; even more prolonged, boisterous whistling and catcalls from the left.)

The bearded one: "If you do not shut your mouths this instant I shall have you kicked out like dogs by the police.

"I hold the keys to heaven.

"Read them the house rules." (To an extra dressed as secretary.)

The extra reads.

"Don't stand so close to the wall; we might have to fly the coop." (One voice.)

"Stop twitting on like a bird; don't torture me this way!" (Another.)

"We want our money back!" (Yet another.)

"Meow, meow, woof, woof, woof." (Still another.)

The player slips smugly into the wings, where he is warmly congratulated by his colleagues.

To recount the scene that followed, attributed to some other first-rate company *bagattelliere*, would be a complete waste of time.

It is a word-for-word rendition, a second edition of the first, the very pronouncement you have just heard, only toned down slightly, and could be translated by the following proverbs: you can see a mote in another's eye, but cannot see a beam in your own; when the fox begins to preach, beware of your geese; or perhaps better still by another that common decency forbids me to put into print.

Again the same applause, the same catcalls, the same disrespectful interruptions from the honorable audience and the same never-ending threats from Jupin who carefully refrains from carrying them out for fear of having his Olympian bones broken.

Finally comes the turn of him who is in charge of the musical part of the program, the singer, the lyricist, or, what is much the same, the bore, a player not oft absent in our political theaters, him who—pale-faced and sunken-eyed—commences by pitifully and plaintively intoning tender laments, deploring errant souls, the corruption of passions, and the profound evils that afflict society; in spite of himself he is soon enthralled by the magnetic spell of his own voice, like the *chingolo* bird by the viper, until, drunk on his own tune, he concludes by enthusiastically bursting forth the following *doh*, as if it were all a God-given truth:

"Republic, no; anarchy, yes; honorable republicans, not a one; demagogues and scoundrels, all," calling, as one can see, a spade a spade, until public fury is unleashed upon his head and the deafening noise of two thousand people whistling in his ears drowns out his voice, forces him to put his violin back in its case, and throws him and his music out into the abyss of ridicule where he remains buried for all eternity.

In short, the hawks opt for the dolt of a deputy and the function draws to a close, naturally with blows, with the intervention of the gendarmes and with twenty-four hours in jail for the rabble.

The big shots and pompous asses, authors and promoters of the republican commotion, they are like Jupin: they hold the keys to heaven and what they want to do and do thereupon is to go home, satisfied of a day's work and proud at having been able to offer a display of customs, a splendidly estimable copy of the luxuriously bound book showing the world how we Argentines practice republicanism, to the curious onlookers of societies who watch us.

Act III

This scene takes place in the pampas, at the army encampment of the defenders of the law, illustrious reformers of suffrage.

They symbolize the truth: mocked; justice: violated; the rights of man: trampled; and sensitive to the bloody offense inflicted upon our lady the constitution, new mistress of their thoughts, inspired in the austere rectitude of their principles, overflowing with righteous indignation, they take up the sword, don the breastplate, and rush into battle to chance their fate, declaring a fight to the death and no mercy on the present government, on the vile rabble who have come to power by the basest of indignities, to the discredit of the country and the affront of the nation's native sons!

But raise their visors and you will scoff at humanity and cry for the country.

You shall find therein the bastard face of the political trafficker who, in exchange for satisfying his bootlicking ambitions and upon realizing that the game is almost up, does not hesitate to hoist the red flag of rebellion, embroiling the country in the untold horrors of civil war.

Whom does he command?

A handful of rebellious soldiers, a few thousand miserable gauchos—cannon fodder seized from their jobs and families—and a band of savages, anxious to plunder and murder, though they too, of course, are illustrious reformers of suffrage.

The echo of a divine voice can be heard bouncing off the ranks of the inspired.

"I lay myself before you," it says, "with the aim of giving this vast and beautiful movement some sort of democratic cohesion and national significance *(sic)*.

"The whole republic raises up in arms against this spurious government that has encroached upon the supreme direction of the country's destiny: I shall stand firm to the end with the last of you who stand beside me and I shall conquer or die with you."

Did he conquer?

Si e vieillesse pouvait!

Did he die?

Pas si bête!

Neither one nor the other.

Of course, it was a crying shame and terrible luck that led him to make himself out to be a false prophet and a warrior king in a disgraceful attempted coup against the rulers of the country.

A lemming volunteer, one might say, he was swept along by the crowd.

Was it a sin, an offense?

Sin and offense are for the common man.

This was a crime—and a crime against the state—committed by a man whose will was always carried out by a kneeling entourage, not a man in charge but an oracle who commands.

I proceed.

In charge of an army, he was pitifully defeated by a few random nobodies; hours later he was taken prisoner, at which time he handed over, along with himself, three thousand Argentines, as one might hand over a bunch of grapes, consenting (with truly evangelical docility) to call the de facto government the de jure government, having previously railed against the former; and a few months later, the rulers of the great party of principles, the pure, the honorable, the patriots, the intransigents, became de jure members of the spurious, vile, usurping de facto government.

For shame!

And if you are not keen on these pastoral scenes, if your palate rejects the sickly sweet nectar of bees, the repugnant Arcadian honey, all you have to do is say so.

The national museum of political anatomy has an extensive collection of this type of aborted action.

In any flavor you like.

I can offer you one on the barricades, a one-act farce performed in public that, in spite of the blood spilled, deserves no name apart from that which a stupid, clumsy clown wears on his head.

Just imagine the work of a Boca Wop.

A superficial token, thrown together posthaste from a block of white pine, the cheapest wood, anointed with three layers of paint, armed with a trident, and adorned with a crown, beneath the bowsprit of some coastal boat—the Cóvine Carlotta perhaps—and you will have before you the Nettuno's caulked monstrosity, or what is known as a figurehead.

That's our man.

Same wooden face, hard, stiff, crude, rough, devoid of any delicate touch in the features that reveals the artist's most excellent superior hand; or any vestige of nobility in the soul; or a remnant of generosity in the heart. The same austere, grotesquely frowning brow that Stein copied so faithfully in his "Mosquito" caricatures;* the same monstrously high forehead, passed down from the celebrated imbecile of Amsterdam; the same stubborn, repugnant figure that unwittingly brings to one's lips either an epithet (hurled at its creator when seen on the bow of the aforementioned boat) or an evil curse hurled at the man himself when by chance one bumps into him and finds it resting atop the shoulders of the individual in question.

Utterly incapable of original thought, this run-of-the-mill lawyer is a third-rate compiler of the few books he had the audacity to publish under his name, as they are naught but menial plagiarism, shocking pillages of foreign harvests. They possess everything of the others and nothing of his, except for a veritably atrocious style.

After straining painfully at the effort, the words finally tumble forth, in shapeless groups of eight or ten, staring at each other or turning their backs on one another, standing upright, reclining, or upside-down,

*The most popular political satire in nineteenth-century Argentina.

it matters not, and as soon as they begin to walk they become stunted, like some malformed midget, crying out for a prod.

It's like a squirt of lemon hitting a live oyster.

Likewise, it is bitter, sour, sharp, and produces the same effect in one's brain as citric acid upon the unfortunate mollusk: it shrivels up, frowns, and wriggles to be free of the noxious contagion and to resist the infection of so sickening a literary virus.

Still floating on the surface by luck and by fate, this god of fools has left nothing in his path; his country owes him nothing in exchange for the ills he has wrought and the countless blunders that—in his public life—he continuously committed; the scheme he hatched, for one, in the midst of parliamentary session, and the threat of war in which his innate loutishness wrapped us up, was a brutal act carried out by his lowly instincts.

Common sense seemed, finally, to have finished off so sad a sire, relegating him to oblivion, when all of a sudden a combination of sound politics (in form) and indecent questionable dealings (in content), borne of the cowardice of him who had not the . . . guts to be a man and lead the people when times were tough, somehow managed to free himself of the ostracism in which he had heretofore been living.

Ah, the strange aberrations of human nature!

A truly despised being, worthless, talentless, heartless, virtueless— qualities that are the very stuff of caudillos, features that exalt a man in the eyes of others—he managed to personify the aspirations of a fanatical crowd whose passion drowned out the voice of reason. Having wounded the generous nature of patriotism by exploiting the vilest of flags—that of selfish localism—their eyes saw not, their minds thought not, only their hearts felt, and felt their sacred mother outraged, her honor groped, her freedom chained, her life threatened.

Two thousand men dead, two thousand empty places in homes, two thousand lives stolen from their country and their toils, the blood of two thousand Argentines spilled on the altar of a deformed idol, an offering to the most cynical and vulgar of demagogues, thanks to the millions squandered and the humiliating spectacle offered to America and to the world. I have here the price of a new deadly nightshade potion, the Greek gift of a false brotherly reconciliation, a phony peace agreement, a fallacious harmony.

So?

So, he lives peacefully in his home, protected by the laws he falsified and the constitution he trampeled; he enjoys the rights guaranteed to honorable, innocent citizens; he comes and goes unmolested; he eats, drinks, and sleeps carefree and without remorse, because he feels none nor could one with no conscience feel any, and there is no shortage of men happy to shake his hand and take off their hats to him.

Ah! If he could have lived two thousand lives and been killed two thousand times, perhaps the account would not have been balanced so in his favor.

The last and lowliest of the lives he sacrificed is worth infinitely more than his own.

"Flames are found not in heaven! What use, then, lightening?"

Justice, you old slattern, why is that sword in thine hand?

Enough.

Given that certain deeds incite and certain men become riled, blood flows to the brain in a frenzy, and one loses the desire to write nonsense and rubbish.

Let us move on, once and for all.

In short, Act III closes with the end of the brawl and the triumph of the hawks who still reign over the old lummox.

Act IV

A most serene tranquillity reigns over the land.

The victorious sun casts down its rays, bathing the noble city in a refreshing, peaceful light.

One's mood is relieved and one's soul eagerly, deliciously breathes in the cool mountain breeze of a morning full of promise.

"Let us raise our eyes heavenward; let us part our lips in fervent prayer; we ask you to join us as we humbly bow our heads and pray.

"The time for honest toil has arrived, the time for today's toil, to-morrow's toil, and the sempiternal toil, till the sweat of our brows and the exhaustion of our aching bodies is generously rewarded by the immortal accomplishment of our abundantly wealthy and enormously powerful country!"

The voice of patriotism roars, dreaming, but Ay! the discordant cry of demagogy hastens to drown it out, thundering through the air; the dream fades away and the offended image of the republic takes refuge amongst her kind, thereby abandoning the disputed field to the hydra of anarchy.

"Work! Yes, in good time; but let us benefit from our toils, though

the gain be destructive, as long as from amongst the ruins one personality emerges unscathed: mine.

"What is the nation?

"Any old piece of land.

"What, the men who inhabit it?

"An abject portion of abject humanity.

"The first is a gold mine, exploited by beasts of burden; men can be
bought in the market of life by anyone whose pockets are full.

"Fill them, then, that is the end; the means matter little.

"Conscience, duty, morality?

"Empty words invented by fools. Search out the motive of self-
interest; that is the only morality because it is the only truth."

Thus spake the wheeler-dealer, the vile exploiter whose profession it
is to fleece the public coffers, shielded by a contract and sheltered by
the indolence of some and the corruption of others.

Like a plague of locusts incubating on the political terrain, it erupts
in the heat of its ardent battles, falls starving upon the fields of public
riches that it decimates, and devastates them until they become barren
wasteland.

Allow me, if you will, to use the heel of my boot to trample him,
like a filthy pig wallowing in muck.

To reach out a hand and touch him—even with the very tips of my
fingers—or to flip him over to exhibit his shocking deformity, that I
cannot do; his contact produces the most unconquerable revulsion
within me and I have delicate sensibilities: 'tis my stomach, you see.

He could sell his soul to the devil, not inspired like Faust by the
ardent nature of his desire for all things beautiful, but as Judas sold
Jesus; he has no faith apart from the bad faith with which he seals all
his life's negotiations.

His conscience is a rubber sack; it will hold anything you place within
it, ever stretching, never ripping.

Well known in the market, his reputation, on the other hand, is
firmly established: it is that of an utter rogue.

With no baggage but his cynicism, with no capital apart from his
ruses and man-of-the-party title, he puts his shoulder to the wheel to
gain candidacy by falsifying a few hundred votes; he gets nominated
anything at all, deputy, say, in the last party campaign, by a half dozen
crafty devils such as himself, cronies and connections of his; and
equipped with this bill of indemnity he sets off to tempt fate with his
eyes glued—like those of a starved man in front of a bakery window—

on the rich and well-supplied exchequer's arsenal, that bastard egg that no one has laid and that is emptied by the caracara's sharpened beak or the clever fox's snout.

One sees him arriving at the Casa Rosada's avenues, slipping into the antechambers and setting up camp, benefited by the station his employment affords him, or by the friendship or family relations that connect him to a minister, magnate, or somesuch.

He is fishing for a so-called deal with the government, clean or dirty, that is of no consequence; what he wants is money and there is nothing like this line of business if one wishes to line one's pockets with gold and make a real killing.

He's got more brass than a band and since he has nothing at stake and has nothing to lose, as he possesses neither decorum nor honor, shame nor money, nor even fear of being thrown in jail—jail was not built for people like him—he accepts everything that falls into his hands, from every corrupt branch of business.

And here's the rub.

Are you decided upon exploring this or that river, making service of the coasts, organizing a scientific or commercial expedition?

In El Tigre or Boca some old abandoned wreck of a vessel has lain for several years, in oblivion, unserviceable.

It is bought for next to nothing, for the price of the timber; the shipwright is called to fill it with burlap; the painter comes to slap on a quick coat of black or some white lead aimed at hiding the worm-eaten wood from public scrutiny; it then looks brand-new and is thus offered for sale to the government.

The government appoints a team of experts to examine it; the team of experts proclaims it leviathan and more than capable of taking on the unleashed furies of the elements undaunted; and the government, naturally, rushes to take advantage of the bargain, making its purchase for fifty-thousand pesos.

And then? Then, nothing: the first sandbank it hits splits the thing to pieces like an overripe peach pit, it sinks effortlessly beneath the gentle-flowing waters and remains submerged therein together with the fifty-thousand pesos it cost.

Tableau.

There in the most desolate part of the pampas, the noble yet wretched Argentine soldier ekes out his existence, that stoic fellow, the admirable embodiment of a beast of burden's endurance and Christian resignation.

The country demands his all and he gives his all to the country.

His home and family he abandons, his wealth he loses, his life he endlessly exposes to the traps set by savages fighting in an all-out, merciless war.

And what does he receive in exchange? What prize, what recompense for the desperate solitude in which he suffers and dies for others?

Is he accorded, by chance, any look of compassion if not gratitude? Are the most pressing needs of his life attended to? Is he thrown a blanket to cover his aching bones, stiffened by the glacial Andean winds? Is he given even the miserable soldier's slop, a piece of meat, a handful of greens, and a cigarette, neither asking for nor requiring more?

The country wants it, the exchequer pays for it, but human avarice— embodied in the degenerate soul who speculates on even his brother's hunger and thirst—does not thus comprehend it. Is it some vast project to endow the nation with the great enterprise that it imperiously demands?

Our man racks his brains, goes on maneuvers, and pulls all the strings imaginable. He inquires as to the weak spot of those who are to intervene in the affair (members of parliament, employees, government representatives, etc.) and, depending upon the results of his investigations, he casts out his nets and lays his traps.

If the candidate is thin-skinned and not the type to sit back impassively and allow himself to be manhandled, he makes himself scarce and relies on contacts; he falls back on the perennial tactic of the letter of recommendation, which—with his hat in his hand—he'll have sought from some friend or relation, and in which he implores the recipient not to forget the importance of protecting one's friends, loyal and true party members, etc., etc.

If on the other hand the subject in question is tough as nails, one of those who is not troubled by the finer points of the law, does not understand scruples, oh! then he does not tarry in compliments; he takes the direct route and shoots straight to the heart of the matter, allowing the other to fall flat on his face from the shock of his obscene remarks so that he shall hand over the business with the bright prospect of reaping a fat share of the company profits.

The accounting is quite straightforward: the exchequer pays 100; what he is given is worth 10; the remaining 90 are split between the partners, be they many or few, at a set price per head, depending upon the risks each has run, the quota each has set, or the importance of the pecuniary or industrial capital they introduced into the equation, all of which translated into common parlance means: as far as the dough goes, the most criminally involved get the biggest kickback.

Ah! You lofty ones, you who would remain pure in the midst of the scandalous moral perversion that presently invades us, stop and think, think of the enormous responsibility dragging you down with its weight.

The country will demand a detailed account of the use of that power that you struggled so to attain.

Slander will blight your names and, mistaken for reprobates in history's telling of the tale, you will be justly damned by those who follow.

There is still time: arm yourselves with energy and fight the good fight, make an iron-handed, white-gloved government, but do it now!

Moors and Christians, let those who should fall, fall; let what is written about all men being equal before the law and courts cease, once and for all, to be an insolent lie . . .

And thus closes the fourth and final act of the performance given by Sir People and upon which Sir People does naught but look on from the balcony of his house, protesting—offended—that they try to claim he is the father of such an odious farce, as did Rossini from a box at the *Italiens*, upon disowning his favorite work after it was transformed by the voice of Patti.

Except, of course, that we must pay due respect to art and give credit where credit is due: whereas Patti is a diva, despite the vast sums thrown into the gutter on the theater's subsidy, our playacting politicians are a *massa di cani*.

VII

Let's get back to my trip and my companion.

As I was saying, he was a heartfelt republican.

But as, unfortunately, everything human is created and everything created is imperfect, our man could not help but fall to this inevitable mortal law, and he too paid his dues in this vale of tears.

Nasty aristocratic blotches mottled the pure crucible of his democratic creed.

Though a strong man, he had his weak spots, some the product of time-honored, conservative prejudices; others the consequence of living on his daddy's blessed ranch spawn.

One or two examples:

He would not eat at the same table as, nor take off his hat to, nor shake hands with, nor call "sir" anyone black, mulatto, or Chinese, if clearly identifiable as such.

I proffer this last prudent proviso since many are we whose veins more resemble cesspools than blood vessels, for the number of odd liquids mixed therein and, yet, being accustomed to seeing people happily mixing with the subjects of the highest social circles unconsciously prevents our analysis of the situation to the point of being left gaping when some amateur or other, one of those old villager-meddlers who make it their business to know every *canaille* put on God's green earth from the year one to the present day, points out to our shortsighted eyes the impure halftones, the chiaroscuro bastard whose color we had hitherto neglected to notice.

Small groups of people would begin to talk about So-and-so, gathered round the hearth, or on the Club del Progreso balcony of a summer night.

"So-and-so? Why, he's a mulatto!" the villager rushes to exclaim with the air of a sly old fox and devilish rogue, so killing is his pleasure at being able to tear apart his fellow man, stirring things up in public thus.

"Well, just between us," he adds confidentially, "rumor has it that this little fellow's mother was this and that and the other.

"I shan't even bring up his grandmother; that whole affair was public knowledge.

"Of course that was back when the cathedral had a straw roof..."

Talk about talking a blue streak! Shredding left and right, hacking off bits of the family tree until it is left mutilated and bruised, as though ten tons of rocks had fallen on it. Conclusion: the individual in question is irrevocably mulatto.

"Well, I never!" we exclaim, in our turn, as if we had just fallen from the sky, "You know, not once did it even occur to me."

And only then do we start to hone in on certain surefire signs that never fail: his thick lips, squashed nose, kinky black hair, olive tone, etc., etc.

This sort of mulatto does not, however, form part of those that our republican looks down his nose at.

He could be family himself.

If, on the other hand, we are talking about a guaranteed, unmistakable, universally recognized mulatto, that is when the situation changes.

Manners are out the window: he speaks to him informally, using "*tú*" immediately and without invitation—particularly if the man comes from a humble background—and throws his color in his face straightaway if he so much as piques him even slightly, thereby incurring our man's noble wrath.

He buys a carriage and rather than dressing the coachman in a coat and hat so that the gaucho's clothes are properly fitting or—since he wants luxury—in the frock coat, black trousers, and high hat that befit the puritanism he espouses, he makes a spectacle of the poor man in some carnivalesque, ridiculous, pompous, liveried outfit.

The equipage awaits at the door of the house.

Would you care to examine it?

Four-wheeled, horse-drawn landau, of domestic variety: (Delanoux) forecarriage with a hood that squeaks to high heaven.

Splendid harnesses: gilt, lots of gilt, gilt everywhere.

Of course these accoutrements hang from plain, old-fashioned sheet metal, just like back in the good old days, when the selfsame people who now dress in *grande tenue* and sit on the Colón Theater balconies used to drive through Palermo, polishing Manuelita's apples, wearing gaucho *chiripá* blankets for trousers, donning red insignia,* and being pulled by a horse straining beneath the weight of silver trinkets.

Naturally he had the aforementioned trappings tailored by Astoul, buying the most *clinquante camelote*, the most infamous of drugs manufactured in France or Germany, expressly for export to America, the most expensive and therefore the most tawdry.

Atop the coach box, the driver: tangled hair, mustachios, goatee, and a Hamburg cigarette in his mouth.

Now the livery: mousy brown-colored boots (for want of polish);

*This is a reference to the *rosismo* period (1835–52), which essentially corresponds to Juan Manuel de Rosas's second Buenos Aires government. Both the barracks and Rosas's own estate were located in Palermo, in the north of the city, which was at the time becoming one of the leading focal points for social activities. Manuela, Rosas's daughter, often organized parties and celebrations for Buenos Aires' high society there. Red was the federalist color, especially representative of *rosismo;* emblems and insignia were always red.

checkered trousers tucked into the boots; excessively baggy and poorly fitting greatcoat down to mid-shin; white cravat, as wide as your thumb, like the sort used by the host of a political banquet who attends in full dress; linen gloves, also white, but as filthy and tatty at the tips as those of him whose gloves hold the reins and run until they are ruined by the halters *aux couleurs de la nation;* a pair of red reins; and, finally, a bowler hat of nearly impossible shape, passed down through the generations, like the cravat, slimy with a coating of dirty oil and sweat and that has been previously adorned with a quite hideous, tasseled cockade.

The charioteer, obviously without removing the cigar from between his teeth, creaks the buggy into action as if it were a parade float, gets the team of forlorn horses moving, patriotic tassels fluttering in the wind, tails of the huge frock coat hanging freely from the back of the coach box, and our man and his abundant wife set off to flaunt themselves smugly down Calle Florida and round Avenida Sarmiento.

Now you have the picture: *chic ébouriffant.*

You now know only too well that a godless fate had abandoned me to this fellow.

Let us proceed.

I admit that I am not in the habit of opening my arms to anybody I first meet.

I am an awkward chap when it comes to friendship, this being the only sentiment in which I believe fanatically; the only one that—ever, in my stroll through life's corridors—I have found to be above all the miseries that the human whirlwind stirs up from the selfishness of its corrupt heart, as a torrent corrupts the crystal-clear waters of a lake, unsettling the sludge that had hitherto lain still in its depths.

Love, for instance—a material appetite selfish in essence as are all material appetites: it wants only to be sated.

Eliminate the lust and it dies.

A bastard son, those who sing its praises commit a crime; they renounce its legitimate sister.

When it reaches the heights of generosity, greatness, exaltation, then it is no longer love, but friendship.

It has evolved with the passage of time in the same way that the miser who gives away his riches in the moments before his death is then lauded as a generous man.

Possessing, as I do, a religious respect for friendship, having worshipped her feverishly since childhood, I will not allow anyone to take her name in vain.

This is why, now an old man, I have but a handful of friends and a very narrow circle of relationships that will never extend beyond courtesy, which is synonymous with urbanity.

Acting on these principles—which were at the time effectively seconded by my abject disposition—I settled myself in a corner of the train carriage and closed myself off, locked and bolted the door, as it were, and fell upon the papers attained, moments earlier, from a newsboy in the station, in order to kill time.

I opened the first one on hand and was confronted by the following leader:

"Let's see eye to eye," began an editorial, three columns of breviary, totaling the respectable sum of twenty-three thousand, five hundred, and some-odd letters.

Thrice I glanced from top to bottom at this select bit of militant literature, with the same expression one wears when laying eyes upon a castor-oil purgative after a cucumber salad has left one with indigestion or, if you prefer, the salad itself after the indigestion.

Three consecutive ugh's were released from deep within my chest and, finally, with a deep breath, I raised the little tract—that bottomless well of enlightenment—to my eyes, and resigned myself to swallow the bitter pill.

"When within the articles of the constitution . . ." paragraph one, thirty-some lines; theory, I thought: nevermind that bit.

"The wholesome doctrine in accordance with constitutional precepts clearly sets forth that . . ." paragraph two; more theory, I said to myself: skip.

"From the federalists to the present day, those authors of public law treatises . . ." paragraph three, same length, same likeness; idem the fourth, fifth, and sixth, and so on, until finally—lost there in the distance like some mathematical equation—a most nitpicky application to a most nitpicky case could be gleaned confusedly from this superbly extrapolated evidence: some poor third-rate civil servant had stolen 20 pesos' worth of paper from the Ajó Town Council, if memory serves, and to redress the public's moral outrage, and to teach him a lesson, it was demanded that the full weight of the law fall upon the shoulders of this corrupt state employee.

"Well, my friend," I said, "why not do us all a favor and go to the devil!"

Why not have forewarned your readership so that we could have started at the end, thereby sidestepping the rest like a crab?

He has the gall to demand that we see eye to eye; if I did I should hang my head in shame; his three exhausting columns with ten tons of constitutional law thrown in for good measure were quite a trial, requiring me to work like an ass yoked to a cart, and when I finally took the bait thinking I saw mountains and marvels ahead, *tout simple*, at the last minute, he throws in this ridiculous line about the picayune, vile villain!

Good heavens! At this rate we couldn't be further from seeing anything eye to eye.

Nothing doing, *niente affato* as we say in plain and simple Spanish; steal money and I'll squeal *tout de suite*.

Is he trying, perchance, to prove himself a connoisseur of tedium and start demanding payment in exchange for the narcotics he supplies?

Decidedly, if he wants us to see eye to eye he must begin once and for all—he and his colleagues since they are all birds of a feather—by understanding that when one rises of a morning and is still half asleep, or in the afternoon after a good luncheon and in the midst of digesting, and one grabs a newspaper, it is not with the very laudable yet tiresome aim of enlightening oneself by witnessing some miraculous, nerve-racking act performed on the tightrope of political science.

For that we have Kant, Stuart Mill, and the rest of the gang who, in exchange for cracking their skulls like Blondin on the Niagara, have done somersaults on the peaks of scientific eminence.

We must be satisfied with them, if we are to be satisfied.

What one wants is to see and not to learn; when one wants to learn one goes to school when young and has books when old, and as for him who cannot when young or old, he cares as much about the writer and his tastes as he does about what was all the rage in the forties. He knows nothing whatsoever about it, *pas du tout*, and that's how it should be; what use Greek or Sanskrit to him?

What one wants is to be *au courant* with what is going on, the ins and outs of political, social, commercial spheres, etc., tolerating if one must—and only as an exception—the moderate use of this or that discrete pen-stroke of scholarly commentary on issues of grave importance that justify the tone because of their character. To learn, in a word, the day's news and suchlike, devoid of nonsense and gobbledygook the likes of which we are often forced to see in print.

For instance:

FOREIGN NEWS

"Translated expressly for the (name of paper)."

Whereupon you find a load of old tripe that you've already read you know not where, although you may remember when: two to three weeks ago.

WIRE SERVICE

"From our special correspondent."

And there follows a torrent of nonsensical dispatches which, in spite of being sent by the aforementioned special correspondent, everyone and his mother saw printed word-for-word in the previous evening's paper.

LATE-BREAKING NEWS

Theft.—Neapolitan citizen Giacomo Piazzetta pilfered two oranges from the market downtown.

The pilferer was put behind bars by a police officer who happened to be strolling by at the time of the incident.

Public drunkenness.—Citizen Juan Pérez received free lodging in the slammer after having been found by the police upon the sidewalk of the seventh precinct in a state of inebriation.

Military movements.—Corporal Agapito Contreras, who had been serving in Patagones Prison, has been discharged from the eighth infantry battalion.

Weather report . . .

Appointment.—Intelligent, young Don Juan Lanas has been named porter to Minister X, Y, or Z.

Clean bill of health.—The Spanish ship Inmaculada Concepción de María Santísima has been granted pratique and will now dock, after having obtained a clean bill of health following her obligatory quarantine.

Utterly riveting stuff.

And on and on, interminably.

Newspapers, essentially ephemeral, should be light, current, *au jour le jour*, with enough to sate quotidian curiosity and then disappear like the paper on which they were printed, destined to the short life span that the demands of domestic use accord them.

They are born and die today, to be reborn and die anew tomorrow. They should be formed from moldable clay; forget erecting stone monuments. Such an endeavor is a waste of time, effort, and money; what is more, no one will be beholden; in fact, quite the reverse. Offer the vast majority of the capital's respectable public a light puff pastry and they will pay its weight in gold for the pleasure; but you could not induce them to accept the heavy, traditional chorizo and eggs even with pieces of silver or threats of violence. That was in vogue in '52 at the Fonda Catalana and nowadays is scarcely touched, even at the most rural country inns.

I was thinking all this to myself when I chanced to see from out of the corner of my eye that my companion was keeping close tabs on me, staring at me fixedly, and barely containing his desire to break in, particularly in those instances when (as occurs naturally when one reads) one stops to retrieve an eyelash from one's eye, look out the window, change position, or scratch one's nose.

The fellow I speak of is curious by nature, brazen, and meddling.

He cannot spend half an hour in the presence of another without pestering him with five hundred banal, indiscreet questions that may irritate one to varying degrees depending on one's mood and that force one to struggle in order to refrain from crying "What do you care!," words that fly in the face of common courtesy but nonetheless come from deep inside and struggle to get out, like a dog tied to a chain when an intruder shouts "Great God!" from the parlor.

As long as I was perusing the papers, all was well. I kept such a close watch that my adversary's hopes were dashed entirely. But once I had done with even the classified advertisements in the last of the papers (doubtlessly the best section of our national press, notwithstanding certain other ads destined to initiate tender, naïve damsels into the mysteries of internal medicine), I found myself obliged to acknowledge his presence, whereupon he pounced immediately and unwaveringly.

"Would you care to read this, señor?" he asked, holding out an edition of *El Diario.**

The offer was sorely tempting; *El Diario* was missing from my collection and, in my humble opinion, is the most intelligible and insightful paper of all those published in the land.

To read it, after having dredged through all the others, is an intellectual voyage to the province of pleasure, is the equivalent, *verbi gratia*, of going from the cobblestones of Calle Santa Fe to the tarmacadam of Avenida Sarmiento on the way to Palermo.

Despite the appeal it held for me, a dry and laconic:

---

* Founded by Manuel Láinez and published between 1881 and 1942, this daily newspaper showed the signs of the press's modernization. Láinez, a prestigious journalist and national legislator, is mentioned by name, along with some other members of the Generation of 1880, in chapter IX.

"No, thank you," was my only reply, immediately thereafter turning my back on him.

Do you suppose, perchance, that this initial blow might have put off my opponent?

Nothing of the sort; he returned repeatedly to the fray with the excuse of the heat that made him sweat like a pig (his words), the dust that choked us, the dry air that bothered him, the train that chugged along at a snail's pace, the name of each passing station, etc.; he also repeatedly beat his brow against the wall in an attempt to wear down the utter reserve with which I, in my turn, was firmly entrenched.

It was quarter past eleven when we finally reached Altamirano, the station at which we were, evidently, to luncheon.

Suffering hunger pangs so sharp that they must have been wearing spurs, I jumped down, made a beeline for the inn and took my seat before a filthy tablecloth beside others who, literally one and all, placed their elbows atop the table; ate off of knives used to cut bread and stuffed it into their mouths directly without first placing back down the sharp utensils; had no need for serviettes as they in their stead used the aforementioned tablecloth, whose edge was a veritable mosaic of egg-yolk and grease stains; shouted their orders for steak and fried eggs (their favorite dish) to the waiter; and peppered their meals with execrations that they interspersed liberally into their conversation with fellow diners every sentence or two.

Commending my soul to God and my stomach to the pampas breeze, I prayed and waited.

The meal began with a cauliflower and chickpea potage that stank to high heaven, which as you might guess was a true blessing and a joy.

General approbation with visible expressions of satisfaction all round, and one lone negative vote: mine.

Next came a mass of boiled meat and a stew with potatoes, in the same tenor.

Second veto, in spite of my best intentions.

Then some skinny ribs, charred black by the grill, were passed around.

Third and final veto, and *pour cause*, utterly justified.

Hunger makes hard beans sweet, as the saying goes, but this time there was no such luck. My hunger was exceptional, but the beans so hard, as it were, that it was impossible to sink my teeth into them.

Realizing that the waiter was proceeding, undiscouraged and without further ado, to pass out the dessert:

"What? Is there nothing else to eat?"

"Yes, sir. Quince jelly and cheese," he replied, showing me a smelly, revolting mass that rather more than quince jelly resembled gangrenous flesh with a foul, old hunk of *gruyère contrefaçon.*

"I am not inquiring about dessert; something to eat that is not dessert is what I want."

"Oh! No, sir. That was the last course."

"Can you not make something?"

"There's no time. The train pulled in late and it's leaving in four minutes."

"How about some cold cuts? Couldn't you give me a piece of ham or chicken?"

" 'Fraid not; we've run out."

"Then I'll take the bill."

"That's 25 pesos."

"There you are."

Twenty-five pesos to wind up having fasted for lunch, with one's stomach growling wildly.

"This is highway robbery!" I shouted to myself, cursing and heading back to the train.

And they call that a station buffet!

A dive or a pigsty is more like it, blast it.

What to do?

"Sleep curbs even the greatest of pains: hunger," I repeated mechanically, recalling an Arab maxim. Let us sleep, then.

Yes, but how? Given the rock-hard saddle they call a first-class seat with Sur Railways.

After a short debate with myself, a few moral and philosophical questions about the scandalous usury of British capital, I decided on a horizontal position and tried, in a manner of speaking, to think of nothing; setting the dogs upon my thoughts (a most excellent recourse that I entreat you to consider, should the opportunity arise), I tried to induce sleep with the rhythm of the train in motion.

I had half-achieved my objective, entering into that soporific state in which one loses consciousness of oneself, when lovely aromas began to stir my senses pleasingly.

I opened my eyes and beheld an absolutely charming tableau.

Do you anticipate, perchance, my embarking upon an exaltation, singing the praises or taking up a musical instrument to describe with melodious voice and poetic meter the wonders of the pampas, the imposing panorama, the expansive green landscape, the sweet scent of wildflowers, the blue skies and fresh, coquet breeze, the timid, twitting little birdies, the gentle-flowing, whimsical brooks, or the "gallant flamingo resting on the lagoon amidst green reeds"?

You are thoroughly mistaken: I was not born with a poet's gift nor anything remotely resembling it.

I am neither Guido nor Andrade, Encina nor Gutiérrez.*

Mother Nature, says me, has an old wrinkled visage; the pampas strike me as the most tedious, monotonous corner on God's green earth; I unfailingly detest the smell of flowers, herbs, and other plants; the fresh air leaves me boiling hot in summer and frozen in winter; breezes block my sinuses; birdsong strikes me as the most shrill sound to have profaned my eardrums to date, with the exception of the night-watchman's whistle; I hold brooks to be terrestrial accidents containing currents or pools of muddy and turbulent waters; and, *finalement*, I care as much about lagoons, reeds, and flamingos (ridiculous, silly-faced birds if ever there were) as I do about the king of Prussia.

A very different sight, indeed, had captivated me.

The enemy had advanced his reserves with the aim of taking me by storm and had lain out his heavy artillery in a battle line across the carriage seat: rolled flank steak; the infantry, parboiled chicken; then the light cavalry, in accordance with ordinance: sweets and desserts brought from the culinary arsenal of his most excellent, oracular wife.

"Would you care to join me, señor?" he asked and, doubtlessly noting the disposed-to-capitulate expression I wore, added, "One cannot luncheon in the station; the Neapolitans (for him all Italians are Neapolitans) cook poorly indeed; they took me for a ride once, but I swore they should never manage to do so again and as I travel this neck of the woods frequently, as a preventative measure I always make sure to bring along something to keep hunger at bay."

*Carlos Guido y Spano (1827–1916), Olegario Víctor Andrade (1839–82), Carlos Encina (1838–82) and Ricardo Gutiérrez (1836–96). Poets of the second Romantic generation, they favored descriptions of landscapes and rural life in their work. Guido wrote the flamingo poem ("gallant flamingo resting on the lagoon amidst green reeds") the narrator quotes and then mocks. Cambaceres rejected the lyricism and sentimental tone of this pastoral, highbrow poetry, dominant in the 1860s and 1870s.

"What a clever idea; you are very wise indeed," I exclaimed with exquisite social graces and in a tone very different to the one I had hitherto employed.

"I myself was quite unable to swallow even a mouthful; everything they served was positively odious."

"Well then do stop being polite; come and join me in breaking bread.

"It's not much, but I can offer you some roast, made by my wife; it might not be to your liking," he added, forcing me off my high horse congenially.

"I accept your kind offer with the utmost gratitude."

Oh, what the devil!

I allowed myself to partake with restraint, my hands and feet bound.

Something resembling shame, however, came to upset the calm within my conscience, having pronounced these last words.

I felt humiliated by the defeat of my ego, embarrassed of myself, almost regretted my new role as *hôte obligé*.

It was the last bleat of my expiring pride, fought off by the weaknesses of the flesh.

I sinned, but what can I say?

Man is like woman: "He resists the first time out of strength and succumbs the second out of weakness."

We all have our Rabelaisian quarter of an hour, and this was mine: they laid siege upon my hunger and I surrendered!

Was Esau's crime not worse, wretchedly selling his right as first son, and is Esau not a lauded man who figures greatly in history?

So what, then, if I, who am naught but a poor devil whose name does not even appear on the classical-music appreciation committee, should sell a bit of vanity and self-love for something infinitely more substantial, such as a plate of lentils!

Decidedly, I told myself, *l'idea é bella e il peccato* is far from *grosso*.

I can eat in peace, knowing that no insect will turn my stomach nor shall anything gnaw away at me. Now that Juan María Gutiérrez is dead, why is Pedro Goyena the country's most pleasing *causeur?**

---

*Pedro Goyena (1843–92) was a legal adviser and philosophy teacher who also wrote important articles on Argentine literature. As a Catholic militant, he opposed—both in print and in parliament—the laical reforms imposed by President Julio A. Roca in the 1880s. Juan María Gutiérrez (1809–78) formed part of the Romantic "Generation of 1837" and, in exile during the Rosas government, spoke out against Roca in the press. His compilations and the literary criticism he produced throughout his life were particularly

I am going to tell you a secret.

Wherever Goyena is, he acts like the temperature: he adapts himself to whatever degree of intellectual heat he encounters, studies his audience, feels them out, weighs them, searches out the leader, and adjusts his organ using the common tuning fork.

That is why he never strikes a harsh chord, and seduces men the way diamonds seduce women—with their brilliance. His accomplishments do not reach beyond those of a crude, behind-the-scenes *truc*; his voice is captivating like a siren's but does not present any danger beyond that of leaving one gape-mouthed when listening to him; one will not fall into any chasm other than that of losing track of the time, looking at one's watch at four believing it is two and having needed to snatch a recalcitrant debtor at three.

He talks of the passage of Venus amongst wise men or Apollo of Belvedere and the Holy See amongst artists as offhandedly as he does about affairs of state in political circles, trade amongst merchants, or sheep and cattle amongst stockbreeders.

He performs with topics of conversation as Robert Houdin does with top hats. He leaves the entire audience entranced, hanging on his every word. He amuses people like no one else and (God forgive me for this) I suspect he even amuses himself, when holding forth gloriously about fashion with a dandy.

Nevertheless, you all know him, and seeing him cross the street in his ever-present schoolteacher's frock coat with his hat resting patriarchally upon his ears, you get a good idea of just how much Goyena cares about a jacket cut by Frank or a pair of trousers made by Alfred.

"To choose well is to invent," some say, as if it were a proverb. They remind me of the fountains in Plaza de la Victoria that, if they spout water, do so only because the Recoleta hoses reach that far; and since I, myself, pertain to that group of shriveled prunes, it is quite clear that I must accept it. For who would not take advantage of the circumstances, laying claim to a patent for an invention that required so little toil.

Well if that maxim is true, then I invented Goyena's crimes and, though at first I was as stubborn as a drunk being led to the police

---

noteworthy. Both Gutiérrez and Goyena were distinguished *causeurs;* the latter was not only a great conversationalist but also quite a polemicist.

station, by the end I had worked up such rhythm and gabbed on so, that it seemed my companion and I had grown up together.

I spoke local yokel for two hours, which was the time required to reach Chascomús, where we parted company, assuring each other that it had been a pleasure, exchanging addresses, proclaiming friendship, and bidding each other bon voyage.

Once alone again, neither you nor anyone else will be particularly surprised to learn that nothing befell me and I arrived safe and sound into Juan's open arms, as we had agreed.

VIII

Atop a bed, a man lay reclining: me; opposite, another rocking in a rocking chair: Juan.

"You are five hundred times worse than Saint Thomas," he was saying. "He had to see to believe, but believe he did in the end. Meanwhile you, you are seeing, hearing, touching; the evidence is everywhere and clear as day and still you are stubborn as a mule and hard as nails; I cannot twist your arm."

"Are we back on that again?

"Hard or soft, if you cannot 'twist my arm,' as they say, that is my affair; I prefer to act with discretion; others can do as they please, blast it! But as far as I'm concerned, it seems that I at least have the right to be an exception to the rule.

"I will not marry because I am perfectly certain that there is no woman who could make me happy, just as I myself am incapable of making any living creature in the form of a woman happy.

"Like all things in life, my friend Juan, there is a time for marriage. Man should marry when there is still a vestige of purity in his soul, a cache of dreams to show him the world as it is in a way it cannot be. When the current has yet to push him in any given direction; quick to set sail this way or that, with the rudder in his hand, he is a ship for hire; he believes in woman like a young sailor in the sea, and beneath the faith that blinds him awaits happiness: out of sight, out of mind; and the eyes of a dreamer do not see, particularly when they are the eyes of a husband.

"But if he has made it to that stage in his life known as the forties all alone and—at risk of being a boor—knows what he knows, then the only solution is to carry on, an empty vessel.

"For an old vessel to tack suddenly in search of cargo, and cargo as heavy as woman, is to bring forth a great wave, to chance shipwreck or at the very least perhaps to be obliged to throw the cargo overboard. If the ship is empty, however, it will neither be grounded nor become trapped in deep water, and it is easy to bypass the rocks of life.

"Get it into your head: man's second error is not a matter of reason, but one of sentiments and, what is more, of twisted sentiments distorted by the imbecilic organization of society.

"If you argue for marriage with all its yokes, I dispute it on grounds of absurdity.

"Just ask the animal urges that speak from within you and especially from within woman, a true domestic chameleon, and tell me if it makes any sense to try to force her to satisfy her hunger on the same dish night after night, or even to bring to her lips the same glass today from which she gulped thirstily yesterday.

"But since the coercion persists and this affront to the categorical, explicit text of natural law is committed, at least consider your own taste, assuming it is not worn out from overuse or deadened from abuse; that way it will be easier to train yourself to savor partridge each day. You can marry your heart, but don't marry your head.

"These arrangements known as marriages of convenience, subscribed to by forty-year-olds whose hearts—like old canaries—have not fluttered in years and who, on the rare occasion when they open their mouths, come out with old tripe—or dance a federal minuet at a lancers' ball as it were—are absolute nonsense and a high price to pay; they are speculations in which the fool plays the devil, gambling away the peace of the last years of his life and losing not only his well-being, but his will to live.

"Have you not heard enough? Then I shall add this:

"What about force of habit, the guiding principle of the general public according to Jean Jacques, and of old men according to me. It begins by knocking timidly on the door, then softly sneaks in and takes over one's abode, finally declaring itself mistress of the house; if it catches you alone, it overpowers, ensnares, consumes, and absorbs you, transforms your character, changes your moods until—when you least expect it—you find you have been converted, thanks to the aforementioned lady herself, into some sort of prickly porcupine.

"Thus I stand before you.

"At times I am the devil's own; everything piques and sickens me.

"My friends?

"I'd wish them oceans apart.

"My lady friends?

"A half dozen contemporaries, old gasbags the lot of them, whose mere appearance so vexes me that I cannot bear the sight of them and turn their pictures to face the wall, cuffing the frames as if to keep them from moving, and leave them there for weeks on end.

"My nieces and nephews, darling creatures.

"Another bunch of clowns, I cannot stand to be in their presence for even a minute.

"Of course, Taniete does not even bear mentioning; he seems more of a quadruped imbecile than ever, if that is possible, and you already know how he weathers a storm: he closes the door, sits calmly upon a broken chair behind it, and refuses to open up for Christ himself, come what may.

"Would you believe this? When my feathers are ruffled, this is one of my favorite pastimes. The person who comes to call, whoever it might be, tires of knocking once, twice, thrice, and so on (and I, as I know that whoever it is has come not to give but to receive), and of shouting as many times, and there I am walking on air, happy as a clam, strolling around my office.

" 'Knock from here to eternity if you like; get stuffed, you'll be wasting your time and energy!'

"It's a pastime like any other. Did not Napoleon have his, doodling on every piece of paper that passed through his hands?

"Well, what floats my boat is letting callers bust their knuckles on my knocker.

"Now then, my dear Juan: how could you possibly believe that a man who cannot even stand himself might possibly stand another?

"That is a cross I could not bear!

"To bring a strange being into my home, some Joan of Arc to share my things, my table, my bath, and, far more serious, my bed, in which—armed with her legitimate title—she would attempt to sleep every night and every day without my having recourse to kick her out when it struck my fancy were I not in the mood for her company.

"And all this, quite apart from the time, affections, and considerations that good social graces would require me to dedicate; the sacrifice of my independence; my humiliation in moral and physical slavery, in a word. Would I voluntarily submit myself to that in exchange for a need I do not feel, a woman I do not love, and a lifestyle whose mere contemplation leaves me bandy-legged with dread, just because?

"No, no, a thousand times, no!

"Different strokes for different folks; you have yours, you married and good for you; I have mine, I shan't marry and even better . . ."

"When did you arrive? Yesterday, was it not?" interrupted Juan, standing up. "It seems as though a twenty-four-hour sermon preached on the purest of examples has not been sufficient to convert you, though.

"I shall grant you the eight days you are here with us and then, if you do not march straight out to find yourself a wife, I shall pronounce you the most hopeless milksop under the sun.

"That is my only reply to your sociophilosophical tirade." Then he added, "Get up, you bum! You have an hour to bathe. It is now four o'clock and dinner is served at five."

Then the curtain dropped and my friend Juan abandoned me on the stage, in order to slip into his wife's dressing room.

IX

Banish hyperbole, metaphor, and figures of speech.

Forget the ebony, alabaster, pearls, coral, suns, sylphs, and other nonsense that he who puts pen to paper, be it in poetry or in prose, feels he has the right to pull from his sleeve in praise of the heroines his distorted mind engenders.

There is no woman alive who exhibits hair like ebony, skin like alabaster, teeth like pearls, lips like coral, body like a sylph, or eyes like two suns; at best one could claim that the most lustrous of them shine like grease candles, thank you very much.

Some are worse off and some better, but they have all got their unattractive features, either on view or hidden away.

If you don't believe me, ask a painter if he has ever touched up a nude model and he will laugh.

For some it is the arms, others the feet, this one the head, and that one the torso; but she who shows a beautiful palm wears long underwear to hide her legs and she who "accidentally on purpose"—as they say—lifts her dress to climb the steps pulls the wool over our eyes with regard to her corset.

To ask too much of the daughters of Eve, aesthetically speaking, is to try to make a silk purse of a sow's ear.

Let us be content with the little bud God has given us as a companion; let us be practical and call a spade a spade, as the saying goes.

Dark brown hair, then; dark skin; lively, expressive black eyes with long, curly eyelashes (the sort particularly remarkable in profile); insolently turned-up snub nose; lascivious, fresh mouth with contralto, prima donna-style down above red lips that never miss a chance to reveal two rows of beautiful teeth; pleasing figure, both full and elegant; ugly hands (like nearly all women); small feet; and, from what I could glean yesterday, as she dismounted from a horse, satisfactory calves.

My friend Juan's wife was, in a word, what is known as a fine filly.

Lively, subtle intelligence, average manners, zero education.

As for her moral constitution, I offer you the following scenario from which you yourselves may draw your own conclusions, as did I.

X

Juan.—Once and a thousand times, damn business! Would that one could live on ambrosia like the lucky inhabitants of Olympus.

You see here a young, healthy, happy, capable man whose only wish is to be granted eternal life, hand in hand with the little wife he adores and who adores him (he kisses her).

María.—Juan, please! What will the gentleman think! (blushing to the tip of her nose with incomparable modesty).

Juan.—(Paying no attention whatsoever.) And yet there is no alternative; I must go back, much as I hate to, to breathe the stuffy air of mortals, to see and take part in their miseries, to weigh myself down, like them, with my share of the burden in that human anthill.

In just two weeks, two months of bliss will come to an end!

Me.—What stops you from making it last a year, or two, or three, should you so desire? Are you not wealthy? From whence this pressing need to work?

Juan.—(Pacing with affected importance.) From whence? That's what you don't know, for God's sake!

Listen and you shall learn: from the lofty, transcendental duties that burden me, given that my character is that of a serious man.

You must know that . . . shall I tell him? May I give you away? Do I have your permission, yea or nay? (looking at his wife who, without saying a word, gets up and takes off like a shot).

Juan.—María, María, come now, my darling . . .

María.—(From the next room.) No, no, I won't. How could you embarrass me so?

Me.—(Seduced by the charm that a display of modesty always induces.) See how awkward you are? Allow me to say it. Why the devil do you enjoy making me blush so?

Juan.—It's true. That was wrong. But how can I resist giving you the happy news? My wife, dear friend, is with child. Certain unfailing indications revealed to me last night that I am, beyond any shadow of a doubt, going to be a father, the father of María's child . . .

Do you realize what that means? Can you understand the magnitude of my joy? No, what would you understand, you old egotist, you shriveled soul, you wastrel of a man!

If you were able to open your heart to pure feelings, you would know what is happening to me, it is enough to send me wild with glee (jumping up and down like a child, he throws himself at me, gives me a hug, and grabs my hands, which he squeezes convulsively).

Me.—(Softened and almost tender in spite of myself.) Yes, yes, indeed! I understand everything, but that's quite enough. Let go, you're hurting me; leave me and go and make amends for the damage you've done; go and ask your wife's forgiveness, the poor thing surely deserves it (he goes).

Me.—(Alone.) One cannot deny that women, the devils, sometimes have certain wily ways, even if they themselves do not wish to be wily . . .

Traps laid for their husbands, glue that nature spreads in order to catch bearded jays, that even when it reaches far and wide never ensnares the cautious, untrusting old owl: he won't fall for it. He prefers his humid cave, barren and somber—but where he is unfettered—to the honor of being served up in some Genovese tavern like the garnish on a platter of polenta with quail . . .

C'est égal, I repeated mechanically after reflecting for a moment upon the thoughts absorbing me, these women—the devils—have certain wily ways.

Juan.—(Entering on his wife's arm.) Here we are before you once more.

After the accused had hung his head in shame, imploring royal clemency on bended knee, Her Majesty María I, Queen of Juan's Heart, had come to grant him her supreme pardon.

The peace treaty was signed and sealed; the rebellion's leader would never again attempt to raise his head!

Me.—Let the quarrel not be mentioned again and may there be peace amongst Christian nobility!

Joking aside, and getting back to your affairs, without trying to intrude (to Juan), tell me why the devil are you returning so soon?

I, in your place, would arrange things so as not to need to be present in Buenos Aires, at least not for the time being.

You are happy; enjoy your happiness; let the floods come and let Troy burn to boot! To the devil with it! The days of our lives when we are not condemned to suffer are few and far between.

María.—Could your friend not look after your affairs? He is such a good man that I am certain he would be only too happy to be of service.

Me.—Nothing could make me happier.

If I can help you in any way (to Juan), you have only to ask.

Juan.—I know and I'm ever so grateful, but I'm afraid that's impossible; this is personal business on fixed terms and cannot be concluded without my presence; I must be in Buenos Aires in exactly 15 days.

María.—(Sighing.) Well, if that is how it must be I shall have to grin and bear it, then.

Juan.—What? Really, my love? Does it sadden you so, to leave the ranch?

María.—It does. I am so happy, so contented here that, were it up to me, I should like to live in the country all year long.

Juan.—Alone or with someone?

María.—(With *charmant* sweetness.) That, husband, sir, is not a question one asks. Don't be a brute; you know very well: with you and no one but you.

Me.—And if your husband did not like to be more than a stone's throw from the Plaza de la Victoria?

María.—I would happily live within that stone's throw, sir, for my husband's will shall always be sacred to me.

Juan.—You see! (turning triumphantly to look at me.) Does that not make your mouth water, your body squirm! Does it not drive you mad with envy!

Compare your life with mine; the fulfillment of my aspirations with the appalling emptiness that surrounds you, you lummox. Compare and admit it. You are still in time; seek and ye shall find, not a treasure such as this (he strokes his wife's face as she pulls his hand away), though you might search high and low, I tell you that without vanity or modesty. But you shall find a creature good enough to undertake your conversion, which you will admit is no small feat, as we know; a woman to set your path in life, to give you a mission to fulfill, to enrich your existence . . .

Me.—(Interrupting him.) A woman to tame me, so to speak; is that it?

Juan.—Exactly; to put you on the right path, the only one on earth that can bring about man's happiness.

Me.—I see one small problem there.

Juan.—What?

Me.—As I am not a wild horse, I have no need of taming.

Juan.—(With vehemence and shaking with rage.) But you've turned into something even worse!

Even as a child, you started off on the wrong foot. You had to live fast, always in a hurry, and you embarked on the life that tedium and skepticism corrupt, the life that shrivels one's heart the fastest: the high life.

Just when others were barely reaching adulthood, you'd already become an old man, if not in years then in ideas, and yours were not the fruits of edifying experience that can only be got in time, but the result of the terrible moral school in which you were educated and whose disastrous influences you have not been man enough to shake off; you are left not even with the sad fate of the elderly, who are clear-sighted as to life's ways.

You are a decrepit old fool, and blind to boot.

What you think you see around you are really the hallucinations of your soul, the ghosts of a sick mind, the memory of monstrous images that distorted your retina and then left their obscene ugliness imprinted on it.

That is why you are so doubtful, so untrusting, why you deliberate so, why your spleen verges on megalomania, why you lack faith in your fellow man, live desperately in self-imposed isolation, why your pessimism is absolute, in a word, and you are your own number-one victim.

But if you think I am going to stand back and watch you die like a dog, with not a single Christian soul around you, no one even to give you a glass of water, given over to the mercenary hands of that imbecile Taniete, you are utterly mistaken. I am your friend and I am going to save you in spite of yourself.

The only solution to this evil that is consuming you and slowly poisoning you is to get married and I shall do and say so much, I shall preach endlessly—though you may complain that I am flogging a dead horse—so that in the end you will give in to me.

Like a fruitless weed, I shall pull you up at the roots from the hovel in which you vegetate, like a stinging nettle that gives everything that comes near it a rash.

I shall save you from that place in which you rot miserably, serving neither God nor the devil, and I shall turn you into a man who is good to himself and to the society in which he lives.

In God's name, I shall find you a wife, like it or not, and I shall not quit—get it into your head—until you have ten kids.

Me.—In the name of the Father, the Son, and the Holy Ghost. Amen.

X I

Of all the heroic acts in the book—breaking one's bones (quite common), turning the other cheek (gospel and Voltaire), shaking people's moral foundations (Montesquieu), being harder on oneself than on others (don't know who), etc.—I find that confessing one's own cowardice is the easiest to come to terms with, the most tasteful, the most refined, the one that one can accept most easily.

By this token, even the saddest sod has the potential makings of a hero. All he has to do is open his mouth and say: I am a yellowbelly; there, it's out now and I'll prove it.

Yes, indeed. After the scene you just witnessed and after sleeping on things, I found my strength failing me, my convictions flagging.

Juan and his wife had just blazed a trail through the fortress of my principles and like a house of cards it was now on the verge of collapsing and taking my life's credo with it.

What if it is true, I lamented, what if I've lived my life like a blind man.

Modesty, innocence, love, all the accoutrements might be found in this life and might perhaps be the assets of woman. Woman: half of mankind, confidante of our pleasures, shoulder to cry on, the ultimate of our unbridled aspirations on earth!

Oh! If it were so all would come clear: riches, ambition, honor, power, glory; I would comprehend man throwing it all, once conquered, at the feet of his beloved creature, be she wife or lover!

My feverish imagination then nurtured that golden ideal and made it true.

Lost amongst the crowd, a poor, miserable pygmy—but full of the inspirational faith and the unbreakable will to find it—I embarked upon my journey across the rugged path.

I took a step, faltered, and fell, rising again with a wounded soul, one less hope, and one more incentive.

One by one, with patient and resigned hand, I removed the stones that human vice placed in my path; and when, during this crude task, my sapped strength refused to keep me standing, I fell anew, but became even more zealous—with my sights set straight ahead—and then dragged myself through the dirt, digging my bloodied nails into the ground, leaving behind pieces of my own flesh that had torn off and were lying in my wake.

I battled desperately, relentlessly, the way a deluge sweeps aside every obstacle in its path, the way a prisoner fights the bars of the cell that lock him away from freedom.

The river floods its banks by virtue of the water's force, the prisoner escapes by virtue of his cunning, so why should I, by virtue of my fervent inspiration, not also be able to attain such heights?

Does the condor, wings aside, need any assistance to soar above the snowy peaks?

It was an anguished crusade, one of untold pain and bitterness that the pen cannot transcribe, one that boggles the mind, one that only the fool who spends his life dreaming of the specter of immortality could suffer.

My lofty plan finally scaled the much longed-for summit, triumph crowned my gargantuan efforts, and I looked down upon the world at my feet.

The very beings who—big when I was small—had tormented me with their hatred and overwhelmed me with their scorn were now on their knees before me, tiny and contemptible in their own right.

I was powerful, free, both sovereign and a slave, but a slave to the beloved woman for whom I had fought and conquered and to whom I dedicated my glories in exchange for her love.

La folle imagination ran wild all night.

The dawn's first light, accompanied by the flock's bleating nature—a splendid cross of Negrette and Rambouillet sheep that, by the way, cost my friend Juan quite a considerable sum of money—finally managed to check her untrammeled course, rudely calling her back to the loony bin of reality.

What was left of my charming vision?

What is left of all human farces, real or imaginary: nothing, or almost nothing; in this case, I was left with the right to tell you: I was a coward, I confess, and thus I am a hero.

Judge for yourselves.

XII

María.—(In a tête-a-tête with me, while Juan—a real country sort—is out presiding over the slaughter.) Well, sir, you must be looking forward to returning to Buenos Aires tomorrow!

Me.—Looking forward to it? That depends, señora. Yes and no. No, because it pains me to leave the good company of you and Juan, whom you know I love very deeply; yes, because I have no marked predilection for life in the country.

It is a question of taste; not everyone thinks as I do.

The other day you yourself, if memory serves, deplored not being able to live in Los Tres Médanos year-round, and I imagine you cannot have changed your mind in such a short space of time.

María.—Surely not; I shall repeat now what I said then: I am perfectly happy on the ranch; but that does not mean that I detest city life, especially as I have been separated from *mamá* and my little sisters for over two months now and I do so want to see them and hold them close.

Me.—(To myself, like a man who has just been elbowed.) Hmm! (To her.) But, why not tell Juan? I am sure he would be quick to please you. You could both come back tomorrow, with me, or at least before the date that is presently set.

I could be your intermediary; if you like I shall speak to him about it myself!

María.—No, no, God forbid! Poor Juan! He is so happy and contented here that I would not upset him for anything in the world.

Me.—I see, señora, that you are not as taken by pastoral pursuits as your words the other day led me to believe and that it is, rather, for Juan's sake that you displayed such willingness to become an all-out, *pour tout de bon* rancher.

In any case, that can only be seen in your favor (baiting her); sacrificing oneself for one's husband is the trait of a faithful and affectionate wife.

María.—You are mistaken, señor. I make no such sacrifice nor do I deserve your praises.

I am here for him as well as for myself; but it's all relative.

Sometimes the days drag on forever, especially when Juan is busy managing the ranch and leaves me on my own; I assure you I do not know what to do or how to kill the time.

In the city it would be different; I could go for a stroll, keep myself entertained, go to *mamá*'s house or visit a friend.

Me.—(Dangling the bait.) You are absolutely right, señora. This must be unbearably soporific after a spell and, to be quite honest, I was quite unable to understand your manifest desire to bury yourself alive here in this tomb.

To resign yourself to inhabit a desert. . . . I mean it would be all right for one who has nothing, but not when one owns, as the two of you do, a splendid house in Buenos Aires, with all the luxuries and comforts that wealth provides: carriages, the theater, dances, and promenades.

I might be wrong, but that is the manner in which I have viewed my life and the way I see it for a wealthy young man like Juan and a beautiful, rich young woman such as yourself: drain every drop of pleasure the world has to offer; there shall be time enough to suffer later on and, anyway, later the Lord shall provide!

María.—(Falling for it.) Oh, señor, what a shame it is that you insist on remaining a bachelor, as good as you are! I envy the woman who finds a husband like you!

You can't pull the wool over my eyes! *Je te connais beau masque.*

Poor thing! So you miss your *mamá* and your little sisters, do you? The days drag on, you know not what to do nor how to kill the time, you are bored of your husband yet lead him to believe the opposite, you lie, you deceive him roguishly; and you yourself come clean about it, thanks to what now grows inside you, only two months after the wedding and in the midst of your honeymoon?

Why I'll bet all that malarkey about shame and embarrassment was nothing but refined coquetry; the innocence and naïveté of your tone, feminine wiles, and deceits; the love you swore at the altar, petty self-interest; you wedded for the sake of being wed, for the same reasons you all do it, so you could have a husband and be called señora; you have been one barely five minutes, and already the tranquillity of home life weighs upon you like a ton of bricks?

Magpie in a golden cage, you do not even realize the indignity of your schemes, but I shall do you the favor of pointing it out: agitated and restless you anxiously await the moment your unsuspecting husband's hand opens the door so that you can fly to neighboring roofs, taking with you his peace of mind, his name, and his honor, of which perhaps you think to rob him treacherously!

What a fool! I was on the verge of knocking on Saint Francis's door, of falling into the trap like a novice! Foolish me and poor, poor Juan!

These were the thoughts that assailed me forthwith, borne of the blasted pessimism for which Juan so rightly reproached me.

Oh! Where will it all end?

But let us not lose the thread. Then I thought: it is simply a case of Messalina and Lucretia blended into one . . .

What had the poor creature done or said for me to abhor her so?

Simply wish to see her mother and sisters after a time of absence?

Why, that is the most natural thing in the world!

Be bored to death when her husband leaves her on her own in a big, old deserted ranch house, which she would not mind so if she had just a few Christian souls to keep her company?

Goodness gracious! I must admit it: she is only too right!

But then, why lie and beguile? Why say white to her husband and black when alone with me?

More than that, why not jump for joy at whatever her husband gives her, even if it is bread and onions, as long as he partakes of them with her? Is that not her duty? Should she not devote herself to doing things *comme il faut*?

Decidedly, everything is not coming up roses; there is something fishy about the whole affair and I fear that Juan's much-trumpeted happiness will, sooner rather than later, begin to stink to high heaven . . .

XIII

Mutatis, mutandi, between February and March each year, the public is condemned to read the following, in the style sustained by our short news items:

"Splendid.—Judging by the magnificent preparations and the vast sums of money already raised, the next Carnival will doubtlessly be a splendid one.

"The streets of our opulent city shall be adorned with great show; multitudinous, extravagant floats shall parade through them, and to ensure that nothing is missing from these crazy days of wild abandon, our aristocratic salons, the Club del Progreso and the Plata, as well as each and every theater, will open their doors to the spirited, buoyant maskers.

"This year's Carnival shall be a landmark event. Get ready!"

Those who were not in on the secret would think that the masquerades of Venetian times, the sumptuous Carnival parades of Rome, the magnificent Veglioni at La Scala and the dances at the Paris Opera were chopped liver beside the grandiose Arabian nights of the Buenos Aires Carnival.

But he who knows a hawk from a handsaw sings another tune entirely: he can see the writing on the wall.

The wise man leaves town for three days, to shoot partridge and batitue birds if hunting is his game, shuts himself up indoors with a few books if reading is his cup of tea, or resigns himself to have fun if that is his last resort, watching the parade follow its route along Calle Florida, making an almighty racket at the Teatro de la Opera, or, if he is a member of the haut monde, as they now insist on calling it, attending the Progreso ball; haut monde, here, where we all know who's who: *risum teneatis.*

So then, what does all this hullabaloo and commotion really boil down to?

Let's see.

The local barber and the confectioner, along with the owner of some warehouse or empty room who is interested in renting it out to set up a little water cannon business, all slip a few pesos into the hands of the commission in charge of the program.

With this sum, they get a few dozen faded flags from old Mr. Picard and pay the gas company an arm and a leg for the outdoor lighting.

Add to that the prestige of the Club del Progreso balconies, seven processional lamps borrowed from the altar of Jesus of Nazareth Church in San Francisco, some random rubbish donated by a few private individuals, and there you have it: all the pomp and glory of Carnival's decor.

And that's it. *Ce n'est pas plus malin que ça.*

With the town now suitably decked out, the clock strikes five, the starting time of the solemn parade that begins with the triumphal march of each float group: a third-rate Vedette from somewhere or other; the Enfants de N'importe Qui; the Knock-kneed or Bowlegged Blacks; in short, a collection of dimwits dressed as mummers, and transformed into *soi-disant* musicians, bands of assassins (as Bassi calls them) who deserve—at the very least—to be disbanded immediately and sent, for the affront they commit, to serve in a unit on the frontier for at least five years.

The sweet, darling black kiddies, more than any of the others, bring me true joy.

I cannot even look at their little black faces, their little sky-blue smocks, their little white undies, their little patent-leather boots, their little riding crops, little drums, little bells, and little rattles without my mouth watering at the thought that such grace and salt of the earth is raised up in this land of mine.

Little angels!

They pass by in turns, between this or that wop, dressed as a Turk or a marquis, with an interminable line of horse-drawn carriages filled with twopenny, high-society girls' processions; "My Granny's Girls," or yours, are stuffed into moving carts pulled by crippled horses and covered with weeds and coconut shells, all in the name of festive splendor.

The cacophonous musicians and maskers irritate one's eardrums with the cries and shrieks they emit, which sound just like passing by a squawking cage of parrots, while the loafers strut about in skintight trousers and try to be interesting:

"Hey, *che*, what's new, how's it going? When you gettin' hitched, Don Juan?"

Armed with their corresponding water cannons—surely the stupidest, crassest toys in human creation—some come, some go, round in circles like idiots, from Plaza Lorea to the Retiro, from the Retiro to Plaza Lorea,* for five hours. Then at ten o'clock they each go their separate ways, soaked to the skin and on their last legs but claiming that the parade was magnificent, that they had a rip-roaring time and promising each other that, of course, they will meet up again for more malarkey the following day.

As for the masquerade, it is, of course, the *ne plus ultra*.

I beg you to forgive me if I do not comment upon what takes place in the theaters, skating rinks, ball courts, and other public dens of iniquity.

There are questions of decency and decorum that I find myself unable to commit to paper, in spite of the familiar and even brutal allures of my pen.

Let us turn a new page.

---

*The parade route goes from a square in the west, in an area full of popular cafés and restaurants, to Retiro, in the north. Once a bullring and then, from 1822, a military garrison, Retiro was converted into a train station with a huge square in 1870.

XIV

At two o'clock in the morning, the haut monde of the world takes itself home; it would appear, however, that for our haut monde, the haut monde way to do things is diametrically opposed to that of the haut monde of the rest of the *monde*.

The haut monde in this country does not even consider turning up at a dance until at least two in the morning.

We shall wait, then, until the appointed hour; let us meanwhile go to the Club del Progreso and see what is happening there.

Many men and women; the latter attired mostly—as is their custom—in tacky, vulgar gowns, with no taste, no elegance, nor any affluence; old rags they have thrown on for the occasion, or new rags they have picked up ten to the dozen.

The men, unmasked but disguised nevertheless, go as Don Juan *J'en ai été et je m'y connais.*

Young and old, single and married, ill-favored and good-looking alike, there is not one in a hundred who would not exclaim *ab imo pectore* contemplating himself in the looking glass:

"Something tells me tonight is the night I am going to make up for lost time."

Of course the fact of the matter is that there is more chance of seeing a cow jump over the moon than getting lucky at a masquerade.

Not a bloody chance!

Grace? Spirit? Sparks? Mischief?

Not for love or money. Not a bit of it.

Let us agree, for the sake of argument, to set aside the list of idiocies with which a masker makes her debut on approaching you, lines like: "Recognize me, *che*?" "How's your mother?" "Where did you leave your wife?" "Shameless!" "You scoundrel!" etc., etc.

Allow me, here, to point out that I have seen this scene played out more than once at the Club.

In the immediate vicinity of the orchestra (and take note, as this is the most strategic point, the part of this human pond in which the most fishing is done), they spend the sleepless night like wallflowers on the prowl, without so much as a slap from the hand of God to say: "Take that, you miserable wretches!" and in exchange for dislocating their jaws, Miguel Cané, Lucio V. López, Manuel Láinez, Roque Sáenz

Peña, and others of their lot—rascals and imbeciles one and all—mill about the salons, find themselves chased, assaulted, and fought over by the blessed maskers like flies on a pot of jam.

Tell me with whom thou goest. . . . No comment.

If we were to place ourselves in the doorway between ballrooms and bothered to cast our eyes about, we would find very curious objects of study lurking. But for this we need two things: time, which I possess, and patience, which I do not.

Yet how could one resist the temptation to cite an instance of vice by peeking under the shirts of a few of the Club's heartiest members?

The one who, for instance, if he were not one of the most talented, would certainly be the most unbearably conceited ass on the planet.

His impeccably tailored suits have not one wrinkle or stain, he is perfectly attired from head to toe (not forgetting hand), spends far more than necessary in order to be what is known as a "well-dressed man," and yet he most definitely is not.

For that he needs what cannot be bought at the hatmaker's or the cobbler's; that which the French express in three untranslatable words: *comme il faut*, nature's supreme gift that cannot be acquired: the higher the ape climbs, the more he shows his tail, and all that.

Admire this gentleman's jacket in the tailor's shop-front window and you would exclaim:

"Beautiful, well-cut, fine material!"

But then you see it on the client, and the trousers clash wildly with the jacket, which does not measure up, does not match, is loud, and makes him look like a Sunday market stallholder who sets up shop by the cathedral when one o'clock mass lets out.

This fine sir orders his shirts from Longueville or Charvet and, naturally, he receives shirts such as those only Longueville and Charvet can make.

Do you think, by chance, that the expense does anything for him?

You are wrong; on a hanger in the wardrobe, a doomed white tie or a set of sparkling stone cuff links wait to dress up their owner at three o'clock, when he goes to plead a case, and turn Charvet's oeuvre into a cheap two-franc rag.

In short, one could say his sense of style was hanging by a thread, but never that he wore his threads with style.

I said he was intelligent and I shall repeat it, a most fostered intelligence, but that does not prevent his having lasted, *long feu*, which, plainly put, means that the plan backfired.

Dizzied by his scholastic achievements, celebrated, pampered, deified as a student first, he then came as a wee lawyer to think that the republic was the university or the bar; the world was his oyster, and without first testing the waters he dove in, headfirst.

What had to happen, naturally, happened: he hit his head on the bottom with such force that ever since, poor man, he has been a bit soft there.

You see, in order to be a good lawyer, dear doctor, all one needs is a knowledge of the law and a wealth of honor, qualities that to be sure I find in you; but to be a public figure, that is another kettle of fish. That unavoidably requires what Adolfo Alsina had, what Aristóbulo del Valle has: brains, brawn, and brass.*

You did not do a degree in politics because you lack the last two of these attributes, thanks to something even fools have, something quite trivial but also substantial, the garnish for the main course: common sense, in which you are most pitifully lacking.

Otherwise you would never have tried, and certainly not with such bad timing, to be a dandy and a governor and a president and a Don Juan—a role to which you are ill-suited—instead of a serious, circumspect man, distinguished lawyer, or illustrious member of the Supreme Court, which is the prize you would never have taken your eyes from had you understood what you had to gain and realized on which side your bread was buttered.

Don't get too big for your boots.

You could have been one of America's leading legal models, but now, because you changed your tune, because you wanted to gallop through the fandangos of life instead of sticking to the slow, reposed rhythm, you dance more in time with the likes of bad blood such as your own; you have cracked your head on the pillar of public opinion and, like a poorly positioned rocket that bounces off Recoba Vieja Arch on Independence Day, you too have now bounced out of court completely.

---

*Political leaders with wide-reaching popular support during the last thirty years of the nineteenth century. Adolfo Alsina (1829–77) was governor of Buenos Aires and vice-president under Domingo F. Sarmiento (1868–74); head of the autonomous Buenos Aires party that challenged the national government by declaring independence from the provinces, he was in charge of defending the frontier against the Indians in the 1870s. Aristóbulo del Valle (1847–96), a noted orator and journalist, held several parliamentary positions; he strongly opposed Miguel Juárez Celman's liberal government at the end of the 1880s and led the so-called "1890 revolution," which led to his removal from office.

Beg pardon; let's move on to a new subject.

Tall, thick-necked and of apoplectic constitution, displaying a risible air of quixotic self-importance in the salons, this next man is one of the association's most outstanding members.

His strut, which by the way is not in time to the lyre, in spite of an entirely *sui generis* hip-sway and a certain lilting cadence, has always reminded me of the trot of those heavy, slow-moving, old Chilean nags, the ones who wind up able to do nothing but stand about.

My word! Why does he walk in this fashion? I often asked myself, until one day, seriously intrigued, I asked one of my lady friends, a graduate in rumorology.

"You who are all-knowing," I said, "do you know why So-and-so walks the way he walks?"

"Oh, it is most amusing," said she, breathlessly.

"Why? Because So-and-so dates from the days of patent-leather boots with colored morocco-leather legs, when men used their feet to seduce the girls; because So-and-so's feet have always been huge and most unattractive, because to make them smaller and conceal his bunions, they say he used to bind them before stuffing them into a pair of boots so tight that to this day the poor man has not managed to rid himself of the plethora of calluses, corns, and ingrown toenails that sprouted in his younger days; because he's over sixty; because there's not much spring left in his step; and because, in spite of it all, he still throws his weight around like someone who can kick up a storm and, naturally, he tries to stave off the decrepitude of old age, now beginning to creep up on him.

"*Voilà.* That's why So-and-so walks the way he walks."

"You are a fount of knowledge," I said to my friend, "a darling bijou of a woman."

We all have our flaws; this man's flaw lies in considering himself the ideal Club president of all time.

Speaking to an assembly; giving his admirable little address recounting the state of the association, announcing that we shall proceed to the election of members to the steering committee, failing as the judge to settle all scores in the case of ties; settling in at one of the dining-room tables to enjoy tinned oyster soup (the latest word in chic supreme, so he says, to come from culinary chemistry), regardless of the fact that Savarin himself would not have invented such a brew, even in jest; formally making his appearance dressed all in white, with pomp and circumstance, casting looks of sovereign protection hither and yon like a monarch holding court; approaching a high-class woman and strolling through the salons with her so that everyone notices and admires him; making a show of his good taste, of which I can of course, by way of example, offer you the blessed balcony lights, etc., etc.; shining, in a word, showing off, standing out as a man of the world and a gentleman of fine taste, that is where it gets him; that is his weak point.

I would wager—and I would win—that if he were offered the choice between the presidency of the republic and that of the Club, he would not hesitate to choose the latter.

To each his own and *meno male*, as the Italians say, because when all is said and done, his own does not do anyone any harm.

This man is, on the other hand, dignified, honorable, gentlemanly, if not very open-handed, so to speak; he is one of those perfectly harmless beings one cannot but love and be charmed by.

He roams the salons, back and forth, to-ing and fro-ing like a squirrel, with a masker on either arm and perhaps two more bringing up the rear, the National Theater's most popular actor.

He is what I shall term, if you allow me, a youthful oldie.

Old because the eighteen hundred and some-odd years our calendar has reached leave over sixty-five from his birth to the present.

Youthful because in spite of the years, nothing about him has aged: not his personality, nor his ideas, nor his habits, nor his heart—always susceptible to feminine charms—nor even his skin, still fresh and taut like that of a maiden in her fifteenth spring.

But what about his beard?

Hold on; I foresaw that objection and victoriously refute it.

It is the blasé man's instrument of flirtation.

It is just like those plump, dark women who drink vinegar to become pale and look languorous and interesting.

Otherwise, why would he not shave?

Without being handsome—far from it—he is a fortunate man, which can be explained thus: lively, audacious, generous, and discreet, he possesses all the requisite characteristics needed to hit it off with the daughters of Eve.

I said discreet and I shall stick to it, though it is a paradox.

If you have had any contact with him, be it solely at the Club, or on the street, more than once you'll have formed part of a little chorus from within which our man takes the floor and holds forth about his amorous campaigns, chronicling his gallant affairs.

Buenos Aires during Rosas's time, Montevideo and Buceo during

Oribes's time; that, he opines, was the greatest stage for his heroic feats.*

It was there that *farfallone amoroso* spent *notte e giorno d'intorno ai giardini, delle belle turbando il reposo*, etc.*

It was there that each and every woman, ugly and beautiful, married and single, dropped like flies, felled by the formidable size of his razor-sharp sword.

It was there that the mysteries of love were uncovered, as it were.

All this he recounts and repeats to those he wants to hear it; he tells it again and again, savoring the sweet memories of his golden years with indescribable delight.

But I'll wager you have never caught him with his guard down.

I'll wager you have never heard him—not even spurred on by his passion for improvisation—say anything rash, make an allusion, give any indication that might cause you to believe that he was talking of this or that lass, or her over there.

He recounts the miracle but never names the saint, and that is precisely what is known in Cervantes's language as discretion, or I'm a Dutchman.

Yes, but if he is your friend, I hear you cry, tell him not to boast, not to carry on so; before he prattles on he ought see to whom he speaks and, what is more, be a bit cleverer, a bit more sensible about certain things that would be better left unsaid and not broadcast to the four winds accompanied by trumpets, whistles, and horns, else he might find his flesh lashed by the whip of ridicule.

D'accord, mais que voulez-vous?

Not all old dogs can learn new tricks.

An old man with a limp dies lame, and that is all there is to it.

Nevertheless, I am sure you will agree that the whole business makes not the tiniest bit of difference and that these minor shortcomings brought on by vanity are quite excusable, given all the talents that make up a through-and-through gentleman in both style and substance.

---

*Reference to the period when Juan Manuel de Rosas governed Buenos Aires, and Uruguayan President Oribe laid siege to Montevideo and Buceo, the capital and port of Banda Oriental, a Spanish territory. Oribe, who ruled only from 1835 to 1838, tried to regain power with the help of his ally Rosas by laying siege to the capital from 1843 to 1852, but he never managed to take the city.

*From Mozart's opera *Le Nozze di Figaro*.

After having knocked about willy-nilly, eating life's bitter bread (or, as Señor Frías used to call it, the nasty, bland roast of exile), this man—notable for his noble sentiments, the steadfast integrity of his character, his extraordinary talent and even more extraordinary ugliness—shipped his belongings off to Buenos Aires.

During the years of blithe memory in which the short- and narrow-sightedness of myopic patriotism kept us trapped between Arroyo del Medio and El Salado,* he played his swaggering role as billboard *bagattelliere*, efficiently contributing to the indecent, farcical show that came to ruin that thin-flanked political specimen known as the Republic of Argentina.

With sharp and biting pen, this quarrelsome diarist and troublemaker stood fast in the thick of public life, hitting out right and left at all those who sang from the party hymnbook.

A mediocre writer of romantic prose and verse, he would leave his literary offerings—violet-scented like Pinaud soaps—on the steps of Mount Parnassus, which of course never stopped him from devoting his leisure time to forbidden pleasures and trying his luck, from time to time, with Cupid, a specialty for which he came to gain a tremendous reputation.

Did he deserve it? Was he truly a charmed individual whose moves were so smooth that he could, as they say, sink two shots simultaneously?

Personally, I am not convinced by the toot of his horn, having seen him play only once in his life and—God forgive me!—finding the euphonic effects of his flute to be something of a fluke.

But I have on good faith that the public more or less agreed and that the well-known, aforementioned feats of our new Lovelace were nothing more than canards invented by a rogue and repeated by a fool that spread like wildfire and that no one took the least trouble to verify at the source until in the end they were swallowed whole by the public, like a letter by the letter box.

Be that as it may, it so happens that a deer-like fear took hold of the populace, to such a degree that any woman he laid eyeglasses upon was a goner, and even the most outgoing of husbands trembled with

---

*Arroyo del Medio forms the natural border between Buenos Aires and Santa Fe Provinces; the Salado River begins nearby, in the northeast of Buenos Aires, and runs down toward the center. Being stuck between the two, therefore, leaves little leeway.

fear and found himself gasping for breath when his wife showed disrespect by saying good day to such a dangerous, dapper Dan.

A brilliant, shining star, he appeared on the horizon with the fall of tyranny, crossed the heavens during the segregation of Buenos Aires, and went down with the sun on the Day of the Pavón.*

Today he rests comfortably on his laurels and vegetates within the chrysalis of private life, as he should: we now live in an age in which widows, lost souls, and dimwits, even in good stead, are furtive figures who frighten no one but a fool.

He should be content with his status as a figure worthy of respect, a lawyer who ill knows the law yet defends myriad cases, a subscriber to every daily published in Buenos Aires and a die-hard regular at the Club del Progreso where, since you can't teach an old dog new tricks, come rain or shine, at eleven o'clock he turns up to play his infallible hand of bezique with some other member of the few remaining, until supper (or rather, until the steak and fried potatoes are served, as they are every night, between one and two in the morning).

The strict uniformity of this life program is broken only thrice per year: May, July, and Carnival.

Et pour preuve: there you have him, reclining to the bitter end on one of the sofas in the portrait room.

Come closer if you like; you shall hear a killing exchange, the scandalous heavy fire of poppycock and *sesquipedalia verba*, which he fires off at close range, struggling to offend the sensitive sensibilities of the masker lending him an ear.

You might ask what for, if he is all talk, as they say.

Well, he was born in a foreign land, though his parents are citizens of this one.

Having shown himself brilliantly primed since childhood, with an

---

*The fall of tyranny refers to Justo José Urquiza's forces defeating Rosas's army at the Battle of Caseros on February 3, 1852. Urquiza, governor of Entre Ríos Province, became the head of the Argentine Confederation a few months later. On September 11, 1852, as a result of political measures he adopted, liberal Buenos Aires factions rose up against him, took control of foreign affairs, and refused to recognize the Constituent Congress's legislative authority. The result was Buenos Aires' secession. Almost ten years later, on September 17, 1861, the federal army fought the Buenos Aires army and lost at Arroyo de Pavón, leading to Urquiza's withdrawal from political struggle, the fall of the Confederation and the formation of a nation-state under Bartolomé Mitre, who had been Buenos Aires' governor.

amazingly well-developed . . . physique, his teachers advised his father to give him over to the arms.

Ció é:

Not to those dangerous, barbaric apparatuses that stab, pierce, and prick, but to those fertile tools of progress whose mouths spew forth only jets of cold water: they made a *sapeur pompier* of him, and, for the glory of this noble and hazardous profession, from within his bronze helmet he gave it all he could.

While his intrepid companions fought face-to-face against the elements, liable to drop dead from smoke inhalation, be roasted like steaks on a barbecue, or at the very least get crushed by a section of wall collapsing upon their heads, he, undaunted in his turn, remained fixed unshakably in his place of honor and peril: he mounted guard in the barracks.

His lucky star, in the never-ending vicissitudes of existence, cast him to the Argentine beaches the way adverse fate propels a pilgrim or the way a gardener uproots a cork tree; the noble spirit of his life was thus forever sterilized, his career shattered, his grandiose future truncated.

He put away his useless fire hose and took up a hammer instead. The earth does not tremble here, houses are not made of wood, there was no flowing water at that time, and the only pumps folks worried about were those used to bring up water from the well to sate the sheep's thirst.

So, he held auctions from nine to four and dishonored women twenty-four hours a day.

In case you do not recognize him, his physical description follows:

Tall, with small, pretty feet, really quite bandy-legged, upright posture, skin as soft and pale as vanilla custard, angular face, his hair is light brown, eyes are small, and his expression midway between picaresque and cretinous; considerable nose and, actually, about his mouth I can tell you nothing as it is ever hermetically covered by a pair of enormous moustachios that were fitting for a fireman, but poorly suited to a dandy, and would be absolutely perfect on the face of a florid French fencing master. The French stuck them on for the stage; a bit of glue on the ends and away you go!

At first glance, he is not a handsome man nor anything approaching that, but a certain colorful flair in his ties and a certain musical zamacueca dance step in his stride make him, beyond any shadow of a doubt, the most stylish young man on our social scene.

As an auctioneer, mediocre; just another judicial miser.

As a champion of erotic exploits, oh! You cannot beat him on that count!

There is no person or thing capable, when the flame of sensuality flickers in his flesh, of holding back the white-hot volcano of his venereal appetites.

He has forced padlocks and damsels, scaled balconies, broken windows, jumped from rooftops, hung from cornices, climbed down chimneys, conquered even stones—like in the mind of the poet they have opened themselves to him, entreating him to tread upon them—and now is the time to be bewitched, to smother him in kisses, when he talks of his affairs with that God-given Andalusian wit: how, upon being interrupted, *par example*, at the crucial moment by some inopportune husband, he managed, crouching between the bed and the curtains to spend many long hours biding his time, waiting for a propitious snore, and another, and another, allowing him to beat a hasty retreat, muffling the sound of his steps so as not to sacrifice his sweetheart.

Oh, if the walls had ears; better yet, if they were phonographs, God help us!

Woe betide you, and me, and nearly every Tom, Dick, and Harry around!

Woe betide our reputations and our names!

Forget Buckingham, forget Don Juan, forget Faublas and Richelieu!

This man is a *succès fou*!

But, of course! Out of fear, the husbands befriend him.

Continuez si cela vous fait plaisir.

As for me, I am afraid I must leave you. I see that a woman in a black domino is waving at me and, well, noblesse oblige.

"Is it me you are calling?"

"Yes."

"What can I do for you?"

"Tell me where your friend Juan is."

"At the dance."

"Yes, but where at the dance?"

"Here, give me your hand and I'll show you," I said, like the nice old candy man, opening a vest pocket.

"You rude man!" my interlocutor hissed between clenched teeth. "I warn you," she said vehemently, quickly, "that I am not of a mind for jokes. I must speak to your friend and I want you to help me find him."

V'appoggiate al braccio mio.

We to-ed and fro-ed from pillar to post; the three dance halls, the galleries, and even the men's toilette and the second-floor apartment, which the masker upon my arm searched without so much as a moment's hesitation or any scruples whatsoever; but alas, it was deserted at the time.

"One of two things: either you are a formidable woman, or you have a very keen interest in finding Juan indeed," I said to myself, feeling my curiosity pricked.

After wasting three quarters of an hour uselessly wandering about, I finally succeeded in making out the object of our inquiry, chatting merrily with a group of musketeers, his face aflame, eyes shining, wearing an expression of titillation; in short, he looked like a man experiencing something out of the ordinary, indescribable.

"*Ecce homo,*" I said to my companion, pointing toward the group.

"Oh, I've torn my dress!" she cried almost simultaneously, bending down abruptly, as if she had just stepped on her tail.

"Take me to the toilette, quickly."

"But what about Juan?"

"Yes, yes, I'll speak to him afterward."

Ten minutes went by, then twenty, then thirty, and still my masker did not reemerge.

Does this lass think I'm a toy she can play with? I asked myself and, quite piqued at being stood up so, I was within a hair's breadth of claiming revenge, standing her up in turn, when in one of my to-ings and fro-ings I saw her rush into the aforementioned toilette by the outer-gallery door.

As I had believed her already inside, this unsuspected *truc* was a just motive for shock and suspicion.

What can this mean? I wondered.

She goes in, asks me to wait for her, and now it turns out that she slips in once more, through the back door, rather than come out.

Am I being taken for a fool, unwittingly playing the joker in some scheming plot? Is something fishy going on here?

And what on earth has Juan to do with all this?

Moments later, she emerged, finally.

"Did I keep you waiting long?"

"Three quarters of an hour, as you well know."

Poor dear!" she cried. "I beg a thousand pardons and, since you have been so good, sacrifice yourself entirely by now taking me back to your friend."

"All for the greater glory of God! As you beg rather than command, I shall consent. You appear rather more pleasant now and, judging by the change in your tone of voice and accent, it seems that the root of the ill humor afflicting you earlier must have disappeared."

Indeed, a remarkable change had come over her manner, air, words . . . even the harsh grating falsetto voice seemed to me less screeching now.

Approaching my friend, who was still in the throes of animated conversation with the aforementioned group of musketeers, I tapped him on the shoulder and said:

"This masker has been after some Juan fellow for over two hours now."

My friend turned around, gaped at her, cut short his discourse and, with the gauche air of a man who is up the creek, quickly offered her his arm, and stammered:

"At your service, my little masker."

Why did my friend's reaction to my companion's arrival seem to have the same effect as that of the police arriving unheralded at a den of iniquity?

Having delivered the cloaked bundle to its destination, my deed was done, my role had come to an end; I slipped, therefore, backstage, which is to say I went for a smoke, and damned if I hadn't forgotten the whole business when, round about five in the morning, Juan stopped before me with a masker on either arm: one black domino and one white one.

The most placid of smiles played upon his lips; he had evidently recovered his habitual sangfroid.

"We are pondering a foolhardy escapade," he said, "and want you to kick up your heels, too. So let the four of us go and dine at the Café de París."

"The Café de París? Why not the cafeteria round the way?"

"For the simple reason, my dear fellow, that the cafeteria has no private rooms."

"Do you mean, then, that you are proposing nothing short of a *partie carée*?"

"With all the *cachet de la chose*, though I must warn you that these lovely maskers accept on the express condition that they remain absolutely incognito."

"Bah! Leave it out! I'd rather go home to bed; I'm not in the mood for games."

"What a gentleman! What finesse! Your friend is a paragon of chivalry!" the white domino said to Juan sarcastically.

Either I'm a loon, I thought, or that is not the first time I've heard that voice, and I've heard it this very night.

Something akin to a glimmer of cruelty crossed my cerebral regions.

Resolved to put an end to my doubts, weighing up pros and cons, I brusquely changed my mind and exclaimed:

"I love a wildcat who speaks her mind.

"Your candor is seductive, masker.

"The Café de París, did you say? So be it: the Café de París it is!"

And I graciously offered her my arm.

X V

To say that the plan came off as intended, that the events that followed were what the management promised, would be a bold-faced lie.

I ask you, dear readers, to be the judges.

Once *in situ* I said to myself: let us see what this is all about and who these people are. So in order to determine the lay of the land, while Juan stood beside the table looking over the *plats du jour*, I made myself comfortable on the couch, grabbed my lady by the waist, sat her upon my lap, put my arms round her neck, and without so much as a by-your-leave, attempted to impart an amorous kiss beneath her ear.

"Well, I never! You shameless man! You swine! What do you take us for, French tarts?" my mysterious maiden barked, jumping up furiously and hurling abuse at me from ten feet away.

"*Ché, ché*, take it easy," Juan said to me, intervening in his turn.

"Don't be so barefaced that they can see you coming.

"Treat them with respect; you don't want to scare them off."

What had I done to provoke such outrage?

The most natural thing in the world.

Nothing that was not perfectly correct: I complied with the rigorous rules of etiquette, being the well-educated man that I am.

Enough. Now we know what game to play, and that is what interests me for now, I thought.

If they spook for so little, they must be real rookies.

To anyone with a mildly knowing eye, indeed, they were virtually shouting out that this was the first time they had been beneath a chandelier, in the presence of truffle-stuffed partridge or strawberries with champagne.

Undoubtedly, these were two country girls, clean and prudish, that is to say decent, which does not mean that for all their cleanliness, prudishness, and decency they could meet Father Phlegm's scruples if they tried.

In any case, with that flop of a prelude and two *cagnes* forming the cast, the whole farce was sure to go to the devil.

And it did: the whole ordeal was *un four*, a failure, a fiasco.

The women ate little, drank less, and spoke of a whole host of insubstantial topics without ever unmasking themselves, while poor Juan struggled desperately to be interesting and to amuse me, and I sat there like a fool and cursed the whole damn party.

Voilà tout.

X V I

The effects of just one bad night, for me, are visually equivalent to balling up a wet linen shirt and leaving it to dry; all the wrinkles and creases become most patently apparent and are accentuated in deep, sinuous furrows that run whimsically from side to side, merrily somersaulting or playfully joining up at my eyes like so many capricious little crow's feet.

The abominable toll of time! The only refuge, in said case, open to us forty-year-olds is the refreshing *coup de fer*, and in order to iron out one's folds there is nothing like sleep.

As it was, I was attempting to rejuvenate myself, which is to say I was sleeping, when I heard the voice and gait of Juan, who had walked in and was making himself at home, opening my window shutters and exclaiming:

"Shameless! It is three o'clock in the afternoon and you're still in bed!"

"If you can think of nothing more gracious to do," I grumbled, "than come here and try my patience after a sleepless night, you can go to the devil!

"Stop badgering me and let me sleep. . . . But do make yourself at home. I'm not setting the dogs on you and, while I settle my account with the pillow, you have there before you, should you so desire, something amusing with which to edify and entertain yourself," I added, indicating an open book on my night table.

"Paul de Kock, *The Cuckold?* Ha! Did the devil have nothing better to do?

"Be aware, Señor Sleepyhead, that when I take the trouble to open a book, it is to learn something useful and not to waste my time miserably, reading idiotic, indecent rubbish."

"Don't be foolish, my dear Juan; Paul de Kock is a great man, a subtle wit, and a connoisseur of the human heart.

"Beneath the film of frivolity, under the light veneer, the trivial narration, and the vulgar dialogue, there is ever a seal of truth in his productions that betrays a deep thinker.

"His works—superficial and at times even indecent in style, as you say—are always perfectly serious and moral in substance.

"So please refrain from slander and be kind enough to speak more respectfully of such an élite spirit who is one of the first of our times to portray local customs."

"Who, regardless of his spirit, is naught but an abominable, second-rate artist.

"But let's forget about Paul de Kock, his cuckold, and every other cuckold on the planet for the time being.

"I did not come here to fight some literary battle tooth and nail, but to have the pleasure of telling you that, frankly, last night you behaved like an utter cretin and that you were had most deplorably by our maskers[1] and that, after one more blow like this, your reputation as a clever man will bite the dust."

"Why?"

[1] Me, under my breath: which of the two?

"Why do you think? Because you did not discover their identities, because you were a slow-witted oaf!"

"Hold on a minute: the one in black[2] was your wife."

"Well, well. Not bad, old man! I'll give you a bit of credit for that. And the other?"

"I don't know."

"Seek and ye shall find."

"I seek but do not find; I repeat, I don't know who she was."

"Cat got your tongue?"

"The chicks can have it too, if you like."

"Who else could it have been, you miserable creature, but her inseparable bosom buddy, her dearest and only friend."

"That forty-year-old thing I often see her with in the street?"

"The one and only."

"And how would you expect me to discover her identity, never having exchanged a single word with her in all my life?"

"What? Have you never seen her at our house?"

"Never. Don't forget that I abhor strangers and before coming to call on you, as I have oft informed you, I question your doorman as to who is and is not already visiting *chez toi.*

"Oh, the old spinsters horrify me, that race of skirted harridans, and I shan't deny that your wife's inseparable, bosom buddy, as you call her, instinctively strikes me as unpleasant and distasteful, like a kick in the stomach.

"So don't be shocked by the fact that I never stop in when I know she is visiting."

"That's just like you! Unpleasant and distasteful, without knowing a single thing about her.

"A most excellent creature she is, an angel of a woman and, what is more, an exceedingly convenient attaché for me; my factotum, a second me.

"If the little one falls ill?

"She doesn't move from his bedside; she sits up with him on bad nights and takes all the trouble and puts up with it all.[3]

"If I go out in the day on business or at night . . . well, just because?

"She is my representative, staying in like a loyal patriot, or worse, like my wife's lapdog, keeping her company. She watched her grow up

[2] One of them.
[3] And what the devil is your wife doing all this time?

and her affection for her is as maternal in emotion as it is canine in adhesion, and it would, I am certain, keep anyone from touching her, even with a gloved hand.[4]

"I assure you that on more than one occasion I have been tempted, in payment for her eminent services, not only to declare her heroically distinguished and meritorious, but to give her a necklace bearing the inscription: *Cave canem!*

"This woman, this saint, nothing less than an angel, is the very being whom you compare to a kick in the stomach.

"I hope you now see how unjust you are . . ."

"Hush up, will you, in the name of God, hush up! If you carry on I will surely shed a bucket of tears in repentance!"

"Laugh if you like. As for me, I have nothing but sincere esteem and deep appreciation for Señorita Concepción."[5]

"Because she looks after madame and the baby, or because she keeps guard while you go off to play hooky?"

"Both."

"I like your impudence.

"At least you are frank about it.

"So, this is what it has come to, after a year and a half of marriage?

"His excellency allows himself to take this path, but deigns to cover his tracks for appearance sake, like an operetta god?

"You're out on the town at night but make sure your wife is not home alone in your absence?

"Not bad, sir, not bad; others do worse; they take the middle road and whoever comes along behind them . . .

"Oh! Dear Juan, what a moral leap we've taken, what an immense distance now separates us from that time when your entire life revolved around your wife and your one and only desire was to live with her year-round at Los Tres Médanos.

"Bah! Why should it surprise me?

"It had to happen, of course; all you're doing is yielding to the unfailing laws of human nature.

"Do you know what Madame de la Sablière replied to one of her relations who flung her fickleness in her face, saying that at least animals only love once a year?

" 'Precisely,' the good woman exclaimed, 'because they are animals.'

[4] Don't be so sure . . .
[5] Get that on record.

"And Madame de la Sablière was a very practical woman.

"All good things come to an end, you know. *Tout passe, tout lasse, tout casse* . . .

"Your love for your wife, that fire you thought would never be extinguished, is now flickering low, if it has not been extinguished already.

"Sick of the pure pleasures to be found at home, you search out the impurities of an adventuresome life; bored with partridge you now waste your hunger on cheap birds.

"Take care, poor Juan, take care so as not to fulfill the third part of the saying, don't be the one to break the fragile cup of your happiness with your own clumsy hand!

"There, you've let it out now; the moment has struck, the real issue's arisen at last!

"That is the problem with methodical men, walking around with their heads in the clouds, bouncing like balls from one wall to the next.

"Utopian fools who, by dint of wanting everything to be black or white, staring at the sun or closing their eyes, end up blind, never realizing the world is lead-gray.

"Man marries or doesn't, fine; but if he does, he must understand that it is like a shackle or, better yet, like a rawhide horse harness that never splits, even at the cinch."

"Those are absurd, ridiculous, enormous exaggerations in the most extreme cases.

"It's fine that man marries and together with his wife traverses the path of life, but really! Up to a certain point!

"Man is like a horse: from time to time he needs to take to the fields, twitch his tail, frolic, and roll around in the mud, if there's no sand around."

"If man is like a horse, then of course woman must be like a mare, who switches her tail, frolics, and rolls around as well.

"What would you say if your wife used your logic?"

"Stop right there! Man is man and woman is woman; she dons skirts and he wears the trousers."

"Oh, how we men, made in the image and likeness of our Lord, mete out justice in this vale of tears!"

"Yes, siree! That's right! Even from a juridical point of view, even considering all the kind attentions, the respect, the deferences, anything you think a woman might deserve, why damn it! One cannot be eternally hanging on her apron strings like an organ-grinder's monkey.

"That would be an offense to human dignity.

"Educated men behave in another fashion, they proceed with tact, with a certain delicacy, they know how to respect certain things, how to deprive themselves of certain things; otherwise they are not gentlemen but boors.

"In short, my dear friend, he who loves his woman well should have many—or at least two—as long as he keeps up appearances, of course, which is what society demands and what I shall comply with; unless some inopportune soul surprises me in *flagranti delicto* and, tapping me from behind, presents my lawful wife, *ex abrupto*, before me.

"Got it, Fabio?"

"Well, that inopportune soul could hardly have imagined that a married man, a serious, discreet man such as you claim to be, would speak of such things in a ballroom."

"What's wrong with that?

"I was among friends and one cannot always control the loose tongue one derives from satisfied self-love, particularly after downing a dozen glasses of champagne.

"Imagine! While you and María[6] were looking for me at the Club, I had sneaked off like a fox[7] with a ravishing little lady who has been driving me wild and who I've had my eye on for over two months now.

"It's quite a story, an eventful affair, full of spice and delicious adventures that I couldn't resist the pleasure of recounting.

"So there I was, just getting to the sauciest part of my tale, when the two of you dropped like a bomb and left me utterly dumbfounded.

"You see, it was quite an episode."

"No, what I see, my dear Juan, is that you stuck your neck out, that your conduct is reproachable, that you neglect the duties that you yourself imposed, that it might land you in some exceedingly hot water, and that you are indubitably heading for trouble."

"What the hell do you mean, neglect duties?

"Why? Because I enjoy myself? Am I not young? Am I not rich? Where is the harm, then?"

"In your wife, in your son."

"What have my wife and my son got to do with it?

"My wife, poor thing, is a saint and I love her dearly; leave her in peace.

"And you have no cause to bring my little boy into this; I adore him;

---

[6] María, huh?

[7] and she like a snake

103

I love him to pieces; he has everything he could wish for and always will as long as I am alive.

"So it seems to me that I fulfill my duties as a father honorably and that even the most exacting soul would find no fault in my conduct."

"Of course; with clothes to wear, a roof to sleep under, and food on the table, you're already in heaven.

"*Quantum mutatus ab illo!*"*

"You are becoming tedious and irritating with your preaching ways," Juan said, getting up.

"I shan't stand for any more of it, I'm leaving, you've driven me away."

"And what you have driven away from me is sleep, with your stories and your bragging.

"You easily might have carried on somewhere else and chosen another confidant for your roguish behavior, another audience before whom to perform your devil-in-disguise act, another illustrious victim of the formidable solo you've so gallantly lavished upon me."

"Speaking of disguises: Do you want to accompany me to a society masquerade tonight, taking place behind closed doors, in a private home? Just get a mask off one of my *amigos* and you'll be right as rain . . ."

"Deliver me, oh Lord, from such nonsense!

"What I want is to sleep."

"Well! You try to do your bit for the country, and look! Goodbye, you useless old fool!"

"Goodbye, lady-killer, womanizer, Don Juan."

"Juan," I cried a moment later, raising my voice.

"What?"

"Come here; listen, don't go yet."

"What do you want?"

"I want to know when you are going to marry me off. Have you finally found me a woman, *as-tu mon affaire*? Or is that no longer your cup of tea? Has your enthusiasm waned?"

"Go to hell!" my friend shouted from the staircase.

---

*How changed from what he once was!

XVII

Then I milled it over and over, thinking either I'm a fool or this is what's happened: Juan goes to the dance with his wife and that old bag, damn and blast her.

Juan takes off at an appointed time, to go make mischief, but not before his wife makes off with identical plans.

So the old dame stands watch and, alarmed at seeing neither hide nor hair of Juan and fearful of giving the game away, goes on maneuvers, bumps into me and sets me on the trail, uses me like a butterboy and thereby makes me an unconscious accomplice to this wicked scheming.

It turns out to be a false alarm; the double indignity is consummated in blessed peace and tranquillity, the husband returns to the dance and the immaculate, chaste wife to her husband's arm.

The proof?

Oh, the proof is quite compelling; if that were not the case, the old woman wouldn't have changed from her white domino into a black one that matched Juan's wife's gown. Nor would she have had me scouring the place like steel wool, in search of her man.

Once we found him, she would not have pretended to ruin her frock in order to slip into the toilette and, certainly, Juan's wife would not have slipped in through the back door, crouching down like a miner on his way down the pit, in an attempt to pull the wool over my eyes!

Where was she coming from?

Verdict: my friend Juan is a . . .

I fell asleep.

XVIII

"Taniete."

"Acher servuss."

"Ah! *Sapristi! Je veux en avoir le coeur net.*"*

*I want to get to the bottom of this.

"Hunh? I don' understand."

"Really? You don't say, man; what's not to understand? Well, don't fret if you don't understand as I wasn't speaking to you but to another."

"Yessir." (Looking around for that other.)

"Come here and listen to me; I don't want to be obliged, as I normally am, to repeat myself a hundred times."

"Righty-o."

"Are you a trustworthy man, Taniete?"

"My papers is in order; they's papers what prove my honerbilty.

"I got one from the vilge priest what I served for sev'n year as a servant, and sometimes as sexton when the opertunety rose. I got one from the mayor, what the whole of city hall can undorse . . ."

And then, staring at me, fixedly:

"Sides, you oughtta know already, being as how I's always here to serve you," my illustrious Taniete added, with a gesture that conveyed the following notion: You can go and jump in the lake.

"Well, that, particularly the last one, would be an indispensable testimony to your irrefutable integrity.

"But I'm not asking if you're an upstanding citizen just as I ask not if you are a thief.

"What I want to know is if you feel able to take a hand in a certain delicate matter, to hunt around, to follow a trail, keep your eyes peeled, see, comprehend, in short, to stop being yourself for once in your life and—and this is what matters most—not to talk about the whole matter with a single, solitary soul.

"Are you game?"

"If it's pol'ticks, I ain't gettin' 'volved; no gov'mint intrigues."

"Why is that?"

"Lord above! 'Cause they might beat the bejesus outta me, like they did another guy I knows from back home what got himself a job as a off'cer of t'law."

"Oh, isn't it marvelous! Your fellow countryman also decided to come good! And who, may I ask, asked your friend to plunge into Argentine public affairs, being himself Galician?"

"Zackly! That's what I said!"

"Alright, don't get over-excited, keep calm, hey? It's nothing to do with revolutions, overthrowing the government, or even public disorder.

"The matter, Mr. Don Juan, concerns skirts: women.

"Can I count you in?"

"Ah! Yup, you can count me in, yessir!" Taniete exclaimed, winking at me with a picaresque smile.

"I'm a expert on that; Father Lestemoño trained me good on that. Lord mercy, that sure was one goddamned priest! If he'd a stayed in our town any longer, he'd a stole all the parish girls there was from me!"

"Your priest, I see, was quite cunning; but that is not what concerns me.

"There is a masquerade tonight at the Club del Progreso."

"I'm sure there is, yessir, I ain't sayin' there ain't."

"Shut up. Stop interrupting and listen:

"I want you, from midnight onward, to be on the corner of Calle Perú and Calle Victoria, waiting in a tilbury that I shall rent and you shall drive.

"You will wait there until I come talk to you.

"You will probably have to follow a masked woman, who will be either alone or accompanied, on foot or in a carriage, I don't know.

"At any rate, you follow her, keeping half a block away, more or less, so as not to raise suspicions; don't lose her from your sights, pay close attention to where she goes, see which door she goes in once she arrives at her destination, wait until she comes back out, and then . . . well, that's it; you come home and tomorrow you recount all the details of your foray to me.

"Did you get all that?"

"Yup, I got it, yessir."

"Good, keep your eyes open and your mouth shut: not a peep out of you."

"Donchu worry; I ain't gon' peep."

XIX

At midnight, as master and servant we were in our respective combat positions: I in the Club and Taniete positioned for ambush in his old rust bucket. Just slightly later Juan made his entrance, flanked by his two cronies, who, rather than wearing black and white, were tonight both in brown dominos.

I had not been mistaken; my calculations were quite mathematical.

At 2:30, the witching hour, the ideal time for hanky-panky, one of the brown ladies—slithering like a snake amongst the human grass there present—cleared a path to the gallery and, protected by the general hubbub, the *remue-ménage*, slipped upstairs and from the stairs out onto the street, though not without being seen by me, since I didn't let her out of my sight. Quick as a wink, I slipped out after her, keeping close to the wall.

She reached the corner and turned down Calle Perú, southbound.

I then approached Taniete, filled him in, explained, pointed, repeated what I had explained so as to force him onto the trail, and jauntily strolled back to the Club.

Did I say jauntily? I tell a lie; not so jauntily, but rather thus: I felt a slight sting—not without the veritable qualities of a pang—in the furthest recesses of my conscience. It was like one of those wee little sounds that grate on one's nerves, contort one's features and one's nervous system to such a point of excitement that it becomes fury.

If you would like an example, just follow this formula: scrape a sharp penknife down a pane of glass.

The whole matter, frankly, was distressing me appreciably.

I was uneasy, anxious, feverish . . .

You see, I didn't have the deck stacked in my favor with respect to the rules of good conduct.

It was not, to be sure, banal curiosity that spurred me on, nay, nor any mean motive that moved me to act, nor any crudely malevolent instinct, no.

My soul drank from a far purer fountain, my behavior was inspired by loftier sentiments.

I saw unfolding before me the intrigue of an indecent farce in which the name, honor, and peace of a beloved friend were at play. Shrugging my shoulders, turning my back, and washing my hands of the whole affair would have been enough to make it impossible for me to look at myself in the mirror.

For heaven's sake! That is what my grandfather used to say. But I'm not a Jesuit nor do I agree with their principles.

After all, this was a woman we were talking about, one had to supervise her actions, check up on her, follow her footsteps from the shadows, spy on her treacherously; let's get it out in the open; and the spy (a repulsive vocation if ever there was one) was a man who passed for respectable.

One question still unanswered.

XX

So, how did it go?"

"It went perfeckly."

"Ho, ho! Let's see: tell me all about your campaign. What did the masked woman do?"

"The masked woman," Taniete began, with all the phlegmatic dimwittedness of a Galician, "well, what she done was walk to the market square. Then, once she got there, she got in a cab that a-went down Calle Perú, alla way to the corner of Cochabamba; at Cochabamba it turned and a-went down to Santiago del Estero and then at Santiago del Estero it turned and a-went down to Cangallo and at Cangallo it turned and a-went down to Florida and a-went down Florida to Rivadavia."

"What? Did she not alight at any point?"

"Yessir, she did alit. She alit right there and a-went back to the party."

(Idiot!) "And is that all you saw?"

"Well, what did you speck me to see, being as how it was nighttime and all?"

"A fine mess! Yes, indeed.

"Do you mean to say that they have taken us for a ride, so to speak, that we are still completely in the dark, as blissfully ignorant as we were before?

"Well, a hearty congratulations, Señor Don Juan; now be off with you; you are excused."

"Have patience," I told myself abruptly, stepping back and rolling my eyes heavenward. Two out of three. You've got a swain, lady, and I aim to get my own back."

"Oh! I jus' about fergot to tell you somethin'," Taniete cried suddenly, retracing his steps.

"What?"

"Well, afore it got to Belgrano, the cairge stopped and picked somebody up."

"Male or female?"

"Man."

"And you were keeping that juicy tidbit for yourself? Well, you certainly did keep your eyes peeled!

"Where did he alight?"

"He done alit on Cangallo and headed down ta Retiro."

"And did you not follow him?"

"Me? I stayed in the cairge."

"Why on earth did you do that, if the carriage was returning to the Club?"

"That's true, I ain't denyin' it. But you done told me, 'Taniete, follow the masked lady,' and that's what I done."

"Well, then, quite simply, you are guilty of the blunder of the century.

"We could have discovered the man's identity or, at the very least, where he was headed so we could discover it later; but now, thanks to your imbecility, we remain ignorant."

"If that's the problem, ain't no problem."

"And why not?"

" 'Cause I 'ready know who he is."

"What do you mean, you know who he is?"

"Well, see, when the cairge stopped and the man alit, he was stood there a minute, talkin' to the lady inside."

"And?"

"And it were Señor Don Pepe."

"Señor Don Pepe! Are you quite sure?"

" 'Course I am. He said, 'Night, Taniete,' and I said, 'Night to you, Don Pepe.' "

"We're done for now! Just when I thought you were doing so well! Really! Fantastic, superb, marvelous.

"Why didn't you just offer him a seat and explain the whole business from start to finish?

"It would have been easier.

"Do you know what you'd need, to be able to play a part in this type of affair?

"Why almost nothing: not to have seen the light of day in Galicia, that is, not to have been born a complete ass in the shape of a man. With that and a few other things which I shall omit out of futility, you could have been a dignified rival of Monsieur Lecocq, top dog, the crème de la crème, the sharpest cop in town, the quickest wit ever born . . .

"Get out of here!"

XXI

For the love of God! Why not the cook, if we've fallen for clerks and third-rate hired hands?

It's the same old story, the age-old line, all an act . . .

"Ah! women, women!"

By luck or chance one offers, one fine day, to lend them a hand, to do them a good turn that nine times out of ten they do not deserve.

Fed up with languishing in the land of innocence, sick of being ingénues, of the privations and the abstinence required by the rules of the game for that role, their pretty little heads become filled with the idea of making their debut as leading ladies and playing at being married on society's stage.

Then some poor devil appears on the scene, strolling along aimlessly and unsuspecting, like dust in the wind, an out-of-work actor who possesses real honor, talent, generosity, and wealth and who would make a perfect counterpart.

A trap is set for him, he becomes ensnared, enters into negotiations and, once the foundations have been laid, the contract is signed through trickery and intervention on the part of the aforementioned lovely ladies who have become *corrispondenti teatrali*, veritable *mercanti* in human flesh as Señor Giacchino called them.

Of course, two opposing genres then arise, to suit the taste and vocation of the actress: serious theater, whose stage is limited to the four walls of the house and whose plot is confined to a man known as husband and some youngsters known as sons and daughters; and the whole colossal farce outside the house, whose stage is the world and whose intrigue unfolds amidst thousands of others.

In the former, the protagonist maternal; in the latter, mundane.

The aura about the first is saintly; it cannot be captured without a spark from the holy fire of virtue.

The crown that digs into the second's forehead is a cardboard tiara that can be bought for five cents in some sleazy, old bazaar.

But even chapel music has its flat notes and, besides, it must keep to the times in which we live.

The rotten repertoire, the café-concert, the *chansonnette* in F-sharp, suits modern tastes far better.

"Classicism can go to the devil, then!" our farce actress cries, "long live frivolity and trivia."

She proclaims herself the grande dame, grande coquette, and grande . . . she plays dirty tricks and hits where it hurts, she knows how to get ahead, her adoring fans carry her on their shoulders and, bathed in the cologne of adulation, she attains the heights of artistic glory.

Unfortunately, all good things must come to an end.

Even the brightest sun in the big, blue sky is clouded over in the sunset, like the dregs in a bottle of sherry.

Our heroine, too, turns to sludge, she comes unstuck, crumples, ages, her popularity wanes, triumph turns to tragedy, and she winds up begging work in theaters in the slums, playing the maid.

And who is the victim in all this?

The management?

Lady Luck, the *egregia e gentilissima signora combinazione,* cares as much about the season's takings as she does about the sultan.

The audience?

No, not them either; they have been served up a scandal and greedily gobbled down every scrap.

The farce actress? Hah! Out of the question; she made her choices in life.

The other one, then?

Yes, it is him and only him, the miserable predestined man, the *bagattelliere,* the actor who gives it his all and gets nothing in return except for the laurels and other leaves that shine on his forehead after the recital.

Ah! Women, women!

They have heaven within their homes yet pursue the inferno out-of-doors.

They live in palaces yet debauch themselves in the first tenement house they come across.

They stuff themselves silly on ambrosia and cure their bellyaches eating pig meat.

Ah! Women, women! Wicked creatures!

And the worst thing is that it is unquestionable, blinding, obvious, clear as day, glaring.

What is to be done?

Tell it to the devil!

Above all, let sleeping dogs lie; let us swallow the bitter pill without protest and, if it suits us, walk in their shoes for a day, and if not, show them who is boss!

As long as Taniete's oafish footprints don't frighten off the fox!

At any rate, we shall see.

XXII

Doit-on le dire? As spiritual author of this now-identified farce, that, dear readers, is what I ask you.

That is the question, the great mystery, the tortuous conundrum.

With a snap of my fingers I rid myself of this problem and answer decidedly and resolutely: yes and no; *cela dépend.*

Naturally, he who thinks—like Aristotle—that friendship is a soul with two bodies or believes—like Voltaire—that it is a marriage of two souls must admit that a married soul cannot remain indifferent to the miseries afflicting its companion.

That is why man often meddles in matters that, on appearance, should be of no concern to him but, in reality, constitute the most pressing of duties for a well-placed heart.

The *quid* is in how exactly to go about it.

In the first place, it must be done well.

When it comes to resolving the issue, one must tread very lightly, proceed by the letter of the law, avail oneself of endless legally founded reasons, a body of evidence—so to speak—of the sort that barristers deem foolproof and that reaches, if possible, above and beyond women, to appeal to that arbitrator who, though completely cast aside nowadays, was very popular, as you know, in the courts of yore.

The jury, respectable institution though it may be, is as befitting in these cases as a fish out of water.

Try to think like a judge and use your conscience to say to a husband: "*Vous savez?* You are one."

"Proof, I want proof," he will reply immediately, in the sweet and mellifluous tones of someone asking for your money or your life.

"I know," you will exclaim haughtily, with satisfied air, *ab alto toro*, placing your hand solemnly and melodramatically on your heart, and you will land yourself in hot water indeed.

You will see how, regardless of your good intentions and suchlike, you will be removed from the premises, kicked out as if from a dance, and then kicked—in a certain part of your person—and called swine, villain, and slanderer to boot.

You see, of all of life's pits, there is none steeper or more difficult to climb out of than that of admitting to having been tricked by a woman.

Why?

Because a woman is not like a chicken that two friends share, carefree.

We members of the stronger sex will not stand for nonsense of that sort.

We understand that the chattels belong to us, are for our exclusive use, end of story.

Emboldened by the right that we know to be on our side, backed by the perception of our personal attractions, a perception that never fails, we all—even the crippled, hunchbacked and one-eyed—insist until the day we die:

That is nonsense! Me? There's not a woman on this earth who could deceive me. Though one should add, if only as an aside, that as soon as the poor devil lets his guard down even slightly, there right under his nose, in front of his face, the aforementioned woman is having it on.

And then go and shake the dreamer from his reverie, notify him of the joint ownership, the common usufruct, push him from a hundred feet up, and, of course, the impact on landing will make him jump up wild with rage and howling to the high heavens, like a little boy who's been pushed over and fallen flat on his face while playing chase.

Forget it; to avoid a difficult situation, don't swim in deep water without a float, insure that you have it all down on paper so you can prove the *truc*, and if the man collapses, it is not one's fault but the fault of the pulley, which suddenly gave way and dropped him backstage.

And what of the offspring?

That is yet another matter of vital importance.

If the husband is incapable, or the wife, or both, which really comes down to one and the same thing; if there is a question as to procreation;

if the family tree has not borne fruit, then the issue is enormously simplified.

In that case, other people's interests are not harmed, the children's silver is not stolen, nor does anyone but the patient husband come into play; he who, having been affronted and hurt, might well make a mountain of a molehill, throw the baby out with the bathwater as it were, should he so desire, and his wife too, because, after all, if he does so, he does naught but dispose of a dirty rag, a moth-eaten cloth.

And since making a fool see the light of day is a real man's job, I shall tell him; if he already knows, then because he knows; and if he does not know, then because everyone else knows and because I must defy that saying, invented by some husband who was taken for a fool and whom the neighbors drove mad by teasing every bloody day of the week, miming horns coming out of his head and making other rude gestures.

However, when there are legitimate and genuine offspring, with no deceit or *contrefaçon*, as in the present case in which the Los Tres Médanos monopoly—more than the manufacturer's seal—assures the provenance of the goods, then the going gets tough. Oh! Then the *façenda si fa seria*, one finds the rug pulled out from under one's feet and must endeavor not to fall flat on one's face.

On the one hand, there is one's friend—the daddy—whose fence is being jumped every time a traitor slips in through the back door without the ninny hearing a thing, despite the noise the intruder always makes, even if he takes off his shoes and tiptoes through; after all he is not a ghost, he does not float.

On the other hand, there are the children—the kiddies—that race of dunces who issued from the wedding and, without doing a thing, cost an arm and a leg; mother tends to—ahem—affairs, but they take the cake.

And a good thing, too! They did not pick their mother, I hear you—or society, which amounts to the same thing—bray like ninnies.

This is true, both society and the horses are right; but let's proceed.

Friendship forces one to grab the former, shake him by the arm, and say:

Don't be an idiot! Look!

And then one's head, pleading with one's sentiments for a lucky break, hoping against hope, checking the heart's noble reflexes, cries out in turn:

No, you mustn't bite off more than you can chew, nor repeat libelous slander; you mustn't drag their names through mud that was not of their making, nor condemn them to bear that cross as well as a sign on their foreheads and an insult on their lips.

It's bad enough if the drama unfolds after the curtains have been drawn and the obscene script has been kept behind the scenes and in the theater dressing rooms.

Worse still if the scandalous news is printed in black and white and doing the rounds of the city's plazas and cafés.

In that case, the children's share price takes a nosedive.

Honestly, why attempt to patch things up with warm towels and bandages, if the whole kit and caboodle is notorious and in the public domain?

Indeed, there is no point trying to catch rain in a sieve.

None whatsoever, but let us take heed, notwithstanding, of the fact that from time immemorial, there have been those who hold a low opinion of the public domain and of notoriety.

Many believe that the former is a fool and the latter a liar, a run-of-the-mill play-actor or small-time musician who is ever off-key, just one more member of the band.

They add that one must not believe ninety-nine of every hundred tales told; the world is full of cynics; no one can fool them. To believe something they have to see it with their own eyes, rummage around, and stick their snouts in, if they really want to.

Amongst these common folk, who buy it all in good faith, the above-mentioned stock can still be sold off, though perhaps at rock-bottom prices.

It is the only chance the wretched stockholders have to free themselves from humiliating bankruptcy. To take away that supreme option—a sort of drowning man's last gasp of air—would be like twisting the knife in a victim's gut, giving him that last coup de grâce, in short, playing the hangman, a profession that, I confess, holds no special allure for me.

But, why does the husband shuffle around like a blind man tapping a cane and, in his frenzied tap, batter the cheap leather of his own reputation?

Why, who on earth wanders about showing warts and all, claiming to be an upstanding patriot, a knavish slave to his wife's wily ways, when in fact he's the first to get caught up in foreign affairs, to be put on the spot, to tempt fate and kick against the pricks.

When a man has a wife and children, and even just a mere inkling of common sense, and his wife sneaks off and plays dirty in the heat of the moment, this is the procedure to follow, with slight variations according to one's strategy:

First, one must knuckle down and gag oneself. Then tie a sanitized cord between the bedrooms, thus placing the sinner in quarantine and thereby freeing oneself from all contact with her and from the consequent pestilent contagion.

This, let it be understood, with no tears, no shouting, nor any scenes, after having had a nice little chat with the infidel, during which the foundations of the modus vivendi are laid.

No externally visible changes.

Señor and Señora live together under the same roof, eat at the same table, and carry on baring their teeth amorously at each other in the presence of servants and strangers.

The only paltry novelty introduced is that they no longer sleep in the same bed, which, when it comes right down to it, is but a trifling detail.

The status quo is maintained long enough to avoid stirring up public malevolence, that is, until a plausible pretext utterly unrelated to the *grande affaire* is struck upon, whence the wife is hurled straight to hell, or oneself might go in her stead, ad lib and depending upon which better suits the situation.

And the accomplice?

Ah! The accomplice, that oh-so-crucial character, merits a separate paragraph.

If he is a simple man, an unknown, any old fellow, neither friend nor relation nor *obligé*, then his conduct is perfectly correct.

He goes about his business however he sees fit, God willing; he is within his rights and even the most puritan could not comment upon his conduct. In a word, he is clean as a new pin.

If, on the other hand, one has opened the door to him and shaken his hand; if he is bound by the ties of friendship, gratitude, or blood, which impose duties and not idiocies, then the whole shebang is turned inside out, the roles are reversed entirely, and that gentleman becomes an ate-your-bun, a sort of ragamuffin looking for trouble, *cherchant midi à quatorze heures*, to whom one gives a piece of one's mind if not another thing or two.

One kicks him or shoots him, just because, because he is insolent enough to hold opinions different from one's own about politics or music, or because, on passing, he glanced sideways, or coughed loudly, or stepped on one's foot, or nearly trod upon one's bunion.

That's it, right?

It's all very easy and very sensible and very perfect, if applied off-handedly, *in anima vili;* but actions speak louder than words, and I was on pins and needles.

What if his temper gets the best of him, what if the man gets feisty and kicks up a great fuss, which is both probable and practical?

Well, on to the state of play and proceedings, considering:

1. That dirty laundry should not be aired in public.
2. That sleeping with young men is perilous.
3. That elbowing a fool only stuns him.
4. And finally, that as far as dice are concerned, the safest bet is not to throw them at all; and since the best music is played after the curtain falls and when the audience is threatening to become rowdy and smash one's head in, my conclusion is the following:

    The husband shall not be summoned into the action; he is absolved from the instance.

    The plaintiff shall appear when necessary . . .

All of which means that I must stick with the hand I was dealt; you've got to do what you've got to do.

Sum total: I will not give the game away to Juan, not even if I am hung.

For his sake, for his son's, or for mine?

Friendship, charity, or self-love?

You decide.

XXIII

S eñora:
    I am not a man to mince my words, as you well know, and if you do not know, please deign to accept it as truth.

Forward or backward, I have always followed the straight and nar-row, avoiding superfluous steps and turns.

I abhor the curve, ill-fated implantation of some prehistoric flâneur and cause of many outrages, for the simple reason that the devil finds work for idle hands to do.

The idiosyncrasy of a twisted mind, the result of my upbringing?

There must be something of the latter: my father taught me, long ago, to draw a laughing man and a crying man, using only straight lines, at obtuse or acute angles, depending on whether it was comedy or tragedy, and manufacturing these miniature men, my favorite pastime as a young lad, has probably managed—over the course of time— to alter the profile of my moral physiognomy.

With this salutary warning-cum-preface out of the way, I proceed to the crux of the matter:

Señora: You are, quite simply, a trollop, with all that that term connotes.

I say that because I know, and if your husband knew he would say the same, surely taking advantage of the occasion to slip in a much less flattering word and perhaps even some other instrument with a sharper, more cutting edge.

What do you expect? It is a question of temperament.

Juan is an excellent young man, but like all of us, he has his faults.

Juan has always been quite naïve, he doesn't suffer fools gladly, nor does he understand jokes and tricks, especially those as, ahem, dirty as the ones you play.

Confess, my good lady, because in this case you've got no one to stand up for you.

What good Christian soul would be amused to find his lawfully wedded wife getting dirty in a dung heap and raising a fist full of muck to smear in his mustachios like an ill-trained cat?

Sleights of hand will black your eyes, particularly when they degenerate into tricks as rude as yours; wipe that look off your face.

Oh, very rude indeed, señora, and in the worst possible taste.

Tell me, otherwise, how we can explain the fact that, having a young, attractive, good, honorable, intelligent, rich husband, in short a first-class husband, the wife—in order to really excel herself—parades around like Lady Godiva in broad daylight, gets involved with a common skinflint loafer and goes off at an ungodly hour to soak up the stench and filth of the slums and catch pneumonia and shake her bones on the cobblestones, in the company of this idiot who is poorer than a church-mouse?

Luckily, señora, the steps which have led you astray are ones that your husband neither sees nor hears; the blessed man, like all God's creatures and cuckolds, only stops wandering about in a dream once in a blue moon, without ever even remotely suspecting this, your most brazen of deceptions.

I say luckily because he is a friend of mine and I do not like to see him covered in filth; as a soap-user, myself, I therefore shall proceed, *s'il vous plait* to wash the muck from his person before he awakes, and to this end ask you to lend a dainty hand, to act as croupier in this deal, to hold the washbasin and the candle, as it were, and to stop holding other things during said undertaking.

So:

Sit down at a table, take up pen and paper, and write:

"My darling beau:"

Your friend, Don Pepito, he of the *claire de lune*, is ugly as sin: ergo, you must call him beau.

In illo tempore, when I was but a young chap, Duval's girls—Leonor, Elena, Carlota, Antonietta, in fact all of the Gauthiers—used to call yours truly that, too; it's like clockwork, never fails, and I presume that, belonging to the same tribe, it will be the same with you.

We shall put, therefore, "my darling beau."

"The most dreadful misfortune now threatens us.

"An evil man . . ."

Put evil, señora, do not put anything more; I shan't resent evil.

"Evil man, has discovered our secret.

"Do not write or attempt to see me again, if you do not want to lose me forever.

"From now on you must forget about your poor, little . . ."

And this is the bit that matches up with the beau line:

You are a brunette, but I would bet, and I would not lose, that your lover calls you "Blondie."

Oh, I can see it now!

Not bad, eh?

Laconic, concise, no digressions, no inopportune hysteria.

Bitter pills are best swallowed quickly.

When one goes to have a tooth pulled, one prays to God that the dentist pulls it, crack! quick as a whip.

I too want to wrench from you, in one go, this nail that out of sheer recklessness you have allowed to pierce your body.

Now then, if it seems an uphill battle and you do not feel sufficiently strong to undergo the operation, even with the help of a bit of chloroform, then you are perfectly within your rights to refuse and I, for my part, shall not insist; but I give you due warning, so as to avoid disagreeable reproaches, that said refusal would oblige me to go to your husband with the gossip so that he, who cares about you above all else in the world, might adopt the measures befitting the gravity of the situation or send you packing or declare you insane and lock you up in the asylum or declare you something else altogether and send you to boot camp or force you to change neighborhoods or whatsoever he should like to do.

As far as I am concerned, my role as bird dog is now formally concluded; I shall go home and wash my hands of the whole affair like King Herod, come what may. So much the worse for you. If that is how you want it, you shall carry the blame.

So choose, then, between what I have said and what you write.

If it is to be the latter and you pay me as much heed as one does the sound of rain falling, then I give you my word of honor that, in less than forty-eight hours, Juan will hear from me what sort of woman you are.

If the former, then hurry up and give me that little piece of paper without dillydallying, in a sealed envelope addressed to me, within another unsealed envelope.

The aim of this precaution is to insure that you do not try to make me bring your lover the letter that I fear you might—no offense intended.

Permit me to reiterate that I am honored to be, señora, your most obliged, humble servant.

XXIV

I put down my pen, took off my glasses, put on my hat and gloves, slipped between glove and hand the document I had just written and with whose tone you are already familiar, and decided to pay a visit to Juan, whom I found in a sybaritic posture, sipping coffee, smoking a cigarette, and reading *El Mosquito*, while María stood leaning over her husband's shoulder, looking at the pictures and indulgently scratching her husband's head.

The baby sitting on the table—gooing and gaaing and sucking his fingers for want of something more fertile to suck—rounded off this tender, moving tableau of domestic bliss.

What a picture, for an amateur!

What a lure, for anyone thinking of soliciting the post!

What misery, veiled by the shadows of a lying, rotten outside world.

One would have thought that the earth ended at their doorstep.

He for her, she for him, and both of them for the little whippersnapper.

An idyll, a little corner of heaven on earth, like turkey stuffed with truffles . . .

From the front, that is.

Turn the corner and go in through the back door; *total déconfiture*.

The honeycomb is a dead stalk; paradise, a wasteland of burning rubbish; and the truffles, trash.

All a question of perspective.

Two things I have never been able to pull off well: a toast and a visit.

Every time I have very unfortunately committed the gaffe, the *bévue*, of raising my glass or opening my mouth, it has been to spew forth utter nonsense or to play the role of . . . toilette paper.

The typical "a truly solemn occasion . . . truly . . . truly . . . truly, solemn; yes, ladies and gentlemen."

But let us not get ahead of ourselves nor fall into the trap, as they say; ipso facto, I shall not grant you the right to deem me more of a fool than I already am.

Recall, if you will, instances from your own lives, think about it a moment and you shall see that you are forced to agree with me: there is no intellectual exertion greater than giving a *discours* while drinking champagne.

Either the subject of your speech adheres to the ceremony—in which case you say what has been said or what others will say and thereby fall fatefully into platitude—or you search out something singular to say and come off the rails like some greenhorn and lay yourself open to plebian questions such as:

So what? What is he on about? What in heaven's name has that got to do with anything?

It is difficult indeed not to wind up burning the toast.

Another little game at which I have always been quite inept: societal talents, or what they call playing the role of the salon bachelor, as the rude women say, as if they were talking about a piece of furniture or a decoration, a chimney or a pair of spittoons.

You can infer from my opening remarks that I am about to tell you the sorry tale.

It was back in '63.

Doña Pepa, after having spent many a year in Villa de Luján—though that fact bears no relation whatsoever to the story—went to visit my mother who had been a fellow pupil and a friend since time immemorial.

Naturally, she spoke of me, of how grown up I must be, a little man by now, gracious me, I was nineteen and a bit, of how industrious I must be, and, finally, she said she could not wait to lay eyes on the little lad and give him a kiss.

This was followed, as a final judgment on my days, by a solemn promise to send me over the next day, in order that Doña Pepa should be able to take in the ameliorations that my person had undergone with her very own eyes, thereby appreciating fully my now-improved physique.

I protested, to no avail, against my tyrannical mother's promise, alleging that I was not one to go calling, that Doña Pepa, Don Pepe and their string of daughters meant nothing to me . . . no use, courage had to be plucked up and, at 8:00 that evening, after putting on my Sunday best (a suit purchased in the Temperley clothier's on Calle Merced, to be precise), I had to walk over to where—God willing!—I should have had the moral fortitude to refuse to go!

About halfway there, I suddenly chanced upon one of Dad's old friends; I stepped aside, as was my duty, to let him pass and, on greeting him, I felt one of my feet slip and nearly lost my balance.

I regained it, thanks to the solid foundation I'm equipped with, and calmly carried on my way, assuming that the incident was finished with no further eventualities.

Finally, I arrived.

I knocked once, just once, like a servant, and upon hearing "come in" from the parlor, I entered.

In all, Doña Pepa, three of her daughters, and three young chaps who had come to call were there present.

Kidskin boots with Louis XV heels, low-cut necklines, teeny little gloves for great big hands, and every other imaginable high-life flourish of the times: it was a tour de force of finery unlike anything seen nowadays.

Upon entering, I tripped over the threshold.

I nearly fell flat on my face, bruising myself on the back of a chair.

Charming entrance, I thought. Embarrassed beyond belief, with my mouth dry as a bone and my tongue stuck to the roof of my mouth, I stammered to Doña Pepa:

"Se . . . Señora, I am Sss-Soo . . . So-and-so, the . . ."

"Oh! Little So-and-so, you've grown so tall! How was I to recognize you if you've gone and become a man!

"Did you hurt yourself, little So-and-so?"

"No, Señora, I'm fine, don't be si-silly!" (this, while seeing every star in the sky before me; I had just banged my bunion).

"Well, come in from the hallway, young fellow, and take a seat.

"These are my daughters."

"Señoritas, I'm very pleased to meet you."

"Pleased to meet you, señor."

"Look, Pepe," she continued, addressing her other half, who had just then walked in, tall, old, rancid, and wrinklier than a ram. "Do you recognize this young man?"

"Upon my soul, I do not," answered Don Pepe, after pushing back his glasses and looking me over from head to toe.

"It's little So-and-so, what's-her-name's son."

"Well, I'll be! He looks just like his mother!" the old fool exclaimed, after being informed that, indeed, I was my mother's son.

"I didn't recognize the little gentleman but, with the looks in that family, I could have guessed."

Hardly a moment had passed when suddenly I noticed a horrid smell.

The first thing that sprung to mind was that it must be Don Pepe who was sitting on my left, since old people tend to be a bit boorish and somewhat shameless.

But as great gusts of the stench insisted on assaulting my pituitary membranes as well as those of my neighbors, whose expressions could be seen to be practicing certain muscular gymnastics that can have only one interpretation, I said to myself:

No, I smell a rat; the persistency points to a body . . . of evidence.

And the band played on.

Imagine, if you will, however, the performance that an idiot of my age was to give; like some shapeless ball of dough, neither seeds nor meal, man nor boy, a novice, quick-tempered and ill-mannered, particularly when it came to exchanging words with women.

Who amongst us has not undergone that unbearable period of human awkwardness?

Saying yes sir, no ma'am, I don't know, I'm sure you're right; wadding up one's gloves; crossing one's legs; not knowing where to put one's hands; sitting as still as a flea-ridden dog and truly sweating like a pig. Those are the performances that appear on the playbill during the season when one's voice changes, when one goes from cheeping chick to crowing cock; that is, between the ages of 15 and 20, the abominable years, a sort of fools' bridge, a squaring of the hypotenuse in the mathematics of life.

In addition to the *maté* that was continuously circulating thanks to a ragged-looking mulatta, when the clock struck ten, the aforementioned servant entered bearing a tray on which sat a bakery cake and cups of hot chocolate.

With the lofty aim of reversing the impression I must have made during introductions, now displaying fine manners, it struck me that I should offer the hot chocolate around to the ladies.

I got up, took a cup, and presented it to Doña Pepa, just at the precise moment when the blessed woman decided to drop her handkerchief. Quick as a whip I bent down to retrieve it, whereupon my hand movement edged the spoon resting beside the cup and saucer over just enough to hit the cup, knocking it down in a rain of chocolate that fell over the poor woman and left her utterly soiled.

A black storm cloud passed before my eyes.

Damn and blast it! If there had been a hole around, even if a Galician had dug it, I would have jumped in as fast as you like.

"How clumsy!" snapped Doña Pepa, choked with rage. "Look! Just look how he's ruined my new dress!"

"That fool doesn't know which way is up," said one of the visitors, *piano piano*.

"Poor kid!" added a second.

"What a clod!" chimed the third.

The girls, in their turn, insisted on leaving me unconditionally mortified with their winks, their whispering, and their stifled giggles.

I was on the verge of committing a crime, when the esteemed, the illustrious Don Pepe put an end to my torment with the following eloquent words, addressed to his daughters:

"Come, come: that is quite enough tomfoolery. What happened to this young gentleman is not so ridiculous as to merit your chattering on so."

A moment of religious silence followed this energetic elocution.

With spirits calmed and the personal chocolate incident nearly forgotten, conversation picked up once more, and Don Pepe undertook to engage me in talk of, amongst other things, books and authors.

Elated at the prospect of finally being able to embark upon a topic that I could talk at length about and prove, once more, that one cannot judge a book by its cover, I launched headfirst into the *sujet*.

"Have you read Renan's *La vie de Jésus*?" (the book of the day) I asked him.

"God forbid!" he replied, crossing himself. "Me? Read such improper sacrilege! Why, whatever next?"

"But, señor . . ."

"Forget it, don't come to me with this rubbish they write these days when any lying dog can go and become a supposed man of letters.

"Heresy," he added for good measure, with a look of profound disgust. "*La vie de Jésus*, or nonsense and foolishness like *Les Misérables* or somesuch, by that old fraud, that charlatan, that frog." (Don Pepe was Spanish.)

"Speak to me about the writers of yore, Lope de Vega, Calderón de la Barca, Cervantes, yes, now *they* had talent!"

Of course I replied that, indeed, he was right. That *Don Quixote*, in particular, made me as happy as a king in his castle; that I considered it a masterpiece, a magnum opus, number one. I carried on in this vein, talking about the hidalgo's adventures and becoming more and more enthused by my own words until, completely *monté*, I said:

"You probably won't recall, but there is a certain dialogue between the two squires which alone contains more philosophy than Aristotle, Kant, and Descartes put together . . ."

And, getting up, staring at the bookshelf:

"I'll show you," I said, "as I can see a copy of that monument to human intelligence from here, holding place of honor in your library."

"Don't trouble yourself," said Don Pepe, jumping up after me.

"Oh, it's no trouble at all."

"But . . ."

"No buts about it, you shall see, you shall see," I replied, grabbing hold of *Quixote* before Don Pepe could stop me.

Noting that the book positively would not budge from the ranks of its companions, I yanked hard, and suddenly the panel that formed it gave way (the library had been a cheap decoy). Bam! I fell back, hitting and noisily knocking over the table and lamp with the posterior part of my person, and the panel then lay in a pile *par terre*.

The depths of darkness surrounded us.

This was Troy.

Don Pepe was squawking.

Doña Pepa was shouting.

The girls were shrieking.

The three lads, not a peep.

Why?

Start swimming . . .

This is it, I said to myself, inching toward the door in total darkness, not without first tripping over a few chairs, three skirts, and as many coattails.

The fresh night air had never been more welcome!

With my tail between my legs, abhorring the outrages I had committed in playing so ridiculous a role, I finally arrived home.

I sat down immediately to take off my brand-new boots, which had left my feet like fresh-pressed olives, when, blast it! I pulled off the right one and nearly fell over.

That's the last time! I cried.

This is all I need; to have been the baby, the laughingstock of the party!

In a paroxysm of rage, I cursed Doña Pepa, Don Pepe, their daughters, the chocolate-bearing mulatta, Cervantes, my father's old friend, the filthy dogs who foul the path and even Don Caytano Cazón, who was the chief of police and did not beat them to death.

If they catch me again at another one of those, I burst forth, let them . . . brand me.

I started off on the wrong foot, as you see, carried on in the same vein, and am now even worse than before.

I repeat: I have never been able to dance to that beat, never quite managed to come off as I would wish.

How many times, in my eagerness to appear polished and my desire to prove that I could speak Castilian Spanish correctly if the opportunity arose, did I not only pronounce *caballero, cuadrilla, brillante* with trilling palatal double l's but then also—accustomed to speaking like a normal Argentine whose tongue, no doubt, sought revenge for the cruel torment I was imposing on it—overcompensated by letting loose a *llo* for a *yo* or *aller* for *ayer*, which turned my cheeks as red as a frieze during Rosas's reign.

This is entirely factual, upon my word of honor.

One day, in a circle of ladies, instead of saying that my grandfather had ended up senile, I said he had ended up pe . . . well, you figure it out.

And that is not all.

Once, in Paris, we were having dessert after a meal with people of the *meilleur monde* and they had just served, by the name of Montreuil peaches, something as insipid as the coming-out ball of a German débutante.

Naturally, patriot that I am, it struck me as the opportune moment to deliver a eulogy to Argentine bush peaches.

I spoke of their monstrous size, their sun-kissed color, their fragrance, and their exquisite taste.

Little by little, I was overcome by my feverish love of the land and by too many glasses of *Château Yquem*, and I ended up affirming in the solemn tones of a man who tells no lies that the wild hills produce peaches amongst us the way they do acorns in Europe, that they stretch for leagues over the islands of Paraná River, and that each tree bears so much fruit that one steps on the peaches as if they were cobblestones.

All well and good, up to this point, correct and commendable from the patriotic stance.

But you see, being not quite shrewd enough to improvise in a foreign tongue (it was my first trip abroad), I Frenchified the Spanish verb *pisar*—to step—to a T, making a foray into Molière's tongue with the present indicative, preceded by the indefinite personal pronoun *on*, and thereby saying that one *pisses* (rather than *paces*) upon them, calm as you please. Brr! Simply recalling the occasion makes me shudder.

Needless to say, it raised quite a storm.

And keep in mind that when things have not gone poorly (all things are relative) and by sheer luck I have managed to make a stab at it (even the dimmest of sheep sometimes break out of the pen), it has been others and not myself who have found me to be like a bull in a china shop every time I have teetered on the edge of so-called decent society, that class of people who demand of their patrons a certain *tenue*, a sort of fold-down chair preposterously uncomfortable for a finicky fan of the Voltaires, who likes to smoke a pipe and spend all day in a robe and slippers.

I adore dressing down and painting the town red; a kind-hearted soul, whether male or female, a bottle of anisette, six decks of cards to play bezique, and, of course, my pipe.

There are no two ways about it, just as there is no denying that in my friend's home, in accordance with my honorable past (affirmed by the dire straits of the present), I was utterly unbearable.

I did not miss a single trick, not a one.

Outwardly, the air of a bewildered fool.

Inwardly, the gesticulations of a toad who, feigning ignorance and absent-mindedness, actually has all five senses on the alert—the hypocrite—and is taking aim at flies, awaiting the exact moment when they cross his line of vision so as to flick his tongue out and gobble them up without so much as batting an eye.

My aim, of course, was to quarter the bomb in the thick of enemy lines without having my artillery discovered; this was what spurred me on.

I would pull moves as slick as pool players like Esteban Risso and Cruz Martín, ricocheting balls and sinking shots without so much as skimming the side of the table.

Obviously, the ideal scenario would have involved getting the husband out of the way; he was just an obstacle, like one of those fat men at the theater who stuff themselves into the neighboring stall and obstruct one's view, forcing one to suck one's breath in for the duration of the show.

But how?

My excellent friend was charm personified. It was uncanny; he refused to leave my side for even a moment.

All in vain did I call upon the multitudinous excuses elaborated for just this purpose; nothing doing.

I reminded him that he had promised to lend me a book, not in view of any unfeigned intention of reading it, as it was a tome of recorded travels, penned by a young compatriot—God forbid!—but simply so that he would go off to his den to fetch it.

To no avail: the book lay on the mantelpiece not two steps from where we stood.

I asked for a cigar, and presto!

He reached into his pocket and produced one he declared of capital quality.

Fiasco after fiasco.

Decidedly, my friend Juan, in his dogged determination to give me a royal welcome, as old women say, was turning into quite a thorn in my side, his presence not only making me uncomfortable but trying my patience and cramping my style to boot, hindering my artistic movement and thereby impeding the performance of the show, which was, after all, being put on for his benefit.

My circumstances called to mind those of a *ripiego*, an understudy, the rabble that roam Italian theater squares; *alto primo tenore, primo basso*, or *primo rostro*, mangy rats from the stage box, the *souffre-douleur* that theater companies treat like slaves, putting a monthly *cento lire* in their pockets for their toil, after taking off their cut, which runs 30 to 40 percent.

What is left over is enough, as you can imagine, not only to stay alive, but also to allow one to live in . . . utter destitution.

If a *divo* or a *diva* falls ill, or pretends to (being the jewel in the house crown, like grandma's lapdog), do you think they cancel? Not on your life; the show must go on: police regulations, on the one hand, and the impresario's insatiable *saccoccia* on the other. Cancellation is terminally prohibited.

What to do?

They suddenly remember the illustrious *ripiego*, like devotees of Santa Barbara, and quick as a flash, send off the *avisatore* with instructions to find him and bring him back, dead or alive.

Said *avisatore* is always an excessively practical man; he knows all the cast's hideaways inside and out and therefore has his course set out prior even to embarking on the task.

He raises himself immediately to the heights, which is to say he bounds up, six at a time, the forty-odd steps that take him into the clouds . . . of coal dust, where our Apollo, *giovine di belle speranze ma privo di mezzi,** lives as the unfortunate suitor of one of the muses— the prima donna Eurterpe who, out of sheer wickedness, refuses ever to give in.

In Helicon, neither dead nor alive.

The weaknesses of the flesh have opened a hole in his mythological existence, rushing him, like a condemned soul, from heaven to hell, or to the ground floor trattoria, which is one and the same, and where one eats for 80 cents a head.

There, sometime between the minestrone and the dessert, like Ban-

*A young man full of hope but without means.

quo's ghost, the fateful *avisatore* appears suddenly beside the table, to lightheartedly reel off the following heresy:

"Il baritono d'obbligo sta male; lei deve cantare quest'oggi" (demanding he sing something utterly impossible; let us say, now that we have already mentioned Banquo, Macbeth).

"Come quest'oggi?"

"Ordine dell'impresa."

"Ma, per Baco, ma se il Macbetto," our man cries in desperation, *"Non lo faccio da che lo cantai nella fiera di ... Cremona* (or since hell froze over) *o son dieci anni!"*

"Questo a me non mi riguarda: órdine dell'impresa."

"Ma, che maniere son queste con un primario artista? Non sono un burattino! Così, come un colpo di cannone, senza una prova d'orchestra, né menno di pianoforte?"

"E già, credete chi vi si paga la quindicina (the touchstone; the magic word) *per andare á spasso e vivere d'entrate?"**

And that's it. There is no way out and there is no God.

The poor man has to buckle down and suffer through the ordeal, just one of the tricks of the trade ...

A serious shot of courage and a two-ounce castor-oil purgative, that acts as a filter or some type of still and that he hopes will clear his voice, and then they carry on with the rest of the program, and the rest—I do not need to tell you—is an exceedingly eloquent manifestation of genteel love and respect, fanatical, a *vero chiasso* in which the loveliest thing the enthusiastic audience shouts is *fuori, salame, porco, cane della madonna!*

Like my colleague the baritone, I, too, found myself between the devil and the deep blue sea.

---

* *"The baritone is ill; you must sing his part today."*

"What do you mean today?"

"House rules."

"But, for Christ's sake! Macbeth! I haven't sung that since the Cremona fair ... ten years ago!"

"That's not my concern; house rules."

"Is this any way to treat an artist? I'm not a puppet on a string! There, just like that, without even an orchestra or piano accompaniment?"

"You better believe it, buddy; do you think you're getting paid for running around doing nothing?"

I was obliged to *andare in scena*, to tread the boards without having practiced my lines, without knowing my role and—what is a thousand times worse, given the type of show it was—with the audience within spitting distance, thus open to the peril of having him peep up my sleeve, see what tricks I was up to, and floor me with one punch.

Oh, to the devil with it! I finally concluded.

Caesar had the Rubicon, Napoleon the Arcole Bridge, and the Urquiza squadron had Martín García Island . . .*

Who was to say that I, too, could not get across what I needed to, right before Juan's very eyes?

Especially since the midwife cried: It's a boy!

And putting my thoughts into action, I stood up, headed for the slattern in question with the pretext of bidding her good night and, in a flash, slipped the pill into the hollow of her hand, carefully relaying the following susurration from the tip of my tongue:

"Take this, read it, and rip it up."

*Juan n'y vit que du feu.**

X X V

T he other day, at eight in the morning, with the envelope still moist, Madame Juan served me the menu I had ordered, adding a homemade hors d'oeuvre that, being overly peppered and salted, left me not a little vexed.

Here are the ingredients:

"Between the despicable woman who neglects her duties and the wretched man who threatens to denounce her, one is more vile than the other: you tell me which."

---

*Martín García Island, strategically located where the Paraná and Uruguay Rivers flow into the River Plate, was used repeatedly in the first half of the nineteenth century to launch military campaigns and to blockade the ports of Buenos Aires and Montevideo.

*Juan didn't have a clue.

"Boom, the bombshell; take that!" I exclaimed; it seems that my little friend was very upset.

And the worst thing is that she could well be right, I then thought, because after all, between the despicable woman and the wretched man and so forth, one must be worse than the other, just as the señora claimed.

The question is, which of the two takes the cake; and since I am the one to award the prize judging by the story, I shall try to do so, after studying the case and knowing full well the proceedings.

I would like to begin by conceding for the sake of argument, señora, that when you were taken out of school you were innocent as a babe in the woods and pure as country wine.

That you remained so until you became ripe and were plucked by Juan from the maternal tree, whither you hung from a bough over your garden fence, provoking the neighbor boys' looks and whetting their appetites.

That when you decided to flee the protective wing of your mother, in order to take on other affairs and to travel the path of holy matrimony, you did it for the pleasure of being in the company of your husband rather than for the first-class ticket he bought you on trains and steamers or for the most expensive hotels, in which you held court and sat like a Russian princess thanks to others' efforts.

But allow me to exempt you even further.

I admit that you were hideously deceived by the reports you were given with respect to your companion's personal comportment and that, though believing you had embarked on this journey with a perfect gentleman, in fact you were faced with a perfect scoundrel.

That at the first station the train pulled into, said personage began to show his true colors, leaving you alone in the carriage while he went off to the bar to toss back a few drinks.

That with other ladies there present, he then proceeded to light up a black-tobacco cigarette that smelled like hell itself, stinking out all concerned and provoking an official complaint to the train guard and, as a direct result of said complaint, an argument broke out and descended—thanks to your man—into a fight, in which he shouted that no one told *him* what to do, that he would smoke whatever he damn well pleased because he had paid his money and it was as good as anyone else's.

It is implicitly understood that for the duration of this utterly obnoxious outburst, you knew not where to look and, what is more, prayed in vain to be swallowed up by the earth and disappear entirely.

That this prelude was more than enough and that given the chance you would have been only too pleased, then and there, to pack your bags and bolt like a stallion, especially when in Act II—set in the restaurant of a popular hotel—your husband, the protagonist of this farce, set to eating his fish with a knife, banging his glass on the table in order to get the waiter's attention, and shouting abuse at him for not having served what his discerning palate desired.

That in Act III, which took place in one of the bedrooms of your house, you caught him *in flagranti* in the throes of erotic pillow talk with the servant-woman.

That as befit the situation, you lost your temper and berated him for so barbarous an obscenity, to which his only reply was to snatch the fireplace tongs, brandishing them like executive powers, and crash them down over your person, leaving you with the most incontrovertible proof of his everlasting conjugal love.

So you see, I flatter him no more and even suppose him to be the *non plus ultra* in terms of male caddishness.

Do you think, perchance, that if your husband scuttles around in the gutter that it gives you the right to roll around in the filth, too?

That his being a degenerate, a gambler, a drunkard, and a libertine would grant you the authorization to smoke cigars, wear a knife in your garter belt, and walk the streets?

What about morality?

Ah, but you decidedly fall into the deepest confusion, jumbling everything our blessed Church teaches and orders us to obey, according to Father Astete's catechism,* a book I can only presume you have glanced through at one time or another, if only to memorize it, parrot-fashion.

Recall if you will that our Lord does not come running to comfort us when we violate the blessed sacraments, and that Police General Regulation 6, known as the "Commandment of God's Law," prohibits the rupture of the matrimonial contract under the harshest of punish-

---

* Spanish catechism written by the priest Gasper Astete in question-and-answer format. During most of the nineteenth century it was a bedside book used to educate women in the River Plate.

ments: the rest of one's days in Purgatory Penitentiary or a life condemned to making flagstones in the pits of hell.

I should, in addition, remind you that the nature or class of the forbearing person, as laid out by the principles governing this matter, cannot—by any means—be invoked by the accused as a justification or excuse nor even as an attenuating circumstance of her crime, and that the full penalty of the law is applied, regardless of who the victim is or what he is worth.

So don't come to me, señora, with any poppycock about it being no crime to steal from a thief.

That might be how they do things in Spain, but not in this God-fearing country in which whosoever takes something from someone else against his will is always deemed not only to have done ill but, ipso facto, to have committed a mortal sin and who must therefore have it out with the devil.

Do you know what you have done by getting married?

You have transferred the use of your person, you have signed a rental agreement; that is exactly what you have done, as if you were a dwelling; it is a contract in which you cannot be occupied by any objects aside from those your tenant chooses.

Juan has taken you in order to inhabit you, and as Juan possesses his fortune one can only suppose that he does not want to share you with anyone else, especially when the intruder is not even paying rent and is, moreover, actually cheating him out of it like a swine.

In a word, you are not your own but another's chattel, and having usufructed yourself clandestinely by a third party you fall—under the precepts of the aforementioned Astete Code—into mortal sin, committing the offence of robbery; and therefore you are naught but a thieving sinner who deserves no pardon from our Lord.

And finally I do not wish to allow you or myself to carry on slandering Juan, saying that he has taken to the bottle, that he loves olives, that he has a loose hand with women, and other degenerate notions, even if those are not unfounded, utterly gratuitous suppositions.

Every *seigneur* must be granted his *honneur*.

There is no cause to speak of humiliating acts or degrading vices; Juan is not the type. So let us get right down to the crux of the matter.

What could he throw at you?

I warn you of course that I, for my part, know nothing.

But let us admit for a moment that as a son of Adam, it runs in the family, and he will often be of a mind to close the book of matrimonial duties and decree his time off and his holiday periods.

Where is the harm in that? How can it wound you?

Do you fear, perhaps, that your husband might forget you or love you less?

Nonsense, señora! Men's hearts are very large: there is comfortably room for many of you within them, simultaneously.

Our Lord Father and Mother Nature, in their infinite knowledge, have made it so. Why, look no further than cocks and other quadrupeds for proof of what I say.

I once met a man, *verbi gratia*, who used to spend his nights at his mistress's house, and yet, one fine day, to save his father-in-law from a fraudulent bankruptcy, he gave his entire fortune to his wife.

To his lover his time, to his wife his money; and since time is money, it made no difference which; and since love is measured according to the benefits it brings, then by giving to both of them he loved both of them in equal measure.

Nothing could be clearer.

Women are not the only ones who want everything that catches their eye: man, too, experiences his whims.

Having endless *roba fina* at hand, as the Italians say, we often put on any old *fondaccio*, whatever rag is at hand, without that implying in the slightest that we prefer the latter.

It is quite like the habitué of the Paris café—where, in the worst-case scenario, one eats passably—who in some cheap, rank market-restaurant wolfs down a rancid stew in one go.

Like the patron of Colón Theater who, sick and tired of the Borghis and the Scalchis, grabs 25 pesos and throws them into the street just to savor the pleasure of getting his own back on Pappenheim and Company.

Could it be that you are terrified of being made a fool of, and in an attempt to evade ridicule you go to such pains?

Since when have women been contaminated by men's blights?

You end up with a man who is not a lost cause but simply a bit of a wily character, and suddenly it's all complaints and woe-is-me's.

Poor thing, poor thing! Left and right; she's an angel! And he's such a scoundrel . . . and she's a saint! And then you're all canonized and elevated to celestial heights.

Meanwhile, if bad luck befalls a man—which does chance to occur once in a blue moon—and he ends up with a bit of a free spirit, then there are not enough bugles in the world to broadcast his sorrows to the public.

Good, decent, and honest, he is nevertheless a so-and-so.

Why?

Simply because his wife has her head screwed on the wrong way round and has pulled the wool over his eyes.

And then to claim that we—the bearded gender—have engineered this arrangement, have assembled this apparatus, tuned the instruments, and opened the dance!

Well, hasn't our money ended up in good hands!

We were deemed master builders before we had even learned to hold a spoon.

Before buying the foundations of that tower of rubble known as the social edifice, we should have started by learning the trade, studying the lay of the land, breaking in the oxen, discovering the true colors of woman, seeing if there was any substance there—if it was worth the effort and worth putting our faith in God rather than turning tail and running the other way—before blithely handing over what anyone in his right mind is most parsimonious with: his good name and his reputation.

That way we would have stopped asking for the impossible, stopped trying to perform miracles and, convinced that the *donna è mòbile* as tenors say, rather than giving her the keys to the cash box, we would have placed them in our pockets and done up—as a final precaution— the top button of our jackets.

Yes, indeedy; it's all our fault.

It was quite a blunder, but we made our bed and we shall lie in it.

Now things are as they are and there is naught to be done about it.

A man's honor can be reduced to the following: not stealing and not shooting anybody in the back; the rest is all nonsense and dust in the wind.

Woman's honor is another issue entirely.

Verdict:

In order for you to have any grounds for what you say, you would have had to have started off by not wandering off the set, not playing hooky from the nuptial bed—the only school authorized by the government—where, under its rule and domination, you were bound to fulfill your natural duties fully and not to take to the woods, procuring immoral, private lessons from that night-school flunky, Master Smart Aleck, who has done nothing but steal your money.

Frankly, my dear lady, you would need remarkable aplomb to attempt to defend yourself, given what is on your record!

But, you will be wondering, how are things at home?

If I were not a God-fearing soul, if I were trying to do anything but rectify the situation that you have made such a mess of and avoid— out of the goodness of my heart—any type of future quarrel between you, your husband, and your son, then why on earth, I ask you, would I get mixed up in this tangled web as well, acting as a prompter and feeding you your lines?

I would not; that is clear as the light of day because, in short, personally I do not give a hoot about your affairs.

It would be the easiest thing in the world for me to prove my gallantry to you without having to have it out with the police commissioner.

The very most you could possibly reproach me for is that, turning a blind eye, I would become a sort of . . . how can I put this? . . . like some sort of *accoucheur*, some male midwife, one who consented to ugly behavior, a sort of mudguard, which would inevitably result in a fall in my moral standing. But this prick of conscience is nothing compared to the charming prospect of being punched—or not far off it—which is the fate human gratitude reserves for all those who meddle in business that is not their own.

Much more practical from my personal point of view, much more in line with my character as a 40-year-old bachelor—which means, in essence, a sentimental scrooge—would be the option of adjusting my glasses, looking closely, frowning, and then carrying on regardless:

1. Because certain issues do not merit being stirred up.
2. Because one should never reach out to catch a falling knife or a falling friend.

But such thoughts never crossed my mind; quite the contrary, in fact. You're caught up in the affair and know better than anyone the part I have played in this farce; you know I have not butted in and that I have even, with heroic abnegation, staked and lost many hours of peace and quiet, at the very least, in exchange for getting burned, losing sleep, and suffering bouts of indigestion that could have wrought disastrous consequences on my health.

If you should deign to acknowledge the full magnanimity, the generosity of my conduct, then reflect upon the fact that I am a selfish old man, solely dedicated to entertaining my person, gathering the vastest quantities possible of life's pleasures, for which an absolutely vital pre-requisite is spiritual tranquillity and perfect balance in one's bodily functions.

How does the informer and—to boot—wretch, as you so kindly called me, quickly become an excellent subject quite capable of climbing on deck and taking hold of the rudder in one fell swoop, when he needs to make one who has gone astray regain her course?

Let us see if you like my analogy.

Let us say that you are the lost sheep, your husband the shepherd, your son the lamb, and I the sheepdog who keeps order and prevents the livestock from becoming too fat and idle and, to keep you from being stolen, bites the quadroon attempting to make off with you.

Should you think that comparing you to an ovine creature is taking things too far and that the story in question is better suited to the society pages of some dismal rural tabloid, referring to a peasant from the country, I shan't argue; I beg forgiveness and move on to the do-main of science.

You are, *verbi gratia*, a nose with a great pimple on its tip.

I, the surgeon's hand that will prune the sickening outgrowth.

Of course one cannot make an omelet without breaking a few eggs; the operation will be painful; the pustule must be pierced, squeezed, drained of its viscous humor until the root is discovered, and then the infected area must be bathed in alcohol.

The patient, clearly, kicks the doctor-cum-executioner; but the suf-fering passes, the evil is rooted out, the healing begins, and the curses are exchanged for a chorus of praise:

"No one has an eye like Señor So-and-so's," they exclaim, "he hits the nail on the head every time; it is a miracle the way he cures folk," and so forth.

By the end they put more faith in him than in God.

And so it shall be with you.

Today you hurl a stream of abuse at me because you still feel the heat of the iron; tomorrow, when your ire has passed, you shall see how you praise me to the high heavens and kneel before me to ask my blessing.

You must be the first to sing my praises, you must convince yourself that I am your best friend, and if your condition could be exhibited without offending public decency and decorum, there would be nothing remarkable about coming out with an advertisement for me along these lines:

> "Ravaged by a life-threatening fever, I was lucky enough to fall into the hands of Dr. So-and-so who, convinced that in excess even nectar is poison, immediately applied a caustic that at first made me howl in pain, but then healed me effortlessly.
>
> "I am therefore pleased to do my duty by making public in this advertisement my deepest appreciation to this benefactor of bereaved humanity, even more so because, in his infinite kindness, he refused to charge even a penny for his toils."

Enough calculations.

If you think your deceit has had any effect whatsoever upon me you could not be more mistaken.

This light canter through the streets of common sense has put its poison in my heels.

Decidedly, nothing consumes one quite like reflection: it is the *pepsina nostra*, the ostrich's mouthful of moral indigestion.

One final push, one more step, I thought then, pacing up and down my room, and I shall be able to crawl into bed and sleep like a baby, with a clear conscience in the knowledge that I have carried out God's will.

At that precise moment I was within reach of the servant-bell.

Shortly thereafter, Taniete walked in.

"Go to Señor Don Pepe's," I ordered him, "and request that he stop by before going to the office, as I need to see him urgently."

XXVI

Our man did not dally; half an hour later:
"Please be so kind as to take a seat and read the contents of this letter that I have been asked to deliver to you in person," I said, staring at him fixedly.

First he turned bright red, then a deathly pallor overcame him and he feigned ignorance, stuttering:

"I don't understand what all this means . . ."

"Then I shall tell you," I replied. "This, friend, means that you are a first-class cad . . ."

"Sir!" he exclaimed, standing up in an attempt to put on airs. "I shall not stand for this!"

"Calm down," I replied phlegmatically, taking him by the arm and pushing him back into the chair. "Do not attempt to play-act; it is unbecoming.

"Keep in mind that I am older than you, which means that it would be quite difficult for you to fool me, and take into account that I must be quite determined to have granted you the honor of receiving you in my home in order to settle the score with you.

"So I advise you not to trouble me any more than strictly necessary and to remain calm and collected, as becomes a well brought-up young man.

"When a man," I continued, "starts off as a little scamp learning about life on the streets, touting theater tickets by night, and scavenging cigarette butts at the entrance, and fighting other boys over marbles and coppers by day, while his poor, sick mother languishes in bed suffering;

"When another man, feeling sorry for the miserable old woman and pitying the hard luck that has befallen the poor lad, reaches into his pocket for the former and attends to the education of the latter, makes somebody of him, calls him to his side and gives him a position of trust in his own home, allowing him to come and go as he pleases;

"When this 20-year-old lad, who is at a time when contact with men and the morbid milieu they mix in has not yet had the chance to pervert his heart, behaves like a barbarian, going so far as to make a common prostitute of his boss's wife;

"When all of this occurs, methinks, I have every reason, and then some, to say that the rascal I am describing has all the makings of a perfect knave.

"This is your story, I believe, and that is what I meant a moment ago when I used an adjective that was not to your liking and that, nevertheless, illustrated precisely the behavior in question.

"In fact, it describes you down to a T.

"But what I happen to think of you is by-the-by, incidental, without my having stopped to consider you as a person, since neither your spiritual betterment nor your reform concern me in the slightest or even enter my head, since I do not aim to act as your penitentiary but rather as the safety cord used by acrobats like you to carry off the final leap on the program.

"So I shall give you the lowdown and get right to the heart of the matter.

"Your girlfriend got wise to you. She wants nothing more to do with you, as she explains categorically in the missive I have had the satisfaction of handing over to you.

"As far as that goes, there is no alternative and I advise you to abandon even the remotest glimmer of hope.

"Someone who would not, on the other hand, mind meeting up with you for ten minutes if he knew the great service for which he is indebted to you both is Juan. But as I am not entirely sure whether or not you two would see eye to eye and, as my home-owning character imposes certain urbane duties upon me, I will be courteous enough to consult you on your tastes first.

"Pay attention; I'll be brief."

My interlocutor, staring fixedly at the drawings of a Smyrne, facial muscles twitching, livid, wild-eyed, looked crushed, utterly *aplati*.

In any other situation he would have moved me to pity; in this case he inspired only rage and scorn.

So I carried on, impervious, in this vein:

"If it pains you to renounce your beloved, if it is serious and the flames of passion burn intensely within your soul, then you hold the answer in your hand: don't give her up, but pull your socks up and be prepared for the consequences.

"I shall immediately close and lock the door, call your boss, open it back up again, enter with him, and sure as my name's So-and-so, I'll recount the whole sorry tale chapter and verse, handing him a revolver as I speak, and maybe even another to you just so you don't try to claim you were shot like a defenseless dog.

"If, on the contrary, you do not go the heroic route, if you couldn't give a bean about the woman or if, although she might mean something, your impressionable and nervous character rejects violent emotions and you opt for the happy-go-lucky, merrymaking route, we can also come to an agreement. You can't accuse me of not being accommodating.

"I have foreseen the event and brought along this case, containing one thousand francs in cash, 20-franc denominations, this passport in your name—ordering the national authorities and begging the foreign ones to place no obstacle in the way of your transit—and, finally, this appointment for your distinguished self to occupy the demanding post of Argentine consul in . . . Monaco.

"Go, my young friend, go and join the ranks of those who, with a few honorable exceptions, nobly and worthily represent the republic abroad.

"I recommend roulette in Monte Carlo.

"It's a capital little game.

"Go wild, lose the shirt off your back, have all the affairs you like, get put behind bars, or shoot yourself.

"That way we'll be well looked-after and you will have quite effectively contributed to the rising returns on our stock, laying the foundation for our swelling national credit by putting it up through the roof, all to the great honor of the country and glory of the government that runs it.

"Here is the key," I said, showing him my right hand.

"Here, the money and the documents," I added, indicating the left.

"Now choose, once and for all; I haven't got time to waste."

XXVII

Sganarelle:
*J'aime mieux consentir à tout que de me faire assommer.**

MOLIERE

O vercome by strong emotions, or pretending to be:
  "I swear, señor," young Pepe exclaimed, standing up, "you will never see hide or hair of this miserable wretch again . . ."

He tried to go skipping off, but not so fast that I couldn't catch up to him and stick the package between his shirt and vest, shouting:

"*Eh! Là-bas!* Don't forget your documents!"

To be continued.

*I'd rather be a cuckold than be killed. A line from Molières *The Imaginery Cuckold.*